Only he can tame
this hellion's desires . . .

The Hellion and the Highlander

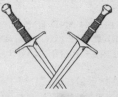

Averill suddenly snatched the compress away and scowled up at her brother. "I suppose you hate me now you know I have a temper."

"Nay, of course not," Will said at once. He then turned to Kade and arched an eyebrow. "Is she still too sweet?"

"What do you mean too sweet?" Averill asked.

Kade turned to peer at the girl. She had pulled the compress away again and her beautiful green eyes were shifting from one man to the other with irritation. The bonnet she'd worn to meet Lord Seawell had been discarded when she'd laid down earlier, and her tresses were now splayed over the bed on either side of her head, fiery locks he'd like to gather in his hands and press to his face. Though her cheeks were flush with color from her temper and her sweet, soft lips twisted with irritation, he'd never seen her look more beautiful.

"Nay," he growled. "I'll have her."

Will grinned and slapped his shoulder happily. "Welcome to the family."

By Lynsay Sands

THE HELLION AND THE HIGHLANDER
TAMING THE HIGHLAND BRIDE
DEVIL OF THE HIGHLANDS

THE RENEGADE HUNTER
THE IMMORTAL HUNTER
THE ROGUE HUNTER

VAMPIRE, INTERRUPTED
VAMPIRES ARE FOREVER
THE ACCIDENTAL VAMPIRE
BITE ME IF YOU CAN
A BITE TO REMEMBER
A QUICK BITE

LYNSAY SANDS

THE HELLION AND THE HIGHLANDER

AVON

An Imprint of HarperCollinsPublishers

This is a work of fiction. Names, characters, places, and incidents are products of the author's imagination or are used fictitiously and are not to be construed as real. Any resemblance to actual events, locales, organizations, or persons, living or dead, is entirely coincidental.

AVON BOOKS
An Imprint of HarperCollins*Publishers*
10 East 53rd Street
New York, New York 10022-5299

Copyright © 2010 by Lynsay Sands
ISBN 978-0-06-134479-4
www.avonromance.com

First Avon Books paperback printing: March 2010

Avon Trademark Reg. U.S. Pat. Off. and in Other Countries, Marca Registrada, Hecho en U.S.A.
HarperCollins® is a registered trademark of HarperCollins Publishers.

Printed in the U.S.A.

10 9 8 7 6 5 4 3 2 1

THE HELLION AND THE HIGHLANDER

Chapter One

"I did tell Father not to get his hopes up, that I did not think Lord de Montfault likely to accept me as a bride, but he would not listen."

Kade heard those words as he stirred from sleep and slowly opened his eyes. He found himself peering up at what might be the patterned draperies of a large bed. The material appeared quite dark, but then the room, too, seemed dark, with just the flicker of flames from a fire that cast dancing light and shadow everywhere.

It was night then, Kade deduced, and he was . . . somewhere. He wasn't sure where, exactly. He was hoping this was Stewart castle, his clan's home in Scotland, but the woman speaking had a very definite English accent, Kade noted as she continued.

"Alas, Father simply does not see what others see

when they look at me." The words were said with a combination of exasperation and sadness that drew his curious eyes to the blurred figure seated next to the bed—a woman, obviously. Not that he could see her well enough to be sure of that, but the voice was definitely feminine, soft and a touch husky. It was soothing and he quite liked listening to it, which was a good thing since it appeared she was speaking to him. At least, there was no one else in the room for her to be addressing.

"I fear he sees me through a father's eyes and simply does not notice how plain and unattractive I am. I suppose all fathers see their daughters as lovely, though. Which is sweet and right, but I do sometimes wish he could see me as I really am. Perhaps then he would not take these rejections so much to heart. I hate disappointing him."

Kade closed his eyes for a moment, hoping to clear his vision enough to see the young woman's face, but it felt so nice and soothing to have them closed that he found himself reluctant to open them again. Deciding he would leave them shut for the moment, he lay still and simply listened to her chatter, letting it flow over him like a sweet balm.

"I was hoping that with you and my brother here, Father would be distracted from his husband-hunting efforts. I do grow weary of being paraded before lords like a prize horse, especially when they all find me so wanting. 'Tis not that I mind the rejection so much, but some are quite rude about it.

Montfault even had the nerve to say outright that he would not wed the Devil's spawn."

She gave a little sigh, and muttered, "Enough on this subject, 'tis a sad one to be sure." There was a silence, then she said fretfully, "Though I am not sure what else I should talk to you about. I have told you every tale I can think of, and surely the details of life here at Mortagne are not very interesting. I fear my life has been most staid and unexciting compared to the adventures you and Will have enjoyed together. No doubt whatever subject I choose will bore you to tears."

Ah, Kade thought. So he was at Will's home in northern England. Well, that answered that question at least. And she had commented earlier that she'd hoped her father would forget his efforts to wed her off now he and her brother were home. That meant she was Will's sister, Averill. Will had spoken often of the lass over the last three years, and the tales had never failed to make Kade smile and wonder about the girl.

He was wondering even more now. Will had never said anything in all those tales that might explain why men would reject marriage to her. And what was this nonsense about being the Devil's spawn? From all he knew, Will's father, Lord Mortagne, was respected and well liked. Kade was suddenly curious to see what she looked like and why she was suffering these rejections she spoke of.

However, it seemed he wasn't meant to find out

just yet, for when he opened his eyes again it was to find that his vision had not improved. All Kade could see was a fuzzy figure seated beside the bed, bent over something in her lap. She appeared to be small in stature, her clothing dark, and her hair a bright, fiery orange in the light from the fire.

Frustration welling up in him, he blinked several times, but it did little good, and he closed his eyes again with resignation.

"I know!" she exclaimed suddenly. "I shall tell you tales of my naughty childhood."

He could hear the wry amusement in her voice and almost opened his eyes to try again to see her expression, but it seemed like too much effort, so he didn't bother and merely lay wondering which tale she would tell. Kade was very sure Will had told him every story there was to tell while they had been held prisoner the last three years. Their days had been spent laboring under the baking sun for their captors, but in the evenings they sat in dark, windowless cells passing the time by talking of home and family. Kade had told Will most of, if not all the details of his own youth and clan and was quite sure Will had done the same. So he was surprised when Averill began to tell an unfamiliar tale.

"I did not have such a naughty childhood really. I was mostly well behaved," she assured him as if confessing a sin. "But when I was six I did try to run away . . . though, 'twas not very successful."

That announcement was followed by a small,

almost embarrassed chuckle. "You see, Will was five years older than I. He was my only playmate and was good enough not to mind having me trailing about after him. We used to play hide-and-go-seek and other childish games together after our lessons were over for the day. But then, when I was five, Will was sent away to train, and I lost my only playmate and best friend."

A little sigh of sadness slid from her lips at the memory. "I was most unhappy, and somewhat spoiled by having had him be so indulgent of me. I begged Mother and Father to bring him back so that I could play with him again, but they were often busy and had little time to soothe a small girl missing her brother. So I decided that if they would not bring him back to me, I should do as I'd always done and follow him.

"First, I asked my father's captain of the guard to please take me to see Will. He, of course, refused, explaining most kindly that my father would not approve. I fear I kicked him in the shins for his refusal. I then ran to my room to have a good cry, and before the tears had dried on my face, decided I would have to run away.

"I planned it all most carefully in my child's mind. I snuck into the kitchens and filched some plums and buns while Cook wasn't looking, then gathered my favorite bed linen—for I knew it might be a long way and I might have to sleep out of doors a night or two—and then I headed out. There are secret corridors built into the walls of

Mortagne—" She paused and there was a frown in her voice as she admitted, "I suppose I should not have told you that. Fortunately, you are not conscious to hear. Still . . ."

Kade strained to listen as she paused again. He was glad when she continued, "Well, you are not likely to recall when you awake anyway, so . . . The secret passages run between the rooms, then join up at a tunnel that ends outside the bailey walls. Will and I were always told that it was the way for us to flee should the castle ever be attacked, and that is how I got out of the castle.

"I took the candle from my room, lit it from the fire in my nursemaid's room—she was old, always cold, and never without her fire blazing even in summer," Averill explained before continuing. "And then I braved the tunnels. They were dark and dirty, with horrible large cobwebs and skittering sounds. I was sure there were small creatures that would attack me at any moment. I almost turned around and hurried back to my room, but I wanted to see Will again, so I made myself continue on and finally reached the end of the tunnel."

A small chuckle rolled through the air around him, and she admitted, "I had the devil of a time getting the outer tunnel door open. However, I did, and a breeze immediately blew in and snuffed my candle, but the tunnel ends in a cave, and enough sunlight was streaming through the entrance that I could see my way out. I left my candle there and dragged my linen behind me out into the open air.

"I remember it being so bright that my eyes stung after being so long in the tunnels, and I was exhausted by all my efforts, so I didn't walk far before stopping under a nice shady tree to enjoy my pilfered food. I planned to continue on my journey as soon as I finished eating, but all the excitement and the food made me sleepy, so I brushed off the worst of the dirt and cobwebs my linen had gathered in my travails and curled up under the tree to sleep. And that is where they found me.

"I gather there was quite a ruckus when they realized I was missing. The servants searched every nook and cranny of the castle, and the soldiers were called in to help look. Father is the one who found me under that tree. I was sound asleep in my dirty bit of linen, cobwebs in my hair and dirt smudges on my face so that he swears he first thought me a peasant girl rather than the little lady I was supposed to be," she finished affectionately.

Kade couldn't resist. He opened his eyes, squinting in an effort to see her better as he asked, "Were you very upset to have been found and brought back?"

"Nay. By that time I was rather relieved," she admitted with a self-deprecating laugh. "It had started to rain, you see, and was growing cold. I was eager to return to the castle and—" Her voice died abruptly, and her head shot up, eyes, no doubt, finding him, then her blurred shape stretched as she stood with a gasp. "You are awake!"

Kade didn't respond. It had pained his throat to

ask his question, and her words didn't require a response.

Averill moved closer to the bed then, but he still could not see her very well as she asked, "Would you like a drink? Or—Oh, I should send for Will. He has sat by you quite often and insisted I find him if you stirred. Wait here."

Kade raised his head to watch her blurry figure bustle away, frustrated by his inability to see properly when her dark outfit blended in with the shadows of the room. The patter of her footsteps and the door opening and closing were the only way he knew she'd left.

Grimacing, he lay back on the bed and closed his eyes once more, wondering why they were playing him false. He had never had trouble seeing before. And why did he not recall how he'd come to be here? And what had she meant by saying Will had sat by him quite often? What—?

The sound of the door opening distracted him from his questions, and he frowned in that direction. Will couldn't have been far away. Probably down in the great hall, Kade supposed, considering the lateness that the dark in the room suggested. He squinted in a useless effort to see better, and called, "Will?"

"Nay, 'tis Averill." Her voice sounded surprised as she closed the door, then she rushed forward, her figure separating from the general blur and becoming a dark wraith crowned with fiery hair as she rushed closer. "I sent a maid to tell Will the news and fetch back a drink. It should be here soon. Are you having trouble seeing, my lord?" The question had barely left her lips when she added, "Do not speak, it obviously pains you. No doubt your throat is dry. Just nod and shake your head for now."

Kade grimaced. She was right. It did pain him to speak though he was sure a drink would help with that. He was more concerned with how he had come to be here and why his eyes were playing him false, but merely nodded to indicate that he was indeed having trouble seeing.

"Oh." She bent slightly over him, and the heady scent of flowers and spices teased his nose, as she muttered, "Will did not mention an injury that might damage your sight. Mayhap the head wound has something to do with it."

She straightened and turned slightly as the door opened again. Kade glanced that way as well to see a much larger figure in dark pants and a light-colored tunic move forward, booted feet pounding on the floor with each step.

"Will?" The question slipped from his lips before Kade could help himself, and he grimaced at the sad croak he produced, not to mention the friction it caused in his throat.

"He cannot see," Averill explained. "It may be a result of the head wound. Or mayhap his eyes are merely in need of liquid as much as his throat to work right. We've managed to get little enough in the way of food or liquid down his throat these last two weeks."

"Aye," Will agreed, moving toward the bed even as Averill moved toward the door.

"I shall see where that girl is with his drink and have her fetch him some broth as well," she said as she left the room. Then Will stepped up to tower over Kade where he lay.

"You look like hell, my friend."

When Kade gave a grunt of disgust at the words, Will laughed and took the seat Averill had been using earlier. "I am glad to see your eyes open at last. I feared that was something I would never see."

"What—?" Kade began, but paused when Will reached out to grasp his arm.

"Save your voice. I'll recount what has happened while you were unconscious, and you may ask questions later."

When Kade relaxed back in the bed, he asked, "Do you recall our boat journey?"

Kade frowned, searching his mind for what he spoke of.

Will obviously noted it, because there was concern in his voice as he asked, "You *do* recall our being captured by Baibar's men and held prisoner for three years?"

Kade nodded. That time was not one he would soon forget. Nearly three years of his life had been wasted in that prison. It had been exactly one thousand and seventy-two days of hell. Kade had counted them off as he'd sat in the dark cell at night, talking to his cellmates—his cousin, Ian, and this man, Will Mortagne. While Will was an Englishman whom Kade had hardly known prior to their capture by infidels while on Crusade, he was now counted among his closest and most trusted friends. Their friendship was the only good thing to come out of the experience.

"And our escape?" Will asked. "Do you remember that?"

Kade nodded again. After three years of hard labor, with sweat stinging in the open wounds on his back from the whips their guards liked to apply, Kade had thought he'd die in that foreign land. He'd seen enough men go that way. Every couple of days another prisoner had fallen, a victim of starvation and dehydration, worked to death and dragged away to be tossed into an open pit where others lay rotting.

Kade had been sure he, too, would end his days in that mass grave. But when his cousin, Ian, had fallen ill, Kade had had enough. He'd lost man after man to the stinking pit, but he was not letting Ian go. He was like a brother; they'd grown up together, and Kade was determined to do what he could to save him . . . or die trying. The plan had been simple, and desperate. At night, after being returned to their cell, he'd had Ian pretend he was dead, not hard since the illness that had claimed him had made him pale as a corpse. Kade had then called the guard.

Two had come, both swarthy and strong, with swords drawn. They hadn't even examined Ian other than to glance at him through the bars before they'd opened the door and ordered Kade and Will to bring him out. Kade had taken Ian's feet and Will his arms, and they had carted him out of the cell, but as they were passing the guard, Kade had dropped Ian's feet and tackled the guard nearest him.

It was surprise alone that had won the day. He'd managed to get the man's sword and keys and tossed the keys to Will to free the others. He'd then taken on the now-unarmed guard and his armed compatriot alone until the others were free to aid him. He still found it hard to believe he'd survived those moments uninjured. But he had, and they had all escaped unscathed.

"And the monastery in Tunis?" Will prodded. "You recall the three months we spent there while Ian recovered from his illness, I healed from my sword wound, and we all recuperated and regained our weight and strength?"

Kade grimaced. While they'd escaped the cells unscathed, they hadn't been so lucky afterward. They were stealing horses on which to flee when Will had been run through by a guard who took them by surprise. Once the guard had been taken care of, Will had tried to be brave and steadfast, clutching the wound in his side and telling them to go on without him, but Kade had ignored that and taken the time to bind the wound the best he could. It had been bad, and Kade had feared losing yet another friend to Baibar's cruelty.

Once they'd reached the safety of the monastery in Tunis, the monks had tended Ian and Will. Ian had recovered from his illness within a couple of days, but it had taken two weeks for Will to recuperate. Once he was up and about, they had spent another two and a half months regaining their strength and working to earn the money for food, clothes, and horses to make the long journey home. It had taken them more than two months to make their way north to France. They'd hired a boat there to carry them across the Channel to England, he recalled.

"But you do not recall the boat crossing from France to England?" Will asked, reminding him of his earlier confusion.

"I remember," he managed, wincing as the words tore at his throat. The boat they'd hired had seemed sturdy and the day fine when they'd cast off, but a storm had whipped up halfway across, and waves taller than the ship had surrounded them. Kade was no coward, but even he had trembled before the powerful walls of water that had tossed the ship about. When they finally saw shore ahead, he suspected he was not the only one to breathe a sigh of relief that it was nearly over. But Mother Nature had not been finished with them yet and, as the captain tried to steer into the harbor, the ship was caught by a wave and dashed against the rocks. Kade had a vague recollection of the screams of men and panicked whinny of horses, then a blinding pain in his head.

"The men?" he asked, doing his throat more damage.

"Stop trying to talk," Will said with exasperation, then sighed. "We lost Gordon and Parlan."

Kade closed his eyes as loss slid over him. Two more men to add to the others lost to the madness of Edward's Crusade. Of the thirty warriors he'd been captured with, only Domnall, Ian, and Angus remained. And Will, he acknowledged. Edward had ordered that the Englishman accompany them on the late-night sojourn to check on the whereabouts of Baibar's men. That order had cost the Englishman more than three years of his life, and while Kade was sorry for his friend's sake, he was grateful for his own. Their friendship had helped him stay sane during their trials.

"But Ian, Angus, and Domnall made it to shore," Will went on firmly. "And I pulled your sorry hide there when I found you facedown in the water. The horses did better," he added dryly. "We only lost one and managed to collect the others as they swam to shore."

Kade grunted. He'd rather have lost all the horses than one more man.

"I took you up on my mount, and we rode straight here to Mortagne. You have been unconscious nearly two weeks now, and—"

"Two—?" Kade began with disbelief.

"Aye, two weeks," Will interrupted, and shook

his head. "I do not know why. You had a bump, but it was not even an open wound. Averill says head wounds are like that though. A small bump can kill a man, while another will survive his skull being cracked open." He shrugged. "She would know, I suppose. Averill was trained in healing by our mother and has aided in tending the ill and injured here since a child. She has fretted over you like a mother hen these two weeks, dribbling broth down your throat several times a day in an effort to keep you from starving to death. She has also been talking to you nonstop. Averill assured me that it would keep your soul tied to your body, so you did not wander to heaven and not return." Will grinned as he added, "Your ears must be ringing from her nonstop chatter. You probably regained consciousness just to shut her up."

Kade shook his head at the words. He had no recollection of anything since the boat broke apart. Though he must have heard her with some part of his mind, for he found himself missing her dulcet tones. As if called by his thoughts, he heard the door open and the patter of feminine footsteps.

"Here we are." That gay voice was accompanied by a gust of the spicy floral scent he'd noted earlier as Averill bustled back in. Her arrival seemed to brighten the room, her cheer helping to wash away some of the bitter memories that had been occupying his thoughts. Blinking the rest of them away, Kade watched her dark, little figure hurry forward, leading what appeared to be at least two maids, possibly three, all carrying items he couldn't make out. He strained in an effort to see better, but the women remained smudgy blurs in his vision, refusing to come into focus.

Kade scowled with frustration and tried to raise his hands to rub at his eyes. They felt gritty, as if he had something in them, though he suspected they were just parched, as was the rest of his body. His head felt stuffed with cotton, his mouth so arid he could not even work up any saliva to oil his throat, and his skin everywhere felt dry and stretched tight, like leather being cured. Still, it was his eyes that troubled him the most at the moment. However, the hands he was trying to lift to rub at the two irritating orbs merely flopped where they lay. He did not even have the strength to raise them. Kade gave it up with a small sigh. He had never felt so weak and helpless in his life, and he wasn't enjoying the experience.

"Here, Will, help me sit him up to drink," Averill ordered.

Kade grimaced as the Englishman slid an arm beneath his back and lifted him halfway upright. He knew he couldn't manage on his own, so didn't protest, but merely waited as Averill leaned down to press the drink to his lips. The liquid, sweet and cool, the finest honey mead he'd ever tasted, poured into his mouth. He would have gulped it down in two swallows, but Averill only gave him a sip, then waited while he swallowed it before tipping the mug up again.

"More," he gasped impatiently, when she did that a third time.

"Nay. You have had little or nothing to eat or drink for weeks. 'Tis best to go slowly at first."

Forcing back his impatience, Kade suffered her slow and sensible approach, and by the time the chalice was empty, had begun to think she had the right of it. While he still thirsted and yearned for more, his belly was churning in a threatening manner.

"How is your stomach?" Averill asked as she set the mug aside.

Kade grimaced for answer as Will eased him back to lie in the bed.

"We shall wait on the broth then, I think," she decided. "Do you think you can stay awake long enough for Mabs to help you clean up? Or do you wish to sleep now and wait until the next time you wake up?"

Kade opened his mouth to assure her that he wasn't at all tired. After all, he'd just woken up, but the words were drowned out by a sudden yawn that made a mockery of what he'd wanted to say.

"Perhaps tomorrow morning then," Averill said gently, as if he'd spoken, and he blinked his eyes sleepily as she tugged the linens and furs up more closely around him. "Sleep. You shall feel better in the morning."

"Should he be tired already?" Will asked, as Kade felt his eyes begin to droop closed. "He only just awoke."

"He will probably stay awake a little longer next time, but he shall tire easily for a while. I am surprised he stayed awake long enough to drink all the mead." Averill's voice was soft and soothing to Kade's ears, lulling him into a state of half slumber. He didn't really want to sleep, but his mind and body appeared to have other ideas, and the soft murmur of their voices wasn't enough to keep him awake.

Chapter Two

Averill woke to the sun streaming through the window and a smile on her face. At first, she wasn't sure why she was so happy. She'd had little enough to smile about since her father had taken it into his head to find her a husband. Most mornings of late she'd awakened feeling nothing but glum resignation about the day ahead, one she expected to be tainted by the poison of rejection as the latest possible suitor turned his nose up at the prospect of marrying her and rode off to find prettier pastures. Not that there had been that many men so far, Averill admitted to herself. There had been only three, but it felt more like thirty when their reactions were so hurtful. She never knew when the next would arrive, so woke up most days dreading that this would be the day.

However, Averill was feeling none of her usual dread this morning. In fact, happiness and good cheer were filling her as she took in the dust motes dancing in the beam of light pouring through the open shutters of her window. She took a moment to ponder that fact, wondering what had filled her dreams to leave her waking so happy, but then recalled that Kade had awakened last night.

Eager to see how he fared this morning, Averill sat up swiftly and thrust the linens and furs aside to leap out of bed. She scurried to one of the two chests against the wall, threw it open, and quickly began digging around for a fresh chemise. This was normally something her maid did for her and, were she to wait patiently, Bess would do it for her today as well, but she simply couldn't wait. Averill had spent two weeks nursing her brother's friend, Kade Stewart. Will had claimed the man had been unconscious when he'd pulled him out of the water, and had remained so, not even stirring during the ride home to Mortagne. He had been sweat-soaked and hot with fever but still as death when they'd arrived; but even after the fever had broken on the second day, he hadn't stirred, and Averill had grown increasingly concerned. She had seen cases before where ill or injured persons fell into a deep sleep and simply never woke up. They had merely wasted away in their beds as their loved ones stood by helplessly.

While Averill had assured Will that would not happen here, now that Kade was awake, she could admit, at least to herself, that she'd feared that might very well be the outcome this time. Still, she had done her best to prevent that from happening: feeding him dribbles of broth several times a day to keep him from expiring from thirst or hunger, helping to wash and turn him every other day so that he would not develop skin irritations that might fester, and talking to him constantly so that he knew he wasn't alone.

She had no idea if her efforts had helped or if it simply wasn't his time yet to go, but Kade was alive and had awakened, and Averill felt she could take at least a little credit for that happy outcome. Now, she wanted to check on her patient and be sure he hadn't slipped back into that unnatural sleep again.

"Oh! You're up."

Averill straightened as her maid, Bess, stepped into the room. The woman was older by twenty years and had pale brown hair streaked with grey and a slender figure. She carried a basin of water and a small strip of cloth, Averill noted, but ignored them, and said, "Aye. Help me dress. I would check on Kade."

"Kade is it?" Bess asked as she set the basin of water on the second chest and moved toward Averill.

Averill felt herself flush at the maid's dry tone. It reminded her that she had no right to be so familiar with the Scottish lord, but after two weeks of telling him everything and anything she could think of as he'd lain sleeping and healing in the bed, Averill felt as if she knew the man. Well, because of that plus all the stories Will had told her about him in the evenings when he'd joined her in her constant vigil. Her brother had told her many tales about their capture and imprisonment as the two of them had sat at Kade's bedside, and it was obvious that Will had forged a strong friendship with the Scot. It was also obvious that he thought highly of the man . . . as did Averill, herself, after all she'd learned about him.

She could only admire and appreciate the way Kade had helped keep Will's spirits up during their enslavement. The Scot was also the only reason her brother was now free, for Kade alone had planned and carried out their desperate escape. He had also dragged her brother to the monks when he was injured, saving Will's life again. Aye, Kade Stewart was a fine and honorable man, a good friend to her brother.

Averill was drawn away from her thoughts when Bess suddenly tugged the chemise out of her hand and tossed it aside. "What—?"

"Ye shall wash up as you do every morning, then ye can dress and go about yer day. Yer Scot can wait," Bess said firmly as she steered her toward the basin and cloth on the chest.

"He's not *my* Scot," Averill said, aware that heat had flushed her cheeks at the words. However, knowing from experience that Bess wasn't one to argue with, she didn't bother trying. She snatched up the clean bit of linen the maid had brought, dipped it in the water, and quickly began to wash herself.

Satisfied, Bess moved back to collect the chemise she'd taken from her, then searched for a gown suitable for the day ahead.

Averill ignored her as she rushed through her washing.

Bess was there waiting when she finished and helped her dress, her actions so slow Averill was hard-pressed not to natter at her to hurry. When the last lacing was done, she released a gusty sigh of relief and immediately made a run for the door.

"Yer hair," Bess barked, bringing her to a halt.

Sighing impatiently, Averill turned back and allowed the woman to fuss with her hair, thinking it all a terrible bother. She tapped her foot impatiently as she waited.

"There," Bess said at last. "You can go down and break your fast now."

"I am going to look in on Kade," Averill said as she moved to the door.

"You may as well break your fast first," Bess said firmly. "Your brother and the three Scots are with him. They'll not welcome your presence at the moment."

"He's awake then?" Averill asked, pausing with her hand on the door to glance back.

"Aye. The lad woke up again at the break of dawn, and Mabs tended to him. He's been watered and fed and had a wash."

"What did Mabs feed him?" Averill asked worriedly.

"Broth, just as you instructed," Bess assured her, and added wryly, "though she says he was wanting something solid in his belly and made a fuss about it."

"His stomach will probably not accept solid food yet," Averill said with a frown.

"That's what Mabs told him. The man didn't believe her until the broth and mead tried to crawl back up his throat. He settled down then and stopped asking for proper food."

Averill nodded, not at all surprised to hear this. She had managed to get some fluids down Kade's throat since his arrival, but it was difficult to feed an unconscious man. After weeks with little more than a few mouthfuls of liquid, even a mug of broth or mead would weigh heavy on his stomach.

"So," Bess said, drawing her attention again, "take yourself down and break your fast while he finishes talking to his men. Then you can check on him."

"Aye." Averill sighed and opened the door.

She really wanted to see for herself that he was awake and well but knew Bess was right, and her presence wouldn't be welcomed. Doubtless, Kade had instructions for his men, messages to send to his kin to let them know he was alive and well, and so on. Will had told her that Kade had a sister named Merry as well as two brothers and a father, and she had no doubt they would all be fretting about his well-being. She had certainly been fretting about Will after hearing not a word from him in the more than three years since he'd ridden off to join Edward's Crusade, and had been overjoyed when he'd ridden into Mortagne's bailey two weeks ago.

The great hall was cluttered with people coming and going when Averill descended the stairs. The tables were almost full with people breaking their fast, servants were rushing around with food and drink, and the air was abuzz with conversation.

Averill settled in her seat next to her father, offering him a smile and quiet "Good morn" as a servant rushed forward to present her with mead and some bread and cheese.

"Good morn, girl," her father greeted cheerfully. "I hear the Scot's awake and well."

"Aye." Averill smiled faintly as she nodded. It had been late when Kade had finally awakened last night, and most had been abed or headed that way when she'd found a maid to take the news below to her brother. Presumably, her father had been one of those already retired.

"Fixed him up right and nursed him through it. You are a good girl, Averill. A man would be lucky to have you to wife," he said, then frowned. "I do not understand these foolish young men today. Any would be lucky to have you, and yet they turn from you as if you are plague-ridden."

Averill sighed at the bewilderment in his voice. He really did not understand, and she felt his disappointment keenly. She cleared her throat, and said quietly, "I have red hair, Father. Many believe that is the sign of the Devil, or of a fiery temper, or promiscuity, or—"

"Bah!" Lord Mortagne interrupted impatiently. "Foolish superstitions. Your mother had your same coloring and was ever a sweet and dutiful wife. She never even looked at another man, and she certainly was not evil or tempestuous or any of that other nonsense."

"And then there is the mark on my cheek," Averill forged on, determined to make him see what others saw. "Some believe it the mark of the Devil as well."

" 'Tis a tiny birthmark," he protested in disgust. "No bigger than a pea. 'Tis hardly even noticeable."

Averill did not argue with him but merely pointed out her final flaw, at least the only other flaw she dared admit to him. "I stammer when nervous so that I sound a fool, and I am always nervous when I meet these men you would wish me to marry."

"Aye, there is that," he agreed on a sigh, apparently having no argument to counter that point, then pointed out with vexation, "but you do not stammer around family and friends."

"Nay," she agreed. "I am not nervous or self-conscious around them."

"Then mayhap if you thought of these men as friends rather than suitors . . ." His voice faded as he saw her doubtful expression, but he gathered himself, and suggested, "Then perhaps we could make you more relaxed ere they arrived, so that you would not stammer."

"How?"

Her father considered the question briefly, his hand reaching unconsciously for his drink. He lifted it, but then suddenly paused and stared at the watered-down ale he favored. His eyes widened, eyebrows rising on his wrinkled forehead, then he gasped with certainty, "Through drink!"

"Drink?" She echoed the word with amazement.

"Aye. Drink always makes the men more talkative and gay. Why should it not work on you?"

"Oh, Father," she began with horror, but the idea had taken hold, and he would brook no argument. She did not even think he had heard her protest as he hurriedly continued speaking.

"We shall try it the very next time. I shall consider whom to approach next, then we shall have you drink down a glass or two of our best whiskey the moment he arrives, before he can meet you, then—" He stood suddenly. "I must go check that list Nathans sent me of the men who have lost or never been matched up with a betrothed and choose the best of the lot to try it on. Oh, this is a brilliant idea. I only wish I had thought of it before."

Averill stared after her father in horror as he hurried away to search out the letter from his friend Nathans. His excitement seemed about equal to her own dismay. This was the very worst idea he had ever had. Have her drink to soothe her nerves ere facing one of those snooty men? Stone-cold sober she was hard-pressed not to strike out at them when they treated her so shabbily on sight. With her inhibitions lessened by drink, she was likely to give in to the temper she took such great pains to hide and do something of that very sort.

Averill let the bit of bread she'd picked up drop back to the table. She had no idea if all redheads had tempers as superstition claimed, but certainly she and her mother had. However, Averill's mother, Margaret, had had it pounded into her from the cradle never to let that temper reign, and she had managed to keep a stern leash on it all the days of her life. Even her husband, Averill's father, was ignorant of Lady Margaret's temper. Lady Mortagne had also remonstrated with Averill from a very young age that she must do the same . . . and she had. Like her mother, Averill was always in control of her temper. Even when the last suitor had sneered to her face that he would never marry a redheaded she-devil with the mark of Satan on her face and lacking the brains God gave most, Averill had controlled her temper. She had not spat in his face and run her claws down his cheek as she'd wished. She'd bit her tongue, literally, smiled sweetly, and went straight up to her room. There, she'd forced herself to lie down and stare at the ceiling until the desire to howl and throw things had passed, and she'd regained control of herself.

However, alcohol could very well steal that control from her and reveal to one and all that she did indeed have the temper redheads were reputed to have, and that while she behaved as she should and presented a sweet disposition to the world, she often wanted to kick people in the shins and run away . . . at least for a while.

Averill grimaced as the thought made her recall the one time she'd lost her temper—the day she'd kicked the captain of the guard in the shin because he wouldn't take her to her brother, then had quite literally run away. That was the one time her temper had been displayed. It was then her mother had started her campaign to make Averill control her temper.

She bit her lip and glanced toward the stairs to the upper hall, suddenly wondering just how much of that tale Kade had been awake to hear. She'd thought him sleeping or never would have told it, but then he'd asked his question . . . At the time she'd been so startled and happy to know he had come out of his unnatural sleep that she hadn't even considered that he had heard the tale of her youthful temper tantrum. She fretted over it briefly but then pushed the worry away. All at Mortagne knew about that incident and thought nothing of it. Only her mother had recognized it as a show of the terrible temper her daughter carried, and she had promptly set out to be sure Averill gained and kept control of it.

Her gaze flickered as Will appeared at the top

of the stairs. Distracted from her worries about her
father's plan, Averill noted the three Scots behind
him. As the men began to descend the stairs, she
felt a smile curve her lips. Morning meal forgotten,
she stood and moved toward the stairs. Now she
could go look in on Kade.

"Close your eyes."

Kade scowled at the old woman, Mabs, and waved
her away impatiently. "I am fine. Let me be."

"Your head aches, doesn't it? This will help," she
snapped, pushing his hands away.

She performed the action as easily as if I were a babe,
Kade thought bitterly, and considering how weak
he was, it was an apt description. While he was
a little stronger this morning and could at least
lift his hands, he was still weak enough that he
couldn't even fend off an old woman. That was a
bitter brew to swallow for a warrior like him, he
acknowledged, as she leaned forward with a cold,
damp cloth in hand.

Kade scowled, but he closed his eyes just sec-
onds before she laid the cloth over them. The harsh
sunlight spilling through his open shutters was
immediately blocked out, and he sighed with relief
as the cool damp soaked into the skin around his
eyes, soothing away some of the aching that had
come on while he'd been talking with his men and
Will.

"Feels better, doesn't it?" the old crow challenged.

When Kade merely grunted, she chuckled her amusement, the sound the closest to a cackle that he'd ever heard. It made him wish once again that Averill was there.

When he'd awakened at the crack of dawn, Kade had been less than pleased to find the old harpy at his bedside instead of Will's sister. Where Averill's voice had been sweet and soothing, this woman's was testy and sharp, and her care had been a bit less than gentle so far. She'd handled him like a side of beef as she'd gone about washing him and rolling him about to change the bedding. The whole experience had been unpleasant and humiliating for a man used to fending for himself, and he was quite sure that had Averill been here to tend to those tasks, it would have been a different ordeal entirely.

Even worse, after all that, all the old woman would allow him to consume was broth and mead. Kade wanted solid food. He wanted to start rebuilding his strength. However, when he'd said as much, she'd merely announced that Lady Averill had ordered that he wasn't yet allowed solid food. Apparently, the maid was loyal to Averill and her orders. Certainly, none of his griping or demands had moved her to go against them.

The sound of the door opening caught his ear, and Kade almost held his breath as he waited to hear who it was. A small smile of relief almost graced his lips when he smelled spice and flowers and heard Averill's soft voice greeting Mabs. The soft patter of her footsteps followed.

"Oh, dear," she exclaimed, sounding as if she were right next to the bed. "Why the cold compress? Are his eyes still bothering him, Mabs?"

"Nay," Kade said at once, but the soft growl was drowned out by Mabs's voice as she said, "Aye. After being closed so long, they are not yet adjusted to the light. Keep the cold compress on him as long as you can today. 'Twill help speed his healing."

Kade scowled as he heard Averill's murmured agreement, then listened as the women moved off toward the door. They were talking softly, but after a moment they fell silent, and there was the sound of the door opening and closing.

"Well." Averill's voice flowed over him as soft and sweet as he remembered. There was a quiet rustle as she seated herself, and Kade smiled and inhaled the scent that drifted to him on the air. And then she asked, "Are you feeling better this morning?"

Kade lifted his hand, intending to remove the cloth covering his eyes so that he could see her, but she caught it and urged the hand back down to the bed.

"Best just to leave the compress for now. It may help your eyesight return more quickly," she said. As soft as the words were, there was steel beneath them, and her grip on his hand was firm before she released it. She then patted it, and added, cheerfully, "Besides, there's nothing worth seeing here anyway, just a bed, a chair, the fireplace, and some sunlight."

"There's you," Kade said quietly, and it brought a soft laugh that had a wry edge to it.

"Believe me, I am hardly worth risking a headache to see," she assured him.

Kade frowned at her words, recalling waking to her lamenting over her father's efforts to marry her off and the cruel insults of the men he'd chosen. It made him more curious than ever to see her, but he left the compress on for now, biding his time. Strength and skill with a sword were not the only reasons he had been a renowned warrior before being captured and imprisoned. Intelligence was an important factor and, despite his illness, he still had that. Kade knew when to bide his time and await his moment, and this was one of them. He didn't wish to make Will's sister uncomfortable or upset her, so he would await his chance, Kade decided, and turned his attention to her, as she asked, "Are any of your men riding out with messages for your family?"

When he hesitated, she added, "Will told me that your mother passed on before the Crusades, but that you have a sister, two brothers, and a father still. He didn't wish to write and give them false hope until we were positive you would recover, but I am sure they must be very anxious to hear news of you."

Kade's mouth tightened slightly at the suggestion. He doubted his father and brothers had been sober enough even to wonder about him the last three years, but his little sister was another matter entirely. Merry would be fretting over him.

"I sent all three men," he admitted, then explained, "I had more than the one task for them to perform."

"Ah," she said, and proved her understanding of the male mind by asking curiously, "Did they fuss about leaving you here alone?"

Kade smiled faintly at her intelligence, for indeed they had fussed at leaving him here at Mortagne without someone to watch his back. He considered denying it, but decided to give her the truth. "Aye, they fussed like old women, insultin' yer brother mightily, I'm sure, but I insisted they go." Grimacing, he added, "I doona need them hangin' over me while I recover, and I'm safe enough here in Will's home. I trust him."

"And he trusts you," Averill said softly.

Kade nodded silently, not doubting it for a minute. They'd had to learn to trust each other while enslaved. It was how they'd survived, by watching each other's backs. He, his men, and Will hadn't been the only prisoners in their jail. There had been others, former residents of towns and cities that Baibar had razed. Most of the populations were killed, he'd been told, but some had been kept to perform manual labor for their new "masters," men who had fed them little but dribbles of gruel and rotten vegetables, and had worked them quite literally to death under the hot desert sun.

Wanting them weak and malleable, the food had never been enough for everyone, and men had been killed by their own prison mates for little more than a crust of bread or a mouthful of swill. But the number who died at the desperate hands of one of their own was nothing next to those who were beaten and worked to death. Kade had quickly stopped counting the men who had died under the baking sun.

"Will said the escape was your plan."

He smiled wryly but didn't tell her that the plan had come to him quite suddenly, and his only regret was that it hadn't come to him before that. Had he come up with it sooner, more of his men would yet be alive.

"Will said you threw the keys to him and ordered him to let the other men out, then took on both guards yourself with the stolen sword while he did," Averill continued quietly. "That was brave."

"That was desperation," he countered dryly, and admitted, "After our time in prison, I was in no shape to fight two on me own."

"And yet you did," Averill said simply.

Kade shrugged where he lay, his ego not allowing him to explain that it was sheer good fortune that had helped him in this instance. Before he'd been captured and starved for three years, he would have taken on three men or more without a thought or worry . . . and been the victor, but he knew it was only the fickle hand of fate that had seen him through their escape alive. Had Will not managed to free the others from their cells as quickly as he had to help him in the battle, they would no doubt all be dead right now.

A yawn suddenly claimed Kade, stretching his mouth almost painfully wide, and he raised a hand to cover the wide maw, bumping the cold compress upward as he did. When the yawn ended, he let his hand drop back to the bed without straightening the cloth and murmured an apology for his rudeness.

"Rest," Averill said, standing and leaning forward to straighten the compress for him. He caught a quick glimpse of her face as she did, then the compress was back in place, and she murmured, "Sleep is the best medicine for you right now. We can talk more later. . . or perhaps I can read to you to help you pass the time."

Kade didn't say anything as he listened to her settle back in her seat. His mind was too full of confusion at the moment. He had woken this morning to find his vision much improved. No doubt that was thanks to the liquids he'd consumed. His sight was almost back to normal, and the face he'd glimpsed just now had been pretty. Not exceptionally so, but certainly nothing to sneer at or turn away from in disgust. It left him a little bewildered and quite a bit angry on her behalf. What was the matter with these Englishmen that they would turn down a sweet woman like Averill? He wondered sleepily, then thought the answer might lie in the question. They were Englishmen.

Chapter Three

When Kade next awoke, it was to find Averill gone and Will seated at his side.

"Thank God you are awake. I thought I should go mad with boredom."

Kade raised an eyebrow at the irritated words and turned his head to better see his friend, his cheek coming up against the almost dry cloth that had previously been over his eyes. He reached up weakly to grab the thing, and Will immediately leaned forward to snatch it from him. He then stood and moved to a chest near the bed to dampen it again. "I came to tell you that Domnall, Ian, and Angus had left, but you were asleep. Before I could leave, Averill insisted I must sit and watch over you while she went below to have the nooning meal.

She is fetching back something for you to eat when she returns."

"I dinna need watchin'. I'm fine now," Kade growled, and frowned at how husky his voice still was.

"Aye, well, you were so sick we feared we would lose you. I suspect she will fret until you are back on your feet."

Kade grunted at the possibility, and waved him weakly away when he moved to replace the damp cloth over his eyes. "I dinna need that any longer."

Will hesitated. "Averill insisted you do. She said you were suffering headaches."

" 'Tis gone," Kade said, though a slight pounding still lingered on the edges of his consciousness. It was mild enough, however, that he would do without the cloth.

"Hmm."

When Will still stood there, looking as if he were debating whether to listen to him or Averill, Kade tried to distract him by asking the question that had plagued him into sleep. "Why are these men yer father is bringing around rejecting Averill?"

Will's eyebrows flew up, and the hand holding the cloth dropped to hang at his side as he considered the question. Kade saw the irritation marking his features and waited patiently.

"Her hair is part of the problem," Will said at last.

"What the devil is wrong with her hair?" Kade asked with amazement.

"I suppose you haven't really seen it, but her hair is orange," he announced with a grimace that suggested it was less than desirable.

Kade scowled at the description. The quick look he'd gotten of Averill had shown him lovely long hair made up of blond, strawberry blond, and fiery red tresses that all culminated in a bright mass of flame-colored hair he'd quite liked. It was not orange.

"I think it's fine," Will added. " 'Tis even pretty in a certain light, but red hair, especially orangey red, is not very popular among the English. There are some superstitions about it being the mark of the Devil and so on." He moved his hand as he spoke, unconsciously slapping the damp cloth he held against his leg in a repeated sign of irritation. "And then there is the birthmark on her cheek, which the superstitious also consider a mark of the Devil."

Kade frowned as he considered the flash of Averill that he'd seen. There had been a red mark on her cheek, a very small, red, strawberry-shaped spot one could almost mistake for a dimple. Hardly something any reasonable man would imagine was the mark of the Devil, but then he'd learned long ago that superstition was rarely reasonable.

"And, of course, she stammers," Will added on a sigh, drawing Kade's startled glance his way.

"Stammers?" he asked with surprise.

"Aye. Have you not noticed?" he asked, showing some surprise of his own.

"She's no' stammered while talkin' to me," Kade assured him.

"Really?" Will asked with sudden interest, the hand holding the cloth going still. "That is odd. While Averill does not stammer around family and friends, she always does when in the company of strangers, at least until she gets to know and is comfortable with them."

"Hmm," Kade murmured.

"Perhaps she does not stammer with you because you have not seen her yet," Will suggested. "If so, that would prove what I have always suspected."

"What is it ye've always suspected?" Kade asked.

"That she goes shy and quiet and stammers when she speaks only because she is self-conscious of her looks," Will said, then quietly admitted, "She was teased terribly as a child about both her hair and her birthmark. So much so that she avoided the other children and would play only with me." He sighed and turned to set the damp cloth on the chest beside the bowl of water. "If so, she will no doubt leave you to Mabs's tender mercies and avoid you, too, once she realizes that you can see properly again."

Kade scowled, not at all pleased at the idea of having only Mabs to tend him and keep him company until he was up and about. Not that he planned to lie abed long, but he had never been a very good patient and had always found an enforced stay in bed bothersome. The idea of spending the next few days with only Mabs and the occasional visit from Will to pass the time was not a pleasing one.

"Give me that compress." Kade held out his hand, only to pull it back with a frown when he saw how it shook weakly.

"What? Why?" Will asked with surprise.

"Because yer sister promised to read to me when I woke, and I'll no have her knowin' I can see and scared off because some stupid Englishmen have made her self-conscious about her looks. Put the damned compress back and let her think I am still havin' trouble with me eyes."

Amusement curled Will's lips as he moved to retrieve the damp cloth. His back to Kade, he asked curiously, "So is it that Mabs is dry as dirt and bossy? Or that my sister is sweet and you enjoy her company?"

"I've hardly been awake long enough to ken whether I enjoy yer sister's company," Kade pointed out dryly, though that wasn't entirely true. The room had seemed a bit brighter the two times he had been awake while she was there. Even the arrival of Will last night, and then him and his men this morning had not been as soothing as the few short moments when Averill was present.

"I suppose," Will acknowledged as he turned back with the cloth. "So I shall ask you that question again in a week or so and look forward to your answer."

Kade merely grunted, then stiffened in the bed

at the sound of the door opening. Without thinking, he turned to glance over to see who was entering and caught a quick glimpse of Averill. Her hair was unbound and flaming around her pretty, pale face as she entered, carefully balancing a tray in hand. His attention had just turned to the dark green gown she wore, and he was noting how it suited her coloring and emphasized her plump figure, when his vision was obscured by the cloth Will suddenly dropped over his face.

"There," the Englishman said loudly. "I am sure your vision will correct itself soon enough. Just keep the damp cloth on it and be patient for now."

"Are his eyes still troubling him then?" Averill's soft voice asked as the door closed. Her footsteps moved closer to the bed.

"'Tis still blurry," Will lied, sounding terribly glib. "I am sure 'twill improve as he regains strength though."

"Aye. I am sure you are right," Averill murmured, but she sounded concerned, and Kade felt a moment's conscience at tricking her like this. He even considered taking the cloth away and telling the truth, but then he thought of the old woman, Mabs, and being stuck with only her for company between quick visits from Will, and he let the lie stand.

"I see you have brought him his nooning repast," Will commented, as the scent of what Kade suspected would be more chicken broth reached his nose. His stomach immediately rolled over, letting him know it was hungry. However, he was hardly pleased at the prospect of another liquid meal. He needed solid food to rebuild his strength and was about to say as much when the other man added, "Bread and cheese, too? Is he ready for solid food, do you think?"

Kade could hear the teasing in his voice, but found himself rising to the bait and snapping, "Too right, I am."

Will chuckled with satisfaction, the sound moving away as he headed for the door. "Then I shall leave you to your meal and take myself off to the lists."

"I shall join ye soon," Kade promised.

"I am sure you will, friend," Will said, and the door closed, leaving the room silent but for the rustle of Averill's gown as she moved around the bed.

"How is your head?" she asked, the question accompanied by a sound he suspected was her setting down the tray.

Kade's hands itched to remove the cloth over his eyes, but he restrained himself, and admitted, "It aches a bit, but no' like it did."

"Then perhaps we can remove the cloth from your eyes long enough for you to eat," she murmured, and he felt her fingers brush against his face as she reached for the cloth. Kade blinked his eyes as she lifted it away and turned to set it back by the bowl of water. His gaze slid swiftly over her, taking in the hair so many disliked, then moving to the birthmark on her cheek. It was all as he recalled: a fall of glorious flame-colored waves and a tiny strawberry on her cheek. Neither what he would have considered ugly or disfiguring. And then she turned back and paused. Sucking her lower lip into her mouth, she nibbled at it worriedly, then asked, "C-can you see me?"

Kade's eyebrows rose at the tiny stammer and the way she lifted one hand as if to cover her birthmark. Recalling Will's suggestion that she might avoid him if she thought he could see her, he cleared his throat, and pointed out, "Will told ye that me vision is still blurred."

"Aye." She relaxed, her shoulders almost sagging with her relief, then smiled widely, appearing quite beautiful in that moment. "I just thought—Never mind, it does not matter," she interrupted herself, and turned to the tray of food she'd brought with her. "I brought you both broth and some watered-down ale, but also some bread and cheese. I thought if the liquids stayed down, you might like to try more solid food after."

"Aye." Kade sighed at the very thought. He'd rather just stick with the solids but had already learned that his stomach—like the rest of him—wasn't as strong as he would have liked.

"Here." She turned back with the broth in hand but paused and frowned, then set it aside and turned back to bend over him. "Let me help you sit up."

Kade grimaced at the need for aid but allowed her to help him sit and arrange the pillows behind

him so that he was upright to eat. She then retrieved the broth and held it to his lips, allowing
him to sip a bit.

"Your men have left for Scotland," she commented as she waited for him to swallow before
offering more. "It took hardly any time at all for
them to pack and make ready."

Kade smiled wryly around the mug she held to
his lips, knowing they'd had little enough to pack.
They'd arrived with nothing but the clothes on
their backs after three years in their prison and
left with little more. They would ride to Stewart
with the message of his well-being, then stop to
collect his chest from his uncle's on the way back
to Mortagne.

"Cook packed them some food to take for the
journey," Averill commented as she raised the
broth to his lips again. "She said they were very
polite for Scots."

Kade nearly burst out laughing at the—he was
sure—unintended insult, but his mouth was full of
broth, and he caught himself at the last moment to
keep from spitting it all over her.

"I am sorry," Averill murmured, seeming to realize what she'd said. "I just meant . . . well, most
Scots are a short, taciturn bunch, a-and—"

"'Tis all right," he said quickly, catching the
slight stammer and trying to ease her discomfort.
"Most Scots *are* a rude lot . . . But Domnall, Ian,
Angus, and I were all raised and trained by Ian's
da, me uncle Simon. While he's a lowlander, his

wife was English and 'twas from her we learned our manners."

"Oh." She smiled uncertainly, then cleared her throat, and asked, "How is your stomach? Could you manage any solid food, do you think?"

Kade glanced to the bowl, surprised to see that it was now empty. He lay still for a moment, paying attention to his stomach as she set the bowl aside and turned back to await his answer. While the broth he'd had that morning had left him feeling full and even a touch queasy, this time he felt fine. A bit full, but without the queasiness, so he murmured, "I'm thinkin' I could manage some solid food."

Averill smiled and reached for the cheese and bread on the tray. This, too, she fed to him, breaking off a bit of cheese, slipping it between his lips, then offering him a drink of mead in between it and a bit of bread. While he wanted to eat it all and rush his healing along, he managed only half the small bit of bread and cheese she'd brought before he professed himself too full to eat more. He was disappointed that he'd eaten so little, but she seemed to think he'd done well and assured him he'd be back to normal in no time at that rate.

"Shall I read to you now?" Averill asked several moments later as she closed the chamber door behind the maid she'd called to remove the tray.

"Aye," Kade said at once, then commented curiously, "In Scotland, 'tis rare fer a woman to ken how to read."

" 'Tis rare in England as well," she acknowledged. "However, Will was my only friend as a child, and I followed him everywhere, even into the classroom. When his teacher decided I was a quick learner with a fine mind, he stopped protesting my presence and set about teaching me as well." She smiled wryly, and added, "When Will left to train in swordplay and such at Lord Latham's, I think father kept our teacher on just to keep me busy. I continued my lessons for several more years and am proficient in English, Latin, French, and Spanish, as well as sums."

She settled back in her seat beside the bed and picked up an old, worn book he hadn't noticed lying on the chest, then admitted on a small sigh, "Unfortunately, intelligence is another strike against me in my father's hunt for a husband. I have been warned repeatedly to keep my learning to myself."

Though he knew what she said was true, Kade shook his head at the stupidity of it. He would think it a fine thing indeed to have an intelligent wife. His mother had been educated as a girl, and it had come in quite handy when she'd been forced to take over the running of Stewart from his father. That man had a problem with drink and was quite often too deep in his cups to manage it. She had taken on the chore without protest, then had seen to it that his sister, Merry, was educated as well. Kade had no prejudice against an educated woman.

He let that thought drift away as Averill began

to read. It quickly became obvious the story was one she'd read often and knew almost by heart. He wasn't surprised. Books were an expensive item and, wealthy as Mortagne appeared to be, he doubted even here, there were many books to choose from.

Relaxing back in the bed, he closed his eyes and allowed her voice to flow over him. One part of his mind was enjoying the life she gave to the characters and the tale she was recounting, while another part marveled that he was here, safe and comfortable in a soft bed, well fed, with a woman's sweet voice filling his ears after so long as a prisoner in a foreign land, with an empty belly, a hard stone floor for a bed, and little hope of ever enjoying anything else.

I could get used to this, Kade thought, and smiled slightly to himself.

Chapter Four

"Here you are, then."

Finished with her wash, Averill set the damp linen in the basin of water Bess had brought to her and turned to take the gown Bess held out. She froze, however, her hand drawing back when she saw which one it was. Eyes widening with horror, she breathed, "Nay."

Bess grimaced sympathetically. "Aye, your father said to dress you in your finest."

Averill closed her eyes, knowing what that meant. He only had her dress in her finest when she was going to be paraded before yet another prospective husband. The dark red gown Bess was holding out was indeed her newest and finest. It was also the one that had seen her repeated humiliations at the hands of rejecting suitors. Obviously, her father had decided on whom he wished next to approach about marrying her, and the suitor was arriving today.

She supposed she shouldn't be surprised. It had to happen sooner or later and more than a week had passed since the last would-be husband had rejected her so cruelly. That had occurred the day that Kade had awoken from his long sleep.

Despite her upset, Averill found herself smiling at the thought of her brother's friend. She had spent the better portion of this week in Kade's room, reading to him, talking to him and—after the second day—helping him walk to one of the chairs before the fire in the morning and back again at night so that he wasn't always stuck in his bed.

Kade was much improved from when he'd first woken. He no longer looked as pale and thin as he'd been on first awaking, and was even beginning to talk of joining Will at the lists. The only thing that hadn't improved yet was his sight. While Averill was concerned about that for his sake, for her own she was somewhat relieved, for she was not looking forward to his reaction when he was able to see properly again. Right now she was nothing but a voice and a blurry image to him, and she worried about what he would think of her when he saw her for the first time.

"Come now," Bess said bracingly. " 'Tis not as bad as all that. Mayhap this one will accept you to wife."

Averill let her breath out on a sigh and allowed

the maid to help her dress. Drink or no drink, she doubted very much if this time would end in anything but rejection either, but since her father had gone to the trouble of bringing the man here, she supposed she would have to go through with yet another humiliating inspection and rejection by a prospective husband.

Kade was hanging from the bed frame when the door suddenly opened. Freezing, he turned his head guiltily to see who had entered. Relief coursed through him when he saw that it was Will.

"You are exercising," his friend said with amazement as he pushed the bedroom door closed and crossed the room. "How long has this been going on?"

Kade grimaced but eased himself down. He released the top frame of the bed as his feet settled on the floor, and admitted, " 'Tis the third mornin' I've done so. Though," he admitted dryly, "the first morn I was no' able even to lift meself all the way up once."

"Hmm." Will nodded solemnly. "You have lost a goodly portion of the weight and strength we worked so hard to regain after escaping our prison."

Kade grunted at the observation and moved to sit in one of the chairs by the fire rather than return to his bed. He had started out trying to rebuild his strength the first day he'd had solid food. Averill had gone below to eat her dinner. She'd offered to send Mabs up with his meal, but he'd convinced her not to "trouble" the maid, that he could wait until she returned if she would not mind bringing it. The minute she'd left, he'd slid from the bed and tried to walk. Kade had only managed to take a few steps—and that while holding on to the bed—before his trembling legs had forced him back into bed. He hadn't given up, however, and was up again the next chance he got, forcing his legs to carry him a few more feet.

After the third day of solid food and walking, he was strong enough to pace his room several times, though he hadn't let anyone know. He'd then started trying to reclaim the muscles in his upper arms as well. As with his legs, it was slow going.

"Does Averill know?"

Kade shook his head quickly. "Nay, she'd fuss."

"Aye, she would," Will agreed with a wry smile. "She would fear you were rushing things and probably have you tied to the bed."

Kade smiled faintly at the idea. Averill could be the sweetest creature he had ever met, but when it came to the matter of his recovery, he had found her surprisingly stern.

"Mind you, she might be less concerned did we tell her you were able to see properly again."

Kade sighed at the words. They were true, and he couldn't deny it but found himself surprisingly reluctant to risk admitting he could see. The worry that she might avoid him once she knew was enough to make the idea unattractive to him. The girl had become the bright spot in his otherwise long and drab days. Kade enjoyed the hours they spent chatting of this and that, and was reluctant to see it come to an end and have her become uncomfortable and shy in his presence.

Though he would have to soon, Kade acknowledged to himself. The last week had seen him regaining enough health and strength that he was growing impatient to leave the room and begin working in the lists with Will. He wanted to build his strength back up to where it had been ere he and the others had been captured and imprisoned. But he also wanted to sit by the fire at night and enjoy the talks he normally had with Averill without her being self-conscious and shy.

"Where is she?" he asked suddenly. Hers was usually the first face he saw in the morning. She had taken to breaking her fast with him so that he need not eat alone. Will normally did not show up until after eating, and it was only for a quick visit before he headed to the lists.

"She is below," he answered. "She was instructing her maid, Bess, to bring you some mead, bread, cheese, and pasties when I headed up."

"Her maid?" he asked with surprise, ignoring the way his stomach rumbled at the mention of food. His appetite had been the first thing to return to normal. "Is she no' coming?"

"Nay, and 'tis lucky for you she is not, else

she would have been the one to find you up and about."

Kade shrugged that away, but explained, "I didna realize it was so late. 'Tis still quite dark out."

Will glanced toward the open shutters with a frown. "A storm is threatening." He grimaced and turned back to Kade to add, "In more ways than one."

"Oh?" he asked curiously.

"Father has arranged for another lord to arrive today to look over Averill with an eye to marriage."

Kade sat back in his chair, a scowl flickering over his face. "He'd best be kinder than the last oaf."

"Aye," Will agreed. "I nearly rammed his teeth down his throat when I heard what he'd said to Averill. There was no need to be so cruel." He scowled at the memory, then added with disgust, "And with Father's new grand plan, I fear this one could be a complete debacle."

"What is this new plan?" Kade asked curiously, then guessed, "Cover her hair and hide the birthmark with a smudge of dirt?"

"How did you know?" Will asked with surprise.

Kade snorted with disgust. Leave it to an Englishman to try such a trick. The man was not thinking straight. Averill would be the one to pay when the covering was gone and the dirt cleaned away and the groom discovered he'd been tricked. Besides, what message did this give to Averill?

That her father agreed with these men? That even he thought her looks unsightly?

"He means well," Will said sadly. "In truth, he is worried over his health and wants to see Averill settled and happy before he dies. He promised our mother on her deathbed that he would." He shook his head. "Unfortunately, he equates a woman's happiness with bearing babies and does not consider that an unhappy, bitter husband might be a stumbling block to Avy's happiness." Will ran his hands through his hair with frustration, and added, "And that is not even the worst of his new plan."

Kade raised an eyebrow. "There's more?"

"Oh, aye." Will's mouth twisted with disgust as he reminded him, "She stammers."

"Aye," Kade acknowledged, wondering what the father could possibly do about that, then asked with disbelief, "Has he ordered her no' to speak to the man? Will he present her, bundled up, dirty, and mute and expect to gain her a husband?"

"Not mute, no," Will said dryly. "He is down there right now making her drink whiskey."

"*What?*" Kade asked with disbelief.

"Aye. Father is sure if Averill would just relax around these men, she will not stammer, and he is equally sure whiskey will relax and loosen her tongue."

"Dear God," Kade breathed.

"Aye," Will said dryly. "Averill was trying feverishly to talk him out of it when I was below, but he was having none of that. When I tried to support her in convincing him, he suggested it may be better did I wait up here with you while Lord Seawell and his mother visit."

Kade's eyebrows flew up. "He sent ye to me room like a naughty boy? And ye let him?"

Will flushed, but said quietly, "He is my father . . . and my lord. The whiskey will not harm Averill and, much as this plan of his would suggest he's lost his mind, he has not, so I cannot disobey him. Well, not openly," he added with a grin. "I bribed Mabs and Bess to keep close and come to me if they think I need intercede."

"Harrumph," Kade muttered. He was tempted to intercede himself, but Lord Mortagne had not quibbled once about having Kade land on his doorstep and had provided a bed and care to both him and his men as he recovered and recuperated. And as Will said, the whiskey would not harm Averill. However, he decided, if this latest lord caused problems or hurt her in any way, it would not only be Will going below to tend to matters. Kade would be accompanying him. He might not have regained his full strength yet, but he could stand on his feet and swing a good fist and would be happy to do so for the woman who had spent so much time and care tending to him.

"So," Will said suddenly, "I asked you shortly after you awoke if you liked our Averill, and you claimed you hardly knew her. It has been a week. Do you not find Averill sweet and enjoy her company?"

Kade hesitated, a small frown plucking at his lips, then sighed and reluctantly admitted, "Aye."

Will knew him well enough that he narrowed his eyes, and said, "But?"

"She's almost too sweet," he admitted on a sigh. "There's no spark of passion in the lass. I'm no' a good patient. I get surly and cantankerous and more than once ha'e tried to prick her temper the last few days, but she doesna react at all except to grow sweeter still. 'Tis as if she has no temper at all."

Will raised his eyebrows. "And that's a bad thing?"

" 'Tis unnatural," he said firmly.

Will shook his head. "Not in England. At least, my own mother was just as sweet all the days of her life. 'Tis a trait admired by most Englishmen."

Kade's lips turned down with disgust. "Then yer fools. A woman'd no survive long in Scotland like that." He scowled. "Were bandits to beset Averill, I fear she'd thank them for troubling themselves."

Will chuckled at the suggestion but didn't argue it either. Instead, he sighed. "Then I suppose I should not suggest that you marry her?"

Kade gave a start at the words. "What?"

"Well, you did mention while we were imprisoned that did we ever escape, you would have to find a bride to bear your bairns ere you ever did anything so foolish again as rushing off on Crusade," he pointed out solemnly.

"And yer thinking Averill and I . . . ?" He didn't finish the question but sank back against the bed with a frown to consider the suggestion. But as much as he liked the girl, and while it would save him the trouble of hunting up a woman later, he could not imagine marrying and taking Averill home to Stewart.

Kade had a battle ahead of him when he reached his family's home. A few years before leaving on Crusade, he'd received a letter from his sister spelling out how matters went. Mother had died, and Merry had taken over the running of Stewart. Their father was still laird in name and threw his weight around when drunk, but mostly he was too sotted to run matters, or too hungover to do so. Little Merry was running Stewart and would do so until she wed as she'd promised their mother on her deathbed.

This news had immediately brought Kade home to Stewart, where he'd waited three days to find his father sober enough that he could broach the subject of taking over the task as laird himself rather than leaving it on Merry's shoulders. He had, obviously, broached the subject wrongly. His father had refused even to acknowledge that his wife had for years run Stewart and that Merry had now taken her place. He was the laird at Stewart. He made the decisions, he insisted. He ran the castle and all their people. He was the great Laird Stewart and had every intention of remaining so and Kade could go jump in a loch if he thought he would take the title from him ere he cocked up his toes.

His father had then, with Kade's two younger brothers backing him, suggested Kade get the hell off Stewart land.

Kade had left, and had someone asked him why at the time, his answer would have been the same as Will's for not interfering with his father's plans for his sister. Eachann Stewart was his father, his laird, and was of right mind. But while he'd believed that at the time, and while that might be true of Lord Mortagne, after thinking about it all these last years, Kade realized his father wasn't in his right mind at all. The drink had a hold of Eachann Stewart and was keeping him from being a proper laird, or even any kind of example for his two youngest sons.

That was what Kade was returning to, a possible battle to take over running Stewart, then no doubt a lot of hard work to set the place to rights if his sister's betrothed had claimed her and his drunken father and brothers had been running Stewart into the ground in a whiskey-induced haze these last years. As much as Kade liked Averill and had enjoyed his chats with her since waking, Stewart was no place for a sweet and gentle woman such as her. Dear God, she would not survive a month in such rough surroundings, he thought unhappily, and shook his head. Perhaps he would have risked it were there a little more fire under the sweetness, something to suggest she might thrive despite adversity, but . . . nay, he would not take her there just to see her grow weary and worn down by misery.

"Ah well," Will said on a sigh. "Then I suppose we shall have to hope Father's plan works."

When he grunted but didn't comment, Will turned the topic to other subjects. Kade listened, but his mind was on what might be happening below. Had the latest would-be husband arrived yet? How much whiskey had Lord Mortagne made Averill drink? Was it aiding her in not stammering? Would this would-be husband accept her to bride?

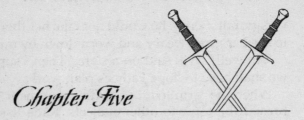

Chapter Five

"My lady, you have a bit of soot just here."

Had Averill not been concentrating so hard on not swaying in her seat as well as keeping down the meal now boiling around in the whiskey her father had made her drink, she would surely have tried to avoid the horrid little Lord Cyril Seawell as he reached out to brush at her cheek. She might even have turned to speak to his equally horrid mother, who sat on her other side. However, she *was* distracted with these other matters, was caught by surprise when he touched her, and instinctively scowled and knocked his hand away with irritation instead.

Really, the man kept *touching* her. Her hands, her face, her arm, even her leg. It was bad enough that he was sitting so close his thigh kept brushing against hers, but he also kept finding excuses to actually touch it with his fingers. A bit of fluff was on her gown, then a crumb of bread had needed brushing away . . . That one had been the excuse for running his hand up and down her outer thigh several times in a rather discomfiting manner.

Averill was having difficulty restraining a desire to punch the odious little man in the nose. And he was indeed both odious and little. He was actually about her own height of just over five feet, but that put him a head and shoulders shorter than both Kade and her brother.

Noting the way Lord Seawell's eyes narrowed at her rebuff, Averill forced a smile and murmured, "Is—It *is* all right, my lord. My maid shall tend it later."

She had to speak slowly to guard against slurring her words, but thought she'd made a good showing of it, so was surprised by the dreaded frown that returned to beetle between his eyebrows. The expression had been tugging at the man's face repeatedly since they'd sat down to the midday feast her father had arranged for Lord Seawell and his mother. It was really quite unattractive, she decided. But then the man himself was rather unattractive as well. Mousey brown hair fell in nasty, lank waves around a face sadly lacking in the fine features that made up Kade's handsome face.

However, Lord Seawell did have at least three times the mass Kade had. Unfortunately, most of it was in his belly. He definitely did not spend time in the lists as Will and her father did. Averill could only imagine that he depended on his soldiers' skills in swordplay, for she doubted he was any stronger than she, and she could not have wielded a broadsword with any competence.

Of course, Averill was not holding any of this against the man. She was sensible enough, even in her present inebriated state, to know that looks were not, and should not, be important. After all, she was ugly as sin with her red hair and marked face, and yet wished to be valued by someone, so was willing to overlook his form and consider the man beneath. Unfortunately, Lord Seawell was falling far short in that area as well. He wasn't nearly as intelligent or entertaining as Kade was. She had spent hours a day for a week talking to Kade about all and sundry, discussing their childhoods, his experiences while imprisoned and afterward in the monastery in Tunis. They had also discussed classic tales such as *Beowulf*, and even politics and religion. However, Lord Seawell appeared to be singularly lacking in opinion or knowledge on most of these subjects, and her efforts to talk to the man had fallen flat after only a few moments.

On the bright side, Averill reminded herself, her father's plan had worked. She hadn't stammered once . . . although she was showing a distressing tendency to want to slur instead.

"Most distressing," she decided.

"What was that?" Lord Seawell asked, leaning closer.

Averill was aware that it was just an excuse for him to try to look down the top of her gown again. He had done so repeatedly since arriving. While the other suitors had barely looked at her after their first glance, it seemed Lord Seawell intended to examine her *thoroughly* before making up his mind. She wondered suddenly if she shouldn't open her mouth so he could inspect her teeth as her father did with horses.

As if thinking of him stirred him to speech, her father suddenly cleared his throat, and said bluffly, "Well, perhaps once we finish our meal, you would join me by the fire for a chat, eh, Lord Seawell?"

"Of course, my lord," Cyril said easily. He then leaned close to Averill, his eyes dipping down her gown again as he murmured, "He wishes to know if I shall accept you to bride."

Averill raised a hand to cover her décolletage and murmured in what she hoped was an adequately interested fashion.

Apparently, it was satisfactory because Cyril straightened and smiled at her, then said, "I believe I shall say yes."

Averill's heart sank.

"And you should be grateful for it, my dear. After all, you have obviously inherited your mother's unfortunate coloring. Though it shows your good sense that you cover it, let us hope you do a better job once we are married."

Averill reached up to her face with alarm, noting that some of the wild, red tendrils had escaped the cloth cap Bess had stuffed her hair into at her father's behest.

"And you have those very tiny, almost nonexistent breasts," he added, startling her into glancing down at her chest. This was a new complaint. While previous men had mentioned her ugly hair, her birthmark and her god-awful stammering as reasons to refuse marrying her, this was the first complaint she'd had about her breasts.

Averill admitted that hers were certainly not overly large, but she did not think they were that small either, and at least they were not so large that she looked unbalanced and likely to tip over, as his mother, Lady Seawell, did. She wondered if that was not why he'd kept trying to look down her top, because he was disgusted by their very lack and trying to find them. Were they so small? she wondered. No one had ever said so before.

"And you do have a tendency to twitter away about nonsensical things," he added with a frown.

Averill answered with a frown of her own. She'd hardly spoken at all after the first few moments, mostly because she'd received little or no response from him. But if he thought the bit of talking she'd done today was twittering away . . . *Dear God.*

"Now Cyril, do not be unkind," his mother chided, leaning in to join the conversation. "Lady Averill cannot help it if she is ugly and sadly lacking a bosom. Besides, 'tis said Lord and Lady Mortagne were very happy, and she was just as homely. No doubt Lady Mortagne was so grateful that he married her that she did all she could to make him happy, and I am sure 'twill be the same with Averill here. She will do whatever you wish out of gratitude. Besides, once you snuff the candle, it will not matter what she looks like, and you can always fill her mouth to keep her from talking. Just think of the dower as you do your husbandly duty," the woman suggested, then laughed gaily at her own cleverness

"Is she right? Will you be grateful?" he asked, his eyes once again seeming to try to climb down to get a better look at those breasts he found so wanting.

Averill stared at him, her mind still stuck on what Lady Seawell had said. Snuff the candle, fill her mouth to keep her quiet and think of the dower? All while she lay there with his tubby little body smothering her in the bed as he panted and heaved over her. Her stomach churned violently, and she bit her lip, breathing through her nose in an effort to settle it. However, when he reached out quite suddenly and actually squeezed one of her breasts as if it were a melon he was checking for ripeness, Averill snapped and plowed her fist into his nose.

The man squealed like a girl, eyes wide, as he grabbed his nose and leapt to his feet.

Despite her churning stomach, Averill smiled the first smile she had since turning to see Bess holding out her red gown.

"Why you ungrateful wretch!" Lady Seawell

screeched, leaping to her feet to rush to her boy. "Cyril. Cyril darling, are you all right?" Grabbing his head, she clasped it to her massive bosom and turned on Averill. "You horrible, ungrateful girl! How dare a mealy-faced, red-haired creature like yourself touch my boy?"

He touched me first, Averill thought, but when she opened her mouth to say so, her rebellious stomach cast out her lunch on the floor at the woman's feet.

"And then what happened?" Will asked.

"Aye, finish it, lass," Kade growled. While he really wanted to go below and hammer Cyril, he also wished to know all that had happened, so he could give him the punishment he deserved. Kade wouldn't want to merely beat the man and find out he should have killed him.

Kade's gaze slid over the woman lying on his bed. He and Will had been talking quietly when Bess had burst into the room and told them that Averill had punched Lord Cyril and all hell had broken out below. He and Will had headed down at once, only to encounter Averill on the stairs. One look at her pallid face and the way she was swaying as she clutched at the rail had distracted him from the shouting below. Leaving her father to deal with Lord Seawell by himself, he and Will had each caught one of Averill's arms and ushered her up the last few steps. Since his room at the top of the stairs was closest, they'd taken her there.

Averill now lay flat on her back on the bed he'd occupied this last week, a cold compress over her eyes as she told them what had happened. Much to his fascination she'd done so not only in slurred words but also in most unsweet ones. Kade found himself unable to take his eyes away from the creature in his bed. She was a changeling. Certainly not the sweet, passionless creature who had hovered over him since his waking. It seemed the girl had a temper after all and had a rather varied and vulgar list of curse words rattling around in her head, for she'd used several to describe the loathsome Cyril Seawell.

"Oh." Averill waved one hand weakly, then released a gusty sigh. "The old cow was ranting on about how ungrateful I was and how I should be kissing her son's feet and bathing them with my tongue in gratitude for even considering me to bride, and I was trying to keep down luncheon and dared not open my mouth to respond. However, I was so exceedingly sick to death of the old bitch's rambling and completely ridiculous rantings—" She paused to sneer with disgust, and muttered, "As if I would lick any part of that addle-pated oaf of a son of hers, let alone his feet."

Will's eyes widened in horror at her words, but Kade found himself grinning as she continued. "And then the old battleaxe snapped, 'Well? Are you going to apologize for such heathen behavior?' and I opened my mouth to tell her to sod off. I got the words out, but before I could close my mouth, my lunch spewed out. I got the skirt of her gown." She sighed at the memory, the bottom of the damp cloth fluttering slightly, then her lips thinned out, and she added, "And I am not sorry. Can you imagine having that mean old harpy for a mother-in-law? Dear God, even without the whiskey to shake my reserve, I could never hold my temper with her."

"But Averill, you do not have a temper," Will protested with dismay, then frowned at the ridiculousness of the claim considering what he'd just heard. "I mean you have never shown a temper before. You have always been sweet and most temperate."

"Because Mother insisted I must be and helped me learn to control it," she said quietly. "The day after I tried to run away and kicked the captain of the guard, she started to teach me to control it."

"Run away?" Will looked shocked. It was obvious he knew nothing about any of it.

"How did she teach you, Averill?" Kade asked quietly. For teaching a five-year-old anything was quite difficult, but trying to make one go against her own nature was nearly impossible.

"Every time I lost my temper, she made me take a bath in cold water." Her voice was almost absent as she said it, with no sign of rancor at the punishment . . . and punishment it would have been, Kade thought grimly. He couldn't imagine anyone forcing a child to sit in cold water. Aside from unpleasant, it was surely dangerous to risk her catching a chill like that.

Averill suddenly snatched the compress away and scowled up at her brother. "I suppose you hate me now."

"Nay, of course not," Will said at once, then grinned, and added, "Actually, I rather like you like this. Where did you learn to curse that way?"

"From you," she said dryly, dropping the compress back over her face. "And from the soldiers who man the wall. They are forever shouting curses back and forth, and I hear it all from my chamber when the shutters are open."

"Hmm, I shall have to take more care in the future and perhaps speak to the men on the wall," Will muttered, but he seemed more amused than anything. He then turned to Kade and arched an eyebrow. "Is she still too sweet?"

Kade turned to peer at the girl. She had pulled the compress away again, and her beautiful green eyes were shifting from one man to the other with suspicion. The bonnet she'd worn to meet Lord Seawell had been discarded, and her tresses now lay splayed over the bed on either side of her head, fiery locks he'd like to gather in his hands and press to his face. Her cheeks were flushed with color from her temper, her sweet, soft lips twisted with irritation, and he'd never seen her look more beautiful.

"Nay," he growled. "I'll have her."

Will grinned and slapped his shoulder happily. "Welcome to the family."

"What?" Averill sat up, confusion on her face. "Whatever are you—" She stopped abruptly, one hand going to her stomach, the other to her head. She closed her eyes with a moan, opened them again, and gasped, "Why will this accursed room not stay still?"

Kade stepped to the side of the bed, pushed her back to lie flat with one hand, then returned the cold compress to her face. "Rest. The room'll right itself do you do so."

She resisted him briefly, but then gave in and allowed herself to flop back on the bed with a miserable little sigh. "I shall never drink again."

Kade waited a moment, but when she stayed still and seemed to drift off to sleep, he glanced to Will. "I'll talk to yer father."

"I will come with you," Will announced, following when he started across the room. Kade had just arrived at the door and reached out to pull it open when sounds from the bed caught his ear. He glanced back in time to see Averill lunge upward, retching violently.

"I'll fetch her maid," Will said at once, hurrying from the room as Kade rushed back to Averill.

"You're awake."

Averill reluctantly reopened her eyes. She'd blinked them open a heartbeat ago, only to groan as candlelight attacked her, sending pain through her head. This time was no better, and she moaned and closed them once more.

"Head paining you?" Bess asked.

Averill opened her mouth to answer but paused on a sigh of relief as a cold, damp cloth was laid over her eyes and forehead.

"Oh, Bessie, bless you," she whispered, as the cool damp began to ease the drumming in her head.

"I have a tonic here when you think your stomach can stand it," Bessie announced.

Averill grimaced at the very thought of consuming anything. On the other hand, it would be nice were her head not throbbing so. She would wait a few moments, she decided. "What time is it?"

"Late," Bess answered abruptly. "Most of the castle has gone to bed."

Averill bit her lip and then asked, "Am I in my own bed?"

A soft chuckle disturbed the air over her head, and Bess said, "Aye, though that Scot fussed about it. He wanted to look after you himself, and did for several hours this afternoon before I suggested 'twas time Will moved you to your own room."

"Kade?" she asked with surprise, then groaned again as recollections began to assault her. Memories filled her mind of his holding her hair back and murmuring soothingly to her in Gaelic as she'd retched up the last of her stomach's contents. "Dear God."

"He was gentle with you, and kind," Bess said, sounding surprised. "He'll be a good husband."

"Husband?" Averill asked with shock, and reached up to tug away the damp cloth to see the maid's face. She saw two of them, both spinning and dancing and slightly out of focus. It made her head hurt, but her stomach appeared fine at least, she noted, and frowned at the woman. "What are you talking about?"

"Kade has offered for your hand, and your father accepted. Actually," Bess added dryly, "he was most grateful for the offer. Your father was lamenting into a mug of whiskey that no one would accept you to wife once this debacle reached court when Kade made his way below stairs and offered for you."

Averill stared at the kind old faces dancing before her, her brain incapable of accepting the suggestion. "He did not."

"Aye, he did," Bess assured her, then asked uncertainly, "Is that not good news? I thought you liked the boy."

"Aye, I do like him," Averill admitted. "That is the problem. I cannot possibly marry him."

"Eh?" Bess's double images frowned with confusion. "But if you like him—"

"Have the contracts been drawn up and signed?"

"The marriage contracts?" Bess asked, and when Averill nodded, she shook her head. "They are doing those tomorrow. Tonight he just asked and your father agreed, then they celebrated. No doubt your father will have a sore head in the morning as well."

"Then it can still be called off," Averill said with relief, and forced herself to sit up. The room immediately began to move around her, but she ignored it and slid her feet to the floor.

"Here now, where do you think you're going?" Bess was on her feet at once, trying to stop her. "And what do you mean, called off? Why the devil would you want to do that? You *like* him, and he you. What—?"

"He cannot see straight, Bess," she pointed out impatiently.

"Well, I'm not so sure about that, but even so, what does it matter? He apparently likes you well enough to offer."

"I would not have him disappointed when his vision clears, and he is able to see me properly," Averill said unhappily, trying to stand.

"My lady," Bess began firmly, pushing her back to sit on the bed. "I am sure he will not be disappointed. In fact—"

"You cannot be sure," Averill argued. "And he should at least know what he is getting."

"Mayhaps, but—"

"I shall just go tell him that my hair is red and about the birthmark and my too-small breasts and—"

"Too-small breasts?" Bess interrupted on almost a shriek. "Where the devil did you get that nonsense?"

"From Lord Seawell," she admitted on a sigh. "He seemed to think they were too small. He was very disgusted and couldn't stop staring or trying to touch them."

"Oh, aye, disgusted he was," she said dryly and rolled her eyes, but she also stepped out of the way. "Go on then. Go explain to the Scot that your hair's as red as a setting sun, that you've a tiny strawberry on your cheek, and that your breasts are too small. But I've no doubt he already knows all this and will still have you."

"Mayhap," Averill murmured as she got carefully to her feet. "But I'll not risk the discontent on his face when he realizes what a poor bargain he made."

"Hmm," Bess muttered, then raised an eyebrow as Averill peered down at herself.

"I am in my nightgown," she said, surprised, though she supposed she shouldn't be. After all, she had been in bed. She was just amazed that she hadn't woken up for it.

"Aye, you are, and I am not going to the trouble to dress you at this hour." She pulled a fur from the bed and hung it over Averill's shoulders. "There ye are, now go on."

"But 'tis not decent," she protested.

Bess shrugged. "What can they do if they catch the two of you together like this but order you to marry?"

Averill narrowed her eyes on the woman. "You would like that, would you not?"

"Aye, I would, and so should you," Bess said firmly. "He'll be a much better husband than any of the others your father has dragged here to Mortagne."

Averill scowled at her briefly, acknowledging that it was true. Kade would make a much better husband than any of the rude, cruel men who had rejected her to date. He was kind, and sweet, and funny, and she enjoyed talking to him, and thought him handsome, and . . . She couldn't bear to see the same disgust on his face as had been on the others. She had to talk to him, but Bess obviously would be of no help. Averill half suspected that if she did go to Kade's room like this, the woman would go fetch her father and bring him to the room to ensure the marriage *had* to take place.

"The morning is soon enough to talk to him," she announced grimly, throwing off the fur and climbing back into bed. "I shall just have to be sure to wake early and speak to him before he and Father can sign the contracts."

Bess relaxed and nodded as she began to tug the linen and furs up around Averill. "A sound idea, and I shall wake you."

Averill snorted with disbelief at the claim but closed her eyes and forced herself to relax.

"Good sleep, my lady," Bess said quietly.

"Good sleep," Averill answered grimly, and listened to the rustle of the woman crossing to the chamber door. She heard it open, and close, then the patter of footfalls as the maid moved away up the hall. She waited another moment before opening her eyes.

The room was dark and still. Bess had taken the candle with her, and it was summer, so there was no fire in the hearth. Unlike her old nursemaid, Averill did not care for a fire in the summer. 'Twas a damned shame, she thought now, for the light would have been helpful.

Grimacing, she sat up and peered around the room, hoping her eyes would adjust. She had no intention of waiting until morning to speak to Kade. She didn't trust Bess to wake her in the morning in time to stop the signing of contracts either.

Her eyes weren't adjusting any, Averill acknowledged with a small sigh, and forced herself to start moving. She knew her room well and should be able to find her chest and don a gown without light to aid her.

Averill found the chest by stubbing her toe on it. Crying out, she grabbed for her foot and hopped twice on the other foot before crashing into the second chest and tumbling to the floor with a curse. She lay still for a moment, taking inventory, but once assured she'd done herself no permanent injury, crawled to her feet and felt around until her hand brushed against stone. It only took a moment for her to realize she'd found the edge of the fireplace. Averill set her hand flat on the rock at the top of the mantel, trailed her fingers over one block, then two, but paused at the third to feel around for the tiny indentation at the bottom. Sighing her relief when she found it, Averill pulled on it, the breath whooshing from her when the wall before her slid away, sending a gust of damp and dusty air puffing into her face.

Wrinkling her nose at the smells of age, cobwebs, and mildew, she hesitated and peered into this new kind of darkness. The yawning darkness before her was so silent and still she could almost believe there was a whole pack of rats or some other nasty creatures in the tunnel ahead, holding their breath to see if she would enter.

Feeling a shudder run down her back at the thought, Averill decided that was most unhelpful thinking and forced herself to move forward into the tunnel. She then turned right toward the room Kade was occupying. He happened to be in a room Averill had used as a playroom as a child. She had often made this journey and thought she knew the way by heart. However, as a child, she'd never done so without a candle, and now thought she must have been much smarter then.

The floor in Averill's room was covered with fresh-smelling rushes that were changed when necessary. The floor in the tunnel was not, and she grimaced at the gritty feel of the dirt and detritus that had gathered over time as it ground into her feet. It made her wish she'd taken the trouble to dress after all. At least then she would have thought to don shoes as well.

Averill no sooner had the thought than she set her foot down on something that was neither stone nor dirt. It was soft under her heel and—with visions of dead rats in mind, or possibly even live ones—she squealed and scampered forward willy-nilly for several feet before realizing how foolish that was and forcing herself to a halt. Standing completely still, she waited for her heart to stop racing, her ears straining for any little scampering sounds that might tell her what she'd encountered. When nothing but the sound of her own breathing reached her ears, she bit her lip and tried to work out how far she might have run.

Had she passed the entrance to Kade's room? Surely she'd not gone that far? Damn! She had no idea where she was now.

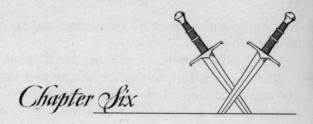

Chapter Six

"Did you hear that?"

Kade raised his eyebrows at Will's question. They had been sitting talking quietly in his room since coming above stairs after celebrating Lord Mortagne's acceptance of his proposition to marry Averill. Will seemed pleased at the coming union, and Kade was feeling rather pleased himself. He liked the girl, he enjoyed talking to her, thought she was attractive, and—now that he knew she wasn't the sweet, weak flower he'd thought—was happy to take her to wife. Any lass who had survived a childhood of cold baths to cool her temper should have no problem with a Scottish winter.

"It sounded like . . ."

"A squealing pig?" Kade suggested, his gaze

moving to the wall where the sound had seemed to come from.

"Aye," Will muttered, and moved to the wall.

Kade watched curiously as he stopped beside the mantel and counted several rocks over. He did something to a stone and eased the wall open a crack.

"What—?" Kade began, but paused when the other man raised a hand for silence. He then got to his feet and moved toward the wall when Will paused to listen, a frown cresting his face. He was next to Will before he heard the voice coming from the crack in the wall. He listened briefly, stiffening when he recognized Averill's voice. She appeared to be talking to someone. Kade had just deduced that she was muttering to herself about never finding his room, or her own for that matter and being lost in the walls forever when Will eased the wall closed.

"What're ye doin'? Averill is lost in there," Kade muttered, pushing on the wall and frowning when it didn't move.

"I thought you would want me to leave first," Will explained. "She obviously wishes to speak to you."

The Englishman turned back toward the wall and reached for the rock he'd touched earlier to open the door, and Kade quickly caught his arm. "Aye. Mayhap ye'd best leave. She may wish to talk about the weddin' and may be embarrassed does she ken ye know o' her creepin' around in the night."

Will nodded, then gestured to the rock he'd

fiddled with the first time he'd opened the door. "There is a lever at the bottom. Pull it up, and the door will open."

Kade nodded, then waited until Will slipped out of the room before turning back to the wall to find the lever in question. Kade pulled on it and the door slid open a few inches. He paused at the sound of Averill's continued mumbling and pushed it all the way open and stepped into the tunnel. He'd expected to see her coming his way, a candle in hand. What he saw was a dark so thick it could have been a cloth over his eyes. The tunnel was also suddenly deathly quiet. He couldn't even hear her breathe.

"Averill?" he said.

"Kade?" The name came out on a whoosh of relief, and he heard the patter of her feet as she rushed forward. She threw herself at him and hugged him briefly. Kade didn't even get the chance to raise his arms to hug her back before she overcame her relief and gratitude, recalled herself, and stepped back with an apology.

"I am sorry, my lord. 'Tis just I feared I would be stuck in here wandering the tunnels forever like some horrible ghost." She paused suddenly and raised sharp eyes to his face. "How did you know to open the tunnel?"

"I heard ye squeal, lass," he said easily.

"Aye, but how did you know—"

"Ye told me about the tunnels that first night I woke," he interrupted.

"Oh, aye," she muttered, and didn't seem to notice that he hadn't really answered her question. She appeared too eager to get inside to worry about it and slipped past him into the room with a little sigh of relief.

Kade followed, pulling the tunnel door closed. Dear God she was a mess. Cobwebs caught in her hair, smudges of dirt on her face and chemise—a very thin, almost gossamer chemise that left little to the imagination, he noted, then forced his eyes away as she turned to face him.

Averill was wringing her hands anxiously, her face screwed up with worry, and then she blurted, "Bess told me that you have spoken to my father about marrying me."

Kade stiffened, but nodded. "Aye. Diya no wish to marry me, lass?"

"Nay," she said quickly. "I mean nay, 'tis not that I do not wish it," she explained impatiently, then added, "But you may not once you know the truth."

He felt his eyebrows rise at her words. "What truth would that be?"

She hesitated, looking completely miserable and really quite adorable with the smudges on her face. "That I am ugly, my lord."

Kade felt himself relax. For a moment he'd worried there was something he didn't know. That even Will didn't know about to tell him—a tendre she held for someone, or a past indiscretion perhaps. He was relieved to know it was nothing like that, just her belief that she was ugly, one instilled in her by others over the years . . . and all because of foolish superstitions.

He'd decided this evening that once they were married he would have to make an effort to build up her self-esteem and convince her that what those other suitors had said wasn't true. It appeared, however, that he would have to do that sooner rather than later. To that end, he cleared his throat, then said, "Yer no ugly."

Averill stared up at the ever-so-sweet man before her and sighed unhappily. She should have known this would happen. He couldn't see her and perhaps didn't wish to believe that what she said was true. She rather wished it wasn't true herself. However, it was, and she'd not allow the man to marry her without first understanding what he was getting.

" 'Tis kind of you to say so, and I do appreciate it," she assured him gently, then pointed out, "Howbeit you cannot see properly and so, of course, cannot see how my hair is an ugly orange, or—"

"I can see yer hair," he growled. " 'Tis no orange. 'Tis a mixture o' blonde and red. I like it."

She blinked in surprise, then realized that he might actually see her hair. He had said his vision was blurry, but that did not affect color. "Really?" she asked finally. "You like my hair?"

He scowled, but nodded, and then—looking exceedingly uncomfortable—added, "It puts me in mind o' a late-summer sunset."

Her eyes went wide at the words. No one had ever described her hair so nicely. A soft smile played about her lips for a moment, but then she sighed, and said, "Mayhap you do not mind the color, but I also apparently have no breasts to speak of."

"Ye—*What*?" he asked with disbelief, and his eyes lowered to her chest, narrowing in an effort to see them better. Judging by the bewilderment on his face, he could no better see them now than he had all week. "What the devil are ye talking about woman? Ye've breasts."

Averill flushed at the disgruntled claim. "Well, aye, I have them, but not bosomy breasts."

"Bosomy?" he asked with confusion.

"You know . . ." She held her hands before her own small breasts as if holding great, heavy melons, and repeated, "Bosomy breasts. Big, womanly ones."

When his expression didn't change one iota, she tried to think of another way to explain, then brightened and said, "They are like plums compared to melons, my lord. Not completely flat, but not large either."

"Plums are nice," he muttered, his gaze still locked on her breasts.

Realizing he still wasn't comprehending, Averill pondered how she was to make it clear to him when he could not see properly. She worried her lip briefly, then recalled how Lord Seawell had groped her and reached for one of Kade's hands. While Lord Seawell's groping had earned him a punch in the nose, *he* was not suffering vision problems and it did seem to her that if Kade could not see them, she would just have to show him. 'Twas better an uncomfortable moment or two now than years of suffering his bitter regret later.

"What—?" Kade began, then seemed to almost choke on the next word as she raised his hand and pressed it against one small breast.

"You see?" she asked unhappily, trying to ignore the strange tingling that had suddenly started in the breast his hand covered. "They are rather small. At least Lord Seawell seemed to think so. I had never noticed it myself. I mean, I did not think them large, but they are not the smallest in the keep, and—" She paused on a sigh. "Lord Seawell seemed to think them lacking, and I would not have you marry me without knowing their size and complaining later."

Kade's mouth opened and closed several times before he managed a strangled, "Er . . ."

Averill sighed with disappointment. It seemed she need not explain her other failings. As with Lord Seawell, the size of her breasts must be important to him, and he was now struggling to sort out how to tell her he had changed his mind. Clearing her throat, she said quietly, "You need not worry that I shall hold you to the offer to marry me, my lord. I would not—"

Averill's words ended on a gasp of surprise as Kade reached out with his other hand, caught her behind the neck, and drew her forward to cover her mouth with his. Eyes wide, she found herself staring at his ear and the side of his head as his mouth moved over her slightly parted lips. It was soft and questing at first, then his tongue slid out and rasped its way into her mouth. Her eyes closed against the riot of sensation stirring through her. His hand was no longer quiescent on her breast, but was now squeezing the orb through her thin chemise and lifting it as if testing its weight.

Averill couldn't stop the moan that slipped from her mouth into his as he then began to pluck at the nipple. Much to her regret, the sound seemed to recall him to the moment, for he broke the kiss. Rather than straighten away from her, however, his mouth trailed away to her ear and his hand continued to knead and pluck at her breast as he whispered, "No' a plum. An apple, and I like apples."

"You do?" Averill breathed, her head tilting of its own accord as he began to nibble at her ear.

"Aye. Verra much."

"Oh." She sighed and leaned unconsciously into the hand at her breast. "I like apples, too."

Kade chuckled, his breath blowing across the skin he'd just dampened, and Averill shivered and instinctively turned her head back to find his lips again. He allowed it, claiming her mouth as she silently requested, his tongue coming out again, this time for a more thorough inspection. As it wrestled with her own, then ran across her teeth, Averill was reminded of the thought she'd had that afternoon that she should open her mouth so Lord

Seawell could examine her teeth . . . which led her to remember that she had not informed Kade of all her faults yet.

Perhaps it didn't matter, she thought hopefully, and moaned as the hand at her neck dropped down to clasp her bottom and urge her lower body against his. She sighed into his mouth and turned her head away to break the kiss. It did matter. She liked Kade and had to be sure he knew what a poor bargain he was making.

"I stammer," she gasped as soon as her mouth was free of his. " 'Tis most—Oh!" She gasped with surprise as he suddenly stepped back and dropped into one of the chairs before the cold hearth, tugging her onto his lap as he went. He tried to capture her lips again, but Averill avoided his mouth and repeated almost desperately, "I stammer."

"Ye doona stammer with me," he said simply and turned his attention to the breast he'd been kneading, tugging the top of her chemise aside so that he could touch and fondle the breast he'd revealed.

"I . . . I . . . Ohhhh," Averill moaned, and clutched at his shoulders as his mouth suddenly bent to her breast and closed over the now-erect nipple. She closed her eyes, swallowing thickly, as heat exploded through her. This was really the most amazing—

Shaking her head, she forced herself back to what she was supposed to be doing. Flaws. Which ones had she listed? Hair, breasts, stammer . . . What the devil was the other—Oh yes! Catching his head, she forced him away from her breast to meet her gaze.

"I have a birthmark on my cheek. 'Tis quite large and ugly and—" Averill paused abruptly as he began to chuckle. Eyes narrowing, she asked, "What, pray, do you find so funny, my lord?"

"You," he admitted gently, then said, " 'Tis no' large or ugly. 'Tis quite small, barely the size of the nail on your baby finger, and at first I mistook it for a dimple. 'Tis adorable."

Averill's eyes widened at this claim, then closed in brief defeat as his lips covered hers once more. It was simply impossible to argue with his tongue in her mouth. Besides, she didn't really want to argue. She wanted him to continue doing what he was doing, kissing her and touching her and— She moaned and sank against his chest as he resumed caressing her breast again, then just as quickly stiffened and broke the kiss again as a thought struck her.

"How do you know 'tis small and shaped like a straw—" She paused and thrust herself off his lap, gasping, "You mistook it for a dimple? You can *see* me?"

"Aye." Kade tugged her back onto his lap despite her efforts to avoid it, then holding her there, he met her gaze, and said, "My vision had cleared by the second morning I was awake."

"The s-second— B-but—"

He covered her mouth with his hand, bringing

an end to her stammering. When she stilled, he said solemnly, "Will said ye were self-conscious of yer looks and might stammer or avoid me did ye ken I could see ye. I wished yer company, so when he claimed I still could no' see, I let the lie stand."

Kade waited a moment for that to sink in, then took his hand away. "Yer hair is glorious, and the birthmark charming, ye doona stammer around me, and I like yer breasts. I'm happy to take ye to wife. The question now is, will ye have me?"

Averill stared at him with disbelief. While she was pleased that he seemed content with the size of her breasts, after so many rejecting her because of her hair and birthmark, it was hard to believe he liked both of those. However, he had no reason to lie that she could think of. Averill supposed he could be trying to prevent her thinking he wished to marry her mostly for her dower. She didn't know why he would bother, however. That was only to be expected, it was why hers was so generous, why dowries even existed at all, to lure a husband. In fact, Averill would have been surprised had someone claimed it wasn't the reason he was interested in marrying her. . . . He was right about the fact that she didn't stammer around him, however, Averill realized quite suddenly, and wondered why that was.

"Avy?" He used the nickname Will had always called her and gave her a little shake, drawing her attention back to him. "Will ye have me?"

"Aye, but—" Her attempt to tell him her final flaw,

that she had a temper, was halted when he kissed her again. Averill tried to keep her wits about her so that she could gasp out the confession the first chance she got, but it was most difficult to think with the upheaval he was causing in her. His tongue was dueling with hers again, and somehow her chemise had got pushed off her shoulders to pool around her waist, leaving her bare from the waist up. His hands were taking full advantage and now covered both her breasts, squeezing and kneading, tugging and pinching so that she moaned and wiggled in his lap. The action made her aware of a strange hardness under her bottom, and she wondered briefly what it was before Kade suddenly broke their kiss to lower his head to her breast again.

"I have a temper," Averill breathed almost dreamily in the brief moment before his mouth latched onto her breast.

"Aye," he growled against her flesh. "I like that, too." Then his tongue slid out to rasp her nipple, and she let the matter go. She didn't really believe he liked her temper, but it mattered little since she always controlled it anyway. She would just have to be sure she did not drink again as her father had made her that morning.

Satisfied that she had confessed all her flaws and that Kade could not now be surprised or disappointed, Averill slid her fingers into his hair and leaned her head back with a moan as he suckled and nipped at first one breast, then the other. She was aware that he had shifted one hand to her back, keeping her from overbalancing, but it was his mouth and his other hand that had her real attention. Kade's mouth was driving her wild as he feasted on her, and his hand was sending little shivers through her as it slid up and down her leg over the chemise, moving closer and closer to the apex of her thighs each time.

Stomach muscles jumping with excitement, Averill instinctively allowed her legs to spread on his lap. When his fingers then reached high enough that they brushed against the very core of her through the gossamer cloth, she groaned and clasped at his head almost desperately as her back arched, hips shifting on his lap.

"Oh, Kade," she breathed, legs closing around his hand, only to open again in the next heartbeat. But when his fingers brushed against her again, more firmly this time, the sensations it caused were overwhelming and even frightening. Panting, Averill closed her legs once more and gasped, "I cannot—"

"Aye. Ye can," he assured her, letting her nipple slip from his mouth to claim her lips even as his fingers drifted away.

Averill felt a moment's regret, but then his hand slid under her chemise, skimming up her bare skin until it reached her core. This time there was nothing in the way as his fingers brushed over the core of her.

He broke their kiss to whisper, "Yer wet fer me."

"I am sorry," Averill gasped with embarrassment

as she became aware of the dampness he spoke of, and for some reason that made him chuckle.

" 'Tis good," he growled, then claimed her lips once more.

This kiss was different than the others. While those had been gentle and questing, this one was hard and demanding. His tongue thrust into her mouth like a sword, filling her and forcing out any embarrassment at the moisture gathering between her legs. His fingers continued to play over her, more firmly now, and when she groaned this time, his mouth caught it, muffling the vibration between them.

Averill moved her hands to his shoulder, unconsciously digging in with her nails. She began to kiss him back fervently, with more passion than technique as her hips shifted instinctively into the caress. She was vaguely aware that the hardness under her bottom had somehow grown larger and more firm, and when Kade groaned into her mouth, Averill worried that her shifting against it was digging whatever it was into his lap and hurting him, but she couldn't seem to help herself. With every caress of his fingers, her body arched and writhed as if moving to music only it could hear.

She was just becoming aware of something easing into her, and stiffening at the alien sensation, when a knock sounded at the door.

Kade stilled, and they both seemed to hold their breath, then the knock sounded again.

Sighing, he broke their kiss and leaned his forehead against hers, breathing, "I'm goin' to kill yer brother."

"Will?" she asked in a whisper. "Why?"

Kade merely sighed again, shook his head, and urged her to stand up as the knock sounded a third time.

When he got to his feet and moved toward the door, she caught at his hand to stop him. "You cannot answer the door while I am here. Wait until I—"

Kade silenced her with a quick kiss. When he raised his head, he said dryly, " 'Twill be Will, and do I not answer, he'll just keep knockin'. I'll send him away."

He moved off before she could protest further, but afraid Bess had realized she'd come to see Kade after all and was coming to try to trap him into marrying her, Averill didn't take the time to argue with him. She snatched the candle off the mantel and scampered for the door into the tunnels.

She raced the length to her room, the candlelight briefly illuminating an old rag doll she'd thought she'd lost as a child. It was obviously the soft thing she'd stepped on earlier, and while Averill felt a moment's relief at the knowledge, she didn't take the time to slow down and grab the dear item. She was in too much of a panic to get to her room and close the tunnel door.

* * *

"Go away," Kade growled when he saw Will standing in the hall. He started to close the door, but Will put his foot out to stop him.

"I just wanted to know—Oh. Were you sleeping?" he asked, surprise replacing the determination on his face as he peered into the room beyond him.

Kade glanced over his shoulder, eyebrows rising when he saw that the room was in darkness. Averill had taken the one lit candle in his room and fled.

"How did she manage that?" he muttered. The light in the room had been wavering but still there as he'd reached for the door handle. The only thing he could think was that she must have closed the tunnel door just as he opened this one.

"Ah-ha!" Will said, drawing his head back around. "So she *was* still here."

"Aye." He scowled at his friend. "And ye interrupted a verra important talk we were havin'."

"Oh?" He arched an eyebrow, looking amused rather than apologetic. Snatching the torch from the sconce beside the door in the hall, he pushed past him into the room. "Tell me all about it."

Kade shifted on his feet, considering tossing his friend out on his rear and going in search of Averill, but then decided this might be for the best. The way things had been going, they were like to anticipate their wedding night were he to be alone with her again.

"Here, put this back."

Kade took the torch Will had used to light another candle and leaned out into the hall to replace it in its sconce. He then pulled the door closed and followed Will to the chairs by the fire. When the other man settled in the very chair he and Averill had been occupying just moments ago, Kade was recalled to what his arrival had interrupted. It made him scowl irritably at his friend as he settled in the opposite seat.

"So?" Will prompted when he didn't speak up at once. "What happened?"

Sighing, Kade relaxed back in his chair and shrugged. "She came to warn me o' her faults."

"Which ones?" Will asked curiously.

"Her hair, her birthmark, her stammering, her bosoms, and her temper," he muttered.

"I have told Averill her hair is not all *that* ugly," Will said with a frown, and Kade rolled his eyes. He was not exactly flowery with words, but even he didn't count "not all that ugly" as reassuring. 'Twas no wonder the girl had no confidence.

"And her birthmark is not—Just a minute, did you say bosoms?" he interrupted himself, as his brain absorbed what had been said.

Kade nodded, amusement plucking at his lips as he noted Will's horror. His tone was dry, however, when he explained, "It seems Lord Seawell thought them too small."

"Oh, for God's—" Will paused, took a breath, and shook his head. "The fool. I have never really noticed, but I am sure Averill's breasts are perfectly fine."

"Aye, they are," Kade assured him, a smile claiming his lips as he recalled the look and feel of them he'd enjoyed just moments ago. Lord Seawell might have a preference for melon-sized breasts, but Kade preferred apples, and Averill's were perfect.

"How the devil would you know?" Will snapped.

Kade grimaced at his outrage and reminded himself that this was Averill's brother. Unwilling to tell him that she had pressed his hand to her breast, or that he'd then done much more, he just shrugged. "I have eyes."

"Hmm." Will scowled at him, then sighed, and said, "I hope you reassured her."

"Aye," Kade said simply.

"What did you say?" he asked curiously.

"I told her I like her hair and . . . everything," he finished lamely.

"Hmmm." Will sat back in his seat to consider that, and asked, "Is she going to marry you?"

"Aye." Kade scowled at the very suggestion that she might not. Now that he'd had a taste of her passion, he wanted more. If the woman refused to marry him, he'd just have to do a little creeping through the tunnels of his own, remind her of the passion they shared, and ensure he was caught doing so. She'd *have* to marry him then. Kade was an honorable man, and wouldn't force her to do anything she didn't want to do . . . except marry him. She'd be happier with him than any of the

English oafs her father kept dragging in to see her anyway, he assured himself.

"Did you tell her you can see now?" Will asked suddenly.

Kade nodded solemnly.

"Was she angry?"

"Nay. At least she didna seem to be," he said, but frowned as he considered that she'd been a bit distracted at the time. He hoped she wouldn't be angry once her brain was no longer fogged with passion.

"Good. Then I shall take myself off to bed."

Kade nodded, but remained where he was as the other man stood and moved to the door. He was vaguely aware of Will's leaving, but his thoughts were now on Averill and what he might expect from her on the morrow.

Would she be angry about the trick they'd played on her about his being able to see? Would she still protest their marriage? Would he be able to keep his hands off her? The only question he could answer with any certainty was the last. He was definitely going to have trouble keeping his hands off her. The woman had been molten fire in his hands, gasping, panting, moaning, and writhing under his touch even as she dug her nails into him in a silent demand for more. Kade was already having to fight a desire to slip from his room to hers and awaken her passion again. Part of him was arguing that they were going to marry anyway, so there would be no harm in doing so, but another part was reminding him that she was the sister of his friend, as well as the daughter of the man who had taken him in and given him a place to mend from his injury. He couldn't repay such a kindness by deflowering Averill under their own roof before they were married.

He would just have to insist they marry soon, Kade thought. Say in a week even. He should be able to control himself and resist Averill for a week . . . Probably . . . He hoped.

Perhaps he'd best just avoid her until the wedding day, Kade decided.

Chapter Seven

"Here we are, lovey. Time to wake up and greet the morning. 'Tis your wedding day."

Averill groaned at that cheerful chirping from Bess. She rolled over in bed and pulled the furs up to block out the sudden glare of sunlight in the room as the woman opened her shutters.

"What's all this?" The maid's voice drew nearer, then the furs were tugged away, leaving Averill blinking owlishly in her bed in nothing but her chemise. "You should be eager and happy, not a layabout on this day of all days."

"I did not sleep well last night," Averill muttered unhappily, but gave in and sat up. Her gaze immediately fell on a pair of maids pouring pails of water into a tub.

"Ah. Too excited to sleep, were you?" Bess asked with a grin.

Averill scowled in response. "Too worried, more like."

Bess's eyebrows flew upward, then understanding creased her face. "Aye, well. I'm sure there's nothing to worry about. Lord Stewart strikes me as a man who knows his way around a bedchamber. I'm sure 'twill all go well enough."

Averill raised stricken eyes to the woman. That was the one worry she hadn't considered during her fretting last night. She'd been more concerned about the way Kade had been acting since that night in his room. After an extremely restless night reliving every moment in his arms, Averill had left her room the next morning to find Kade pacing the hall. He'd grunted a good morning when he saw her and asked if she was willing to go through with the marriage. When she'd shyly stammered, "A-aye," he'd grunted again, then took her arm and led her below. He'd deposited her at the table without another word, then had led her father away to discuss the marital contracts . . . and that had been the last she'd seen of him since.

Averill had learned from her father afterward that Kade had wished to have the wedding within the week, but he'd insisted on waiting at least two. Kade had apparently argued the point, but in the end had given in. He'd also agreed to everything her father wanted in the contract, then had taken himself out to the lists without even stopping to break his fast . . . and the man had been there ever since.

Oh, Averill supposed he must come in to sleep at night, but—if so—it must be very late, for she hadn't seen him within the keep walls since that day. In fact, neither Kade nor Will had turned up in the castle since then, not even for the meals. Averill had been sufficiently worried that she'd slipped down to the lists the first night to find out what that was about. What she'd found was that the men were taking their meals at the lists, the two of them barely stopping to gulp down the food before taking up their swords and hacking away at each other once more.

Averill had clucked and fussed and shaken her head, but she'd also found it very hard to drag herself away and back to the castle that first evening. She'd been unable to keep from haunting the lists since. She told herself it was just concern for her patient but knew that to be a lie, or she wouldn't have been taking such care not to be seen watching the men at practice. And the admiration she'd experienced as she noted the slow return of muscle and weight to Kade was far from that of someone caring for a patient. The truth was she was sneaking about, watching him with cow eyes like a callow youth with a tendre . . . and considering they were to be married, that just seemed ridiculous. In truth, the whole situation did.

It was not that she'd expected him to court her with pretty words and flowers, but she was taken aback by his complete avoidance of her. Averill had never been one to sit about daydreaming about wedding and having children, but had she imagined it, she would have expected there to be a little more interaction between a betrothed couple . . . and she was now worrying whether this was how the entirety of her married life would go—she in the keep and her husband in the bailey and never the two would meet . . . except in the marriage bed at night.

"Come now," Bess said suddenly, catching her arm to urge her out of bed. "You're sitting there looking like you carry the weight of the world on your shoulders. The bedding is not as bad as all that, and is over quickly."

"How quickly?" Averill asked with a frown as she allowed the woman to lead her to the tub, which two maids were filling with pails of steaming water.

"Well now, that depends on the man," Bess muttered.

Averill considered her words, and asked, "What exactly happens?"

The sudden stillness in the room was rather alarming. Bess had turned to stone, but so had the women working over her bath. Each of them exchanged glances with the others that seemed to exclude her.

Bess was the first to move. Letting her breath out on a whoosh, she moved to begin helping Averill out of her chemise, and muttered, "Don't you worry. He'll know what he's about and take care of everything."

"Oh, Bess." Old Ellie, the eldest of the maids filling her tub, scowled at the lady's maid. She then shook her head, tipped up the pail she held to dump the rest of its contents in the tub, and snapped, "You can't be leaving the girl completely ignorant."

" 'Tis not my place to—" Bess began, but fell silent when Ellie dropped the bucket and straightened to glare at her, hands on hips.

"Well whose place is it then?" the old woman asked. "Her poor mother's dead, God rest her soul, and her father won't be explaining anything."

Averill could feel Bess's sigh ruffle the hair on the back of her head and glanced around to see her unhappy expression. Feeling sorry for causing her this discomfort, she cleared her throat, and murmured, " 'Tis all right, Bess. I am sure you are right. 'Twill be fine."

"Nay, I'd best tell you," Bess said unhappily. "It might ease your mind to know what to expect."

"That or scare you silly," Sally, the younger of the two maids working at filling her bath, commented dryly as she emptied her own pail into the tub. She received a stern glare from Old Ellie for her trouble and rolled her eyes. "Well, it will no doubt sound awful in words," she pointed out, and then glanced to Averill, and added, " 'Tis much nicer in the doing, my lady."

Recalling the night two weeks ago in Kade's

room, Averill had no doubt that was true. It certainly had seemed nice to her, and she wouldn't have minded repeating the exercise in the weeks since. However, Kade apparently hadn't felt the same way.

Frowning over that thought, she asked, "Do all men like it?"

This brought a sudden round of laughter from the women.

"Oh, aye," Old Ellie told her dryly. "As a rule, there's nothing they like better."

"As a rule?" she asked. "Then some do not like it?"

This brought another exchange of glances and a few grimaces, then Old Ellie said, "There are one or two who seem to lack an interest, my lady. But they are a rare breed indeed."

Averill was frowning over this when Sally suddenly said, "They are rare, but I met one once. I couldn't get a rise out of him no matter what I tried and didn't know why till I saw the size of his . . . er . . . sword."

"Sword?" Averill asked uncertainly. "Do you mean his—"

"She means his piffle," Old Ellie interrupted, and then snatched up a linen that lay on one of the chests nearby and dangled it before her skirt so Averill could not misunderstand.

Sally snorted. "Aye. Only his was more like this." She picked up the bit of cloth Bess had brought up for Averill to use to wash herself, folded it four times and then rolled it up so it was no bigger than her little finger and dangled that before her legs . . . except it did not dangle.

The maid shook her head sadly. " 'Twas a shame that. A great, strapping fellow with the tiniest wee sword you ever did see. I think 'twas what put him off it. He was anxious about his lack in that area."

"Foolish man," Old Ellie said with disgust. " 'Tis not the size that counts but what they do with it."

"I don't know about that," Sally argued. " 'Twas a wee thing."

"Aye, and a knife is wee next to a sword, but can cut just as well," Ellie said dryly. "Sometimes better."

Averill was just pondering whether Kade might have been avoiding her because his own piffle was undersized, when Bess muttered, "Aye, well none of this is telling her what to expect tonight."

Her maid straightened her shoulders like a soldier heading off to battle, and said, "When they decide 'tis time for the bedding, we women will bring you above stairs, strip you, bathe you, and put you in the bed. The men will then bring Lord Stewart up. They'll strip him and put him in the bed as well, and no doubt take a good gander at you as they do, so prepare yourself for it."

"They will put him in the bed without the bathing part?" Averill asked curiously, and wondered why when Bess nodded. She didn't get to ask, however, as the woman was already rushing on, apparently eager to get the discussion over with.

"We will all leave, then he will . . ." She paused,

licked her lips nervously, then cleared her throat and forged onward. "He'll then probably kiss you, and . . . er . . ."

"Oh, good Lord," Old Ellie muttered when Bess couldn't seem to force herself to continue. " 'Tis easy to tell you had no daughters to tell this to, Bessie."

Bess flushed, then snapped, "Aye, well you've had enough of them. Why don't you explain it to her since you're so smart?"

Old Ellie harrumphed, but turned to Averill, and announced, "He'll kiss you, squeeze ye here and there, then ride his horse into your stable."

"Ride his horse . . . ?" Averill echoed uncertainly.

"His sword," Sally said helpfully.

"Oh," Averill muttered, then, as she understood what her stable must be, "Oh!"

"Aye." The women said as one, and apparently satisfied that they'd explained it, Bess returned to dragging the chemise up and over her head and the others turned back to filling the tub.

Averill scowled with dissatisfaction. The women really hadn't been very helpful at all. Good Lord, she'd known the basics of what was coming. You couldn't live in a castle with so many people all crowded together, a good portion of them procreating in any handy dark corner in the evenings, not to mention procreating and sleeping on the great-hall floor at night, without learning at least that much. Her ignorance lay in other areas.

"Does it hurt?"

The women all stopped and turned to her again, but were suddenly reluctant to talk, it seemed, for a full moment passed before Bess asked a bit irritably, "Where did you hear that?"

"I overheard a couple of maids talking about how it hurt," she admitted.

Bess nodded grimly, but admitted, "It will hurt the first time, my lady. He has to breach the maiden's veil, and 'twill hurt and bleed a bit. But it should be fine after that."

"So long as he isn't one of those who likes it rough," Sally muttered with displeasure.

"Lord Stewart doesn't strike me as one who likes it rough," Old Ellie said solemnly. "But that Seawell fellow . . . now, he had a cruel streak. 'Tis glad I am it's not him you're marrying, my lady."

All the maids mumbled their agreement as they turned back to their work.

Averill tended to agree with them. The man had shown a disturbing enjoyment of insulting her, and his hand when he'd grabbed her breast had been pinching, not soft and seeking like Kade's later was. Thoughts of that night reminded her of something else she wanted to know, and as Bess tested the water, nodded at the temperature, then urged her to step in, Averill asked, "Are your breasts supposed to tingle when he touches them?"

The dead silence then lasted so long that Averill couldn't resist glancing up once she was settled in the water. All of them, even Old Ellie, looked discomfited, and they were all staring at her with wide eyes. However, when she glanced at them, they all turned to Bess, silently handing this one off to her.

"How do you know about that?" Bess's voice was almost strangled.

"I overheard one of the maids talking," she lied in a mutter, ducking her head.

They all sighed, relaxing at the same moment.

"Aye, well," Bess said at last. "I suppose if he does it right, and if you like it, they may tingle."

"Oh Bess, you poor thing," Sally said sadly. "Have you truly never had the tingling?"

Bess flushed and turned away to begin folding Averill's discarded chemise, obviously unwilling to respond.

Averill bit her lip, feeling guilty that she'd caused the woman such discomfort. Bess had been married when she was younger to a man she often spoke of fondly and claimed had been fine and good. Obviously, his fine and good had not stretched to the bedroom. It had taken little more than a kiss and caress from Kade to make her tingle. Hoping to distract them from Bess and ease her discomfort, she cleared her throat and asked her next question. "What about the . . . er . . . the wet?"

"The wet?" they asked as one.

Averill flushed and grimaced, but really wanted to be sure it was normal. Kade had commented on it, after all. Clearing her throat again, she concentrated on dunking the small bit of linen Sally had used to make the imaginary piffle in the water, and said, "Between the legs. Is it normal to get wet there?"

"That—You—How could you—?"

"She overheard the maids talking," Sally answered for her, but there was a twinkle in her eye that suggested she, at least, was no longer fooled that that was the case.

"Oh, of course," Bess muttered. She was silent for a moment, but then paused and looked to Ellie for help.

The old woman rolled her eyes, but said, " 'Tis natural. It greases the way for the sword to slide in your sheath."

It seemed horses and stables wouldn't do for this explanation, Averill thought wryly, but merely nodded. So long as it was normal, she was happy. She'd worried it was unnatural or something. Now that she knew it wasn't, she relaxed a bit, and asked, "How do I please him?"

Old Ellie had picked up her empty buckets, preparing to leave the room, but dropped them abruptly at the question and whirled back. Sally had only just bent to gather her own buckets, but paused, her shoulders shaking with what Averill suspected was silent mirth at her questions. Bess, however, was looking absolutely horrified.

"Please him?" her maid asked weakly.

"Aye, well, you said he would kiss and caress me.

What am I to do to please him in return?" It did seem an important question for her to ask. Kade had made her gasp and moan with pleasure in his arms, and all she had done was hold on for dear life and writhe under his caresses. She wished to be a good wife and would like to please him as much as he pleased her.

"Nothing," Bess said finally. "You just lie there."

"That's all?" she asked doubtfully.

Old Ellie clucked impatiently. " 'Tis no wonder you've no children, Bess. You and Billy didn't have a clue what you were doing," the maid snapped. She then soothed the insult by adding, "You were both young, though, when you married, and not much older when he died."

"They like it when you play with their piffle," Sally announced abruptly.

"Play with it?" Averill asked uncertainly, an image rising up in her mind of dressing it up like a doll and—

"Aye, especially with your mouth. They really like that," Sally said firmly, then added as an after-thought, "And some like their nipples tweaked."

Not dressing it up like a doll then. Well that was a relief.

"And they like compliments on their size while you do it," Sally assured her knowingly. "The more compliments the better."

"What are you telling the poor girl?" Bess gasped in horror, and it seemed obvious that while the woman had been married, she wasn't nearly as experienced as the much younger Sally. It made Averill wonder if Bess had forsaken men after her husband. If he moved her as little as it was sounding, than she supposed she wasn't surprised.

"Oh, leave off, Bess," Old Ellie said gently. "Sally is right. They do like it." She turned back to Averill to warn, "But some women don't like doing it, and a hand is just as good if you're of that ilk."

Averill had no idea if she was of that ilk or not, she still wasn't entirely certain how she was supposed to play with his piffle with her mouth. She supposed Sally could mean in the same way that Kade had played his mouth over her breasts, suckling and nipping gently. Before she could ponder the possibility too deeply, Ellie continued.

"What you do is grease your fingers up good and slick, then take him in hand and pump away at him like you're milking a cow," she announced, only to frown, and say, "Well, not really like milking a cow, but sort of. That should get him good and hard and ready to go."

Averill nodded, her hand unconsciously closing around the linen she held and pumping it a bit. When the woman nodded, apparently done, then regathered her buckets and chivied Sally to leave, Averill murmured her thanks and gasped in surprise as Bess poured a bucket of tepid water over her head.

"We'd best get you washed and out before your

father sends Will looking for you. We've wasted so much time, the priest is probably here waiting on you."

Wiping the water away from her eyes, Averill grimaced as Bess set to soaping and lathering her hair. She tried to relax, but now that the worry about the wedding night ahead had been dealt with—well, as much as it could be, she supposed—she was once again fretting over Kade's avoiding her the last two weeks and worrying that he really had changed his mind about marrying her. If so, she wasn't sure he would say so. He was good friends with her brother and wouldn't want to insult him by rejecting her, she feared. And he probably wouldn't repay her father's kindness like that either. However, she didn't wish to be married to him if he didn't want her anymore. Averill suspected it would be unbearable to be married to someone she liked so much and found so attractive, only to be completely ignored by him.

She needed to talk to Kade.

"The lass is taking her time," Kade said tensely as he shifted in his seat at the trestle table to glance toward the stairs once more in search of his errant bride.

"She will come," Will said reassuringly. "No doubt she is fussing and making herself as pretty as she can for you."

"Aye, but 'tis nearly the nooning," he complained. "How long does it take to make her pretty?"

Will chuckled at his disgruntled words, but pointed out, "They will no doubt wash her hair, then have to brush it dry. 'Twill take some time."

Kade grunted and glanced back to the cider on the table before him, thinking that it was either that or she had changed her mind and was unwilling to marry him. The thought made his mouth shift into a scowl.

"You are hardly looking like a happy groom on his wedding day," Will said with amusement.

"Most husbands are not happy on their wedding days," Kade pointed out. After all, most weddings were little more than contractual agreements between two families, a joining for money, or land, or some other profit. Kade almost envied the men who enjoyed such arrangements. At least they would not be sitting, wondering if the woman they had hankered for and dreamed of for the last two weeks had decided he wouldn't do and was even now climbing down from her window on a rope made of gowns so she might run away. Not that Averill would have to do that, he supposed. She could simply slip away through the tunnels as she had when she was five.

He scowled at the thought and glanced to the stairs again, but there was no sign of her.

"She would no doubt be surprised at such eagerness, considering you have not troubled even to speak to her in two weeks," Will said dryly.

Kade grunted and began to toy with his mug. He was unwilling to tell the lass's brother that the only reason he'd avoided her was to ensure she arrived at her own wedding unsullied. Will would probably punch him did he know the indecent imaginings Kade had enjoyed since the night of Averill's visit to his room. Staying away from her and taking out his frustrations on Will in the lists had seemed the smartest route. It had also been rather beneficial. He was his old self again, filling out his clothes and almost back to full strength. Though it was not his own clothes he was filling. His had been lost in the sinking of the ship, and he'd apparently been dragged from the water in only the shirt he wore under his plaid. Kade had been wearing borrowed clothes since the first time he'd decided to get up from the bed; Will's clothes, in fact.

He glanced at the dark green tunic and braies Will had loaned him and thought that while he looked more than fine in them, it would be a relief to be back in a plaid again. This in turn made him think of his men and wonder why they had not yet returned. He had expected them to arrive in time for the wedding. That was the only reason he had agreed to wait two weeks. Will was a good friend, but it would have been nice to have his own kin standing beside him on this day.

"Here she comes."

Kade glanced around at that announcement from Will, eyes widening as they landed on Averill descending the stairs. She wore a dark green gown

that matched his clothes in color, her hair was unbound and flowing around her head in fiery waves,
her cheeks were flushed, and she looked absolutely
beautiful to him.

Kade stood up and moved toward her, but Lord
Mortagne suddenly rose and waved him back to his
seat as he hurried to her side. He hesitated, tempted
to ignore the man, but it was her father after all, so
he settled reluctantly back on the bench.

"Let us head out to the chapel steps," the priest
said, getting to his feet on the other side of Will.
"Lord Mortagne will bring the bride along."

Kade scowled but began to walk when Will
nudged him. Averill was here. She must plan to
marry him. That would have to be enough.

Most of the castle inhabitants were already out
by the church waiting when the priest led Kade and
Will across the bailey. The old man spent a moment
fussing and arranging them on the steps, then they
all turned to peer back toward the keep in expec-
tation. Much to Kade's relief, Lord Mortagne and
Averill were already halfway across the bailey, but
as she drew closer, Kade was able to see that she
was nibbling at her lip and wringing her hands.

"She looks worried," Will muttered.

"Aye," Kaye growled.

"She is also moving a bit swiftly," Will pointed
out. "Father appears to be having trouble keeping up."

Kade grunted. He had just noted that for himself. Averill was moving at a quick clip that soon became a jog, then a run as she dropped her father's arm, and left him behind to hurry through the parting crowd to pause before him.

"K-kade?" she said uncertainly.

"Aye?" he asked growing wary.

"Averill!"

That shout from Lord Mortagne made her pause and glance around. Clucking impatiently, she hurried back to him, caught his arm, and chivvied him toward the stairs, saying, "I am sorry, Father, but I must speak to Kade. Please hurry."

"There will be plenty of time to speak after the ceremony," the priest said repressively, as a panting Lord Mortagne and Averill arrived at the stairs. "Please take your place beside Lord Stewart, and I will start the ceremony."

Averill ignored him and turned to Kade. "M-my lord?"

Kade frowned at her stammer. She had done it only once before—the morning after the night in his room—but it surprised him that she was stammering now. Taking her hands in an effort to calm her, he raised an eyebrow in question.

"My lady," the priest began in sharp tones.

"Oh, stuff and bother, Father Bennett. I must speak to Kade," Averill hissed impatiently, and caught Kade's arm to urge him down the steps. He supposed she'd hoped for privacy away from the priest, her father, and Will, but all she did was take them down to where the people of Mortagne stood. The servants, soldiers, and guests made room for her and Kade to join them, but then stood, listening eagerly for what she had to say.

"I-I . . . er . . ." She forced a smile for those around them, then cleared her throat and turned back to Kade. "D-do y-you—" She paused abruptly when Kade lifted a hand to cover her mouth.

"Yer stammering," he pointed out quietly when she raised her eyebrows in question.

"Aye. Lady Averill does that sometimes," one of the nearer men said, and Averill lowered her eyes, misery crossing her face.

" 'Tis only when she's nervous or uncomfortable with someone," another pointed out.

"Aye, but she don't normally stammer around Lord Stewart," a woman announced, and Kade glanced over to see Mabs among the crowd surrounding them.

He turned his gaze back to Averill, and asked quietly, "Are ye so uncomfortable with me now ye ken I can see ye?"

"N-nay, t-tis not that," she murmured, then shook her head impatiently. "Tis j-just I—" Her words ended on a gasp of surprise when Kade lowered his head and kissed her. She stood still under his kiss for a moment, but sighed and sank against him as he deepened the kiss.

"Here now," someone said, "the kiss don't come until after the ceremony."

Kade ignored the speaker and the people who hushed him, and kissed Averill until they were both breathless. He then raised his head and asked, " 'Tis just what?"

"I was worried you no longer wished to marry me, but felt you had to because you had already agreed," she admitted in a breathless rush. And didn't stammer once, he noted.

"I want to marry ye," Kade said simply, then caught her hand and turned to pull her out of the crowd that had moved to surround them, but she tugged her hand free. Frowning, he turned back in question.

"B-but you have been avoiding me these last t-two weeks," she pointed out, and he frowned as he noted the stammer was back.

"I told you it would upset her," Will said dryly, and Kade glanced around with surprise to see that the man had joined the crowd around them. Glancing to his sister, Will added, "I did tell him, Avy."

Kade scowled, but concentrated on Averill, and said, "I had me reasons, but it wasna because I'd changed me mind on marryin' ye, lass."

She opened her mouth, no doubt, to ask what those reasons were, but he forestalled her by saying, "I'll explain later. When we're alone."

"Oh." Averill glanced around at the people surrounding them, then relaxed and nodded in acquiescence.

"Can we get married now?" Kade asked quietly.

Averill blushed, her eyes dropping away from his, but she also nodded.

Feeling the tension ease out of his shoulders, Kade took her hand and drew it over his arm, then led her through the crowd and up the stairs to stand before the priest.

Chapter Eight

" 'Tis time."

Averill glanced over her shoulder to see Bess and the other women standing behind her.

Surely it could not be time for the bedding already? she thought with dismay, but the presence of the women seemed to suggest it was.

Feeling her stomach flutter nervously, Averill forced herself to stand and moved away from the table without even a word or glance to Kade. It was terribly rude, and she felt bad for it, especially after how solicitous and kind he'd been through the celebrations that had been going on all afternoon and the better part of the evening, but she simply didn't have it in her to meet his gaze at that point.

It was time for the bedding!

That fact kept screaming through her head as

the women led her above stairs, then stripped her and ushered her into her bath. On an intellectual level, Averill knew she shouldn't be this nervous, especially after the way she'd let Kade kiss and caress her on "that" night. However, that had been wholly unexpected, completely spontaneous, and exciting. There was a vast difference between that experience and this one, where she was being prepared and perfumed like a sacrificial virgin.

Worse yet, while that had been a wholly private occasion that no one knew about, the entire castle knew what was going to happen tonight. They would all be sitting below stairs, continuing to drink themselves silly and no doubt making ribald jokes about what the two of them were getting up to. Besides, this time they were actually going to consummate their relationship. He was going to ride his horse into her stable, sink his sword in her sheath, breach her maiden's veil . . . .

These thoughts rolled through Averill's mind over and over again like a cat chasing a mouse around a table as she was bathed, dried off, and fussed over. They so distracted her that it was with some surprise that she found herself lying in bed as Bess pulled the linens and furs up to cover her.

"There now," her maid said in soothing tones as she straightened. "The men should be along soon. Sally went to fetch them."

Averill had just begun to panic at those words when the door crashed open and a riotous group of singing men began to squeeze through the door carrying Kade overhead. They set him down and continued to sing and joke as they surrounded and began to strip him. Averill bit her lip and thanked the good Lord she wasn't a man, for they were taking little care with her husband. The sound of tearing cloth, and Kade's grunts and curses filling the air was most disconcerting.

This then explained why the groom was never put in a bath, Averill decided as she watched various bits of clothing flying through the air above the crowd of men. The poor groom would no doubt be drowned by the mass of well-meaning, but very drunk companions.

When the crowd of men began to part, Averill realized the stripping part must be done and closed her eyes, steeling herself for the lifting of the linens and "revealing-her-to-all" part Bess had warned her about. It seemed barely a moment later that she felt the linen and furs lift and a cool breeze brush against her flushed and heated skin, then Kade fell into the bed beside her as if tossed there and the linen and furs dropped back over her.

Not eager to meet the gazes of the men who had seen her naked, Averill kept her eyes closed until the laughing voices and pattering of feet faded, and the click of the door sounded. She then breathed out a little sigh and cautiously opened her eyes. The room was empty, as she'd expected, and Kade was staring at her from right next to her in bed.

Averill managed a rather sickly smile and whispered a polite, "Good eve, my lord."

For some reason, that seemed to amuse Kade, and a low rumble of laughter slid from his lips as he dropped to lay flat on his back.

Averill lay still, watching him uncertainly, then he suddenly glanced back to her, and asked, "Are ye hungry?"

She blinked at the question. "Hungry, my lord?"

"Aye. I noticed ye hardly touched yer food at the feast so had yer maid bring up a tray ere the bedding," he explained, then added, "I wouldna mind a bite meself."

Averill hesitated. She *hadn't* eaten much at the feast. Her nerves had been stretched too taut for that as she contemplated the night ahead, but they were no better now, and she wasn't feeling hungry. However, delaying what was the inevitable sounded a good idea to her, so she nodded.

Kade rewarded her with a smile and heaved the linens and furs aside and rose from the bed.

Averill's eyes widened incredulously as she got her first look at his piffle. Surrounded by the men as he'd been and quick as it had gone, she hadn't been able to see much during the undressing earlier. Now that she could see, however, it was immediately obvious to her that his lack of attention these last two weeks was not due to anxiety over size. The man was well endowed. She didn't think he was unnaturally large, but he certainly had nothing to complain about or fret over.

"Are ye comin'?"

Averill flushed as he glanced her way and caught

her staring, then sat up only to pause. She was naked, and while he might not be self-conscious about strutting around so in front of her, she was made of much weaker stuff. After a hesitation to glance around, she tugged the linen out from under the furs, wrapped it around herself in the old Roman fashion, and scooted off the bed.

Someone had started a small fire in the fireplace, something she rarely bothered with at this time of year, but it was cozy and nice. As Averill watched curiously, Kade grabbed the furs from the bed and carried them over to spread them out on the floor in front of the fire. He then collected a selection of fruit, cheese, meat, and bread that had been left on the table.

"Sit," Kade ordered as he settled on one end of the furs. Averill sat opposite him, taking a moment to be sure her toga covered her decently before glancing up to the tray of food he set between them.

They ate in silence at first, Averill merely nibbling at the food, and then—unable to bear the quiet any longer—she reminded him, "You s-said you would explain why you have b-been avoiding me these last w-weeks."

Averill lowered her eyes self-consciously. She hadn't stuttered the whole week while she'd tended him, but suddenly found herself nervous around him now that she knew he could see her. She supposed the present tension of the situation didn't help any either. Aware that Kade was silent, she raised her eyes cautiously and glanced his way as he bit a strawberry in half. He then gestured for her to move closer with the hand holding the strawberry.

After a brief hesitation, Averill gathered her linen close and shifted along the furs until she sat next to him.

"Look at me." The words were almost a growl, and Averill bit her lip and raised her eyes to meet his. The moment she did, he ran the strawberry over her lower lip. She thought he meant to feed her and automatically opened her mouth, but he merely ran it back and forth one more time, then said, "I avoided ye because I kenned did I get close to ye again, I'd want to do this."

Leaning forward, he caught her lower lip between both of his and drew it in, sucking away the juice left behind by the fruit.

Averill sighed and closed her eyes, but then popped them back open when she felt him tug the linen away, revealing one breast. He then let her lip slip from his mouth, and whispered, "And then I'd want to do this."

"*This*" was running the cool fruit over one nipple and lowering his head to draw it into his mouth and suckle and lick away the juice left behind there as well.

Averill swallowed, her fingers tightening in the folds of the bit of linen she still clutched over one breast, and breathed, "Oh."

Allowing her nipple to slip from his mouth, he

raised his head, and asked, "Would ye have liked that?"

When she bit her lip and nodded silently, Kade nodded solemnly back and added, "And then I'd have wanted to do other things, things a man shoudna do to a woman who's no his wife, and so I decided 'twas best did I stay away until after we were wedded."

"W-what other things?" Averill asked daringly. The question brought a smile to his lips, and he dropped the strawberry on the platter, reached for her head, and leaned forward to press his mouth to hers.

Averill sighed, allowing her mouth to slip open for him, then sighed again with pleasure as his tongue invaded. He tasted of strawberry and Kade, a delicious combination, and she found herself releasing her hold on the linens to clasp at his shoulders instead. Cool air immediately drifted across her breasts. It was followed by Kade's warm hands, and Averill groaned as he began to knead and fondle them both. When he urged her back onto the furs with his weight, she didn't resist but merely clutched at his shoulders so that she eased to the floor. The moment he had her flat, Kade shifted, easing one leg between both of hers as his kisses became more demanding. His tongue thrust into her, and his leg pressed upward against the core of her so that she moaned and shifted her legs restlessly on either side of his.

When he broke the kiss, Averill groaned in disappointment, but then sighed and turned her head as his mouth trailed to her ear. He nibbled there briefly, stirring a surprising riot of sensation in her, then began to lick and nibble his way down her throat. Averill gasped in surprise when he reached her collarbone and began to nibble there, the riot turning immediately into an excited mob. Kade didn't stay long there, however, before dipping lower to replace one hand with his mouth.

This time, as he drew the erect and sensitive nipple into his mouth, Averill cried out and clutched at his head as he suckled and nipped lightly. She felt his hand slide down over her stomach, but bombarded as she was by the other things he was doing, hardly paid attention until it slid lower, pushing the linen before it until his fingers could dip between her legs.

Averill cried out again, her hips bucking as he brushed against the sensitive core of her, but unlike the last time he'd done this, she didn't even consider closing her legs, but instead spread them for him. She was aware of his mouth moving away from her nipple, but the fingers of his free hand quickly replaced it to pluck and tweak gently, and to be frank, she didn't care anyway. All of her attention was on the excitement he was stirring between her legs, so it wasn't until his head slipped from her grasp that she realized he was shifting down her body. At first, Averill merely reached for the linen, now lying crumpled beneath and on either side of her, but then he removed the fingers that were giving her such pleasure. Disappointment cleared her mind enough that she became aware that his head was dipping between her legs.

Startled and shocked, Averill gathered her breath to protest, but all that came out was a long "Ahhhh" as he began to lave her with his tongue.

Back arching and hips grinding down into the caress, she stared briefly at the ceiling overhead, then squeezed her eyes closed and let her body do what it would. It was now dancing to its own rhythm, urging him on as he drove her wild. Her eyes flew open again, however, when she felt something gently prod her opening. Averill lifted her head to peer down, but his head was still all that was between her legs . . . as well as his hands she recalled as something began to push into her and she realized it must be a finger.

Despite his having done this before, the sensation was so alien that for the first moment, it made her still and hold her breath, but then he withdrew it and redoubled his attention to the nub of her excitement, and when he eased his finger back in, she began to move again.

Averill's breath was now coming in little gasps as she rode his tongue and finger, and she couldn't seem to grasp a clear thought. Her body and mind were pure sensation now, surfing the crest of the passion he was milking from her. And then he began to suckle as he worked, and the tension that had been building in Averill snapped, drawing a scream of pleasure as her body convulsed and writhed.

Lost in the waves assaulting her, Averill was hardly aware of Kade crawling back up her body. When his mouth covered hers for a kiss, she responded urgently, her arms reaching to clasp him and hold him close. It was then he thrust into her, drawing another scream, but this one of shock and a little pain as he breached her maiden's veil.

Kade froze his body stiff as a board as he peered down into her face. Averill peered back and managed not to grimace as she felt all of the lovely passion he'd stirred quickly draining away. It had been quite nice until he'd ridden his horse into her stable.

"All right?" he growled after a moment.

Averill bit her lip but managed a nod. He let out the breath she hadn't realized he was holding and eased himself out of her. She was just releasing a relieved breath of her own when he suddenly surged back inside. Clutching at his shoulders, she managed not to wince and closed her eyes to avoid looking at him for fear her disappointment and discomfort would show, but then blinked them open again when he reached between them to caress her again. Averill stilled and concentrated on what he was doing, surprised when excitement began to build in her once more. Then he began to move again, but with his caressing her as he was, she didn't mind.

He stopped his caresses a few moments later, and Averill experienced a moment's concern and disappointment, but then he shifted slightly, his body rubbing where his fingers had been as he slid in and out of her, and she groaned at the sensation. Hips arching instinctively, knees rising and feet pushing against the floor, Averill met him thrust for thrust, her breath coming in little gasping pants again as she struggled to reclaim the release she'd just enjoyed. She screamed his name as it struck her, crying out with amazed pleasure as her body shuddered and convulsed around his manhood, then he thrust one more time and shouted out himself, body straining over her as he spilled his seed into her.

Averill grunted when he then collapsed on top of her. He muttered an apology and immediately shifted to the side, removing his weight. Kade then gathered her in his arms and tugged her over to lie half on his chest so that he could run his hands soothingly over her back. Averill wiggled about until she found a comfortable position and settled in with a contented little sigh. However, her contentment did not last long. She thought she should be tired after what they'd just done, but she wasn't. In fact, she felt quite energetic. They had consummated the wedding. She was now completely his wife.

Lady Averill Stewart. She tested the name in her mind and decided she quite liked it.

"Are ye all right?"

Averill smiled faintly as the words rumbled to her ear; the chest she laid on vibrated as he spoke. She then tilted her head to peer up at him shyly, and whispered, "Aye."

In the next moment, she found herself turned onto her back and Kade was getting to his feet. Half sitting up, she watched with confusion as he moved to the bath the maids had left behind. She saw him pick up the bit of linen she'd washed with, dip it in the cooling water, and wring it out, then he turned and moved back to her side.

"Spread yer legs," he ordered.

Averill blushed, but supposed it was silly to be shy after what they'd just done and forced herself to lie back. When she opened her legs to him, Kade washed her with the cloth. He was gentle, but per- functory, and still she felt a tingle that was negated by a slight soreness. Then he was done and up and moving back to the bath again. She watched him rinse the linen in the bathwater, then bit her lip as she watched him clean himself, wondering if she should not have offered to do it for him as he had done for her. Before she had decided, he was fin- ished and returning to her side.

She expected him to rejoin her on the furs, so was surprised when Kade gathered her up in the linen and straightened. Averill quickly caught her arms around his neck as he carried her to the bed, noting that he was definitely much wider and stronger than he'd been on first awakening from his illness. It seemed the two weeks of plentiful food and exercise were speeding him along in his mending.

Kade set her in the bed, kissed her forehead, then returned to gather the remaining furs. He brought those back to the bed, laid them over it, and climbed in beside her before drawing her against his side to rest her head on his chest once more. A little contented sigh slid from his lips then, but he did not go off to sleep as she almost expected. Instead, his hands were roaming restlessly over her body again. One began smoothing down her back to find and clasp her behind, pressing her against his hip. The other slid up and down her side, brushing the curve of her breast. When that hand paused to cup her breast, Averill moaned softly as her earlier passions stirred lazily. She then tipped her head up, silently requesting a kiss.

Kade complied, covering her mouth to kiss her in a way that was at first only gently questing but soon became more ardent. Averill moaned as the first embers of her returning excitement became a blaze, and when the hand at her bottom suddenly dipped between her legs to find her core again, she shifted one leg up over both of his, opening herself to make it easier for him. When he then started to slide a finger inside her, however, she stiffened in surprise at her tenderness there.

Kade immediately stilled as well, then he withdrew his hands, broke their kiss, and urged her head to his chest.

"Sleep," he ordered, his voice grim.

Averill hesitated, then asked uncertainly, "Are we not going to—?"

"Nay," he growled, not sounding happy about it, then added more gently, "Yer sore from the first time."

"Oh," Averill whispered, but couldn't deny it. She was tender. However, her leg was still splayed over his hip and groin, and she could feel that he had grown larger and stiff again. While her body was not ready for another round, it appeared his was. She lay still for a moment, debating whether to suggest they risk it anyway. They could always stop if it was too painful, but then she supposed that would leave them both feeling as frustrated and unsatisfied as she'd felt after that night two weeks ago. She'd lain in bed for hours, her body aching. At the time, she hadn't known what it had been aching for, but now she knew and really didn't want to suffer getting even more excited, then being left unfulfilled. She shifted her knee, accidentally nudging Kade's hardness, and glanced up swiftly at his hiss of indrawn breath.

She was just wondering if he was suffering the same frustration she had that other night and, if so, what she could do about it, when Sally and Old Ellie's advice on how to please him came to mind. Considering what the maid had said, she decided she might be able to ease *his* aching at least.

Averill bit her lip, considering how to go about it. She had nothing to grease her hand with, so the pumping thing was out, but she did have her mouth. Of course, Ellie had said some women didn't like it, but she had no idea if that was true for her. Deciding the only way to find out was to try, she ducked under the linens and furs and began to shinny down his body.

Kade was trying to think away the bothersome erection plaguing him when Averill suddenly slipped from his arms and began to struggle her way down his body. Stiffening, he lifted his head to peer down in confusion, then caught at the linens and furs and jerked them up away from his body to see what the devil she was up to. He froze, however, eyes squeezing tightly closed and furs slipping from his fingers when her hand suddenly found his erection and grasped it firmly.

"Wife?" Kade asked, gritting his teeth against the sensations just her touch was sending through him.

"Aye?" her muffled voice came from under the furs.

"What are you—Jesus!" he gasped, his back raising halfway off the bed in shock as something wet—her tongue, he thought—rasped across the very sensitive tip of his manhood. In the next moment, he sucked in a hissing breath and grabbed at the bed linens, twisting them in his fingers as she licked him a second time.

This was wholly unexpected, he thought vaguely, as she licked him again. And a sort of hell to bear, he acknowledged as her tongue flicked over him once more. The woman had no idea what she was doing, Kade realized with dismay as her tongue rasped over him for a fifth time. And he didn't have a damned clue how to stop her without hurting her feelings.

Her tongue lashed him again, and he suffered it helplessly, aching to direct her, but—

"Oh, my, what a large piffle you have, my lord."

The words came to him muffled from under the furs, and Kade's eyes shot open with a sort of horror.

"Aye, a fine piffle indeed," she added, then licked him again before adding, " 'Tis very . . . big . . . and . . . er . . . handsome."

That was followed by yet another lick, but Kade hardly felt it this time. His upper body was convulsed upward off the bed with sudden laughter. He tried to stifle it for fear of hurting her feelings, but 'twas like trying to stop the wind.

"Why, I would wager it's the largest and handsomest piffle in all of England," Averill added for good measure, then went still as she apparently became aware of the sounds he couldn't keep from slipping out; little choked guffaws and low-pitched snorts. And then his erection was suddenly released and the linens and furs began to move as she shifted to crawl out from under them.

Kade immediately dropped back to lie flat, biting his tongue hard to kill the amusement on his face as she appeared and eyed him with concern.

"Are you all right, husband?" Averill asked, shifting up beside him so that she could peer down into his face. "I did not hurt you, did I?"

Kade bit his lip to hold back any remaining amusement and shook his head quickly.

She frowned, but said, "I thought I heard—"

" 'Twas verra nice, thank you," he got out in tones stretched thin by his effort to keep his amusement from showing. He then tugged her down to lie with her head on his chest, and muttered, "Sleep now."

"But I have not finished—" Averill began, trying to sit back up again, only to gasp in surprise when he tugged her back into place and held her firmly there.

"We're finished fer now," he assured her. "It's been a long day. Time to sleep."

"Oh." She sighed, then settled against him, her hand moving absently across his chest. "Well, I suppose I can finish pleasuring you in the morn when you are rested."

"Aye," he growled, horrified at the very thought of suffering her repeated licks.

Much to his relief, she fell silent then, her fingers stilling. Kade was just relaxing, a smile curving his lips, when she suddenly raised her head, and said, "Husband?"

Kade erased the smile at once. "Aye?"

"How am I supposed to tweak your nipples when they are all the way up here and I am all the way down there?" She dropped her hand down onto the furs over his groin, and Kade no longer had to fight the urge to laugh. The woman had just thumped him in the balls. He closed his eyes briefly, intending to wait until the pain passed, but then her words sank through the pain and he blinked them open again. "Tweak me nipples? Why the devil wid ye want to tweak me nipples?"

"Well, Sally said men like it when you play with their piffles and tweak their nipples," she explained.

Kade was just about to ask who this Sally was when she added thoughtfully, "Mind you, she did not say they had to be done at the same time. Mayhap she meant just that men liked it, too." She considered that briefly, then yawned, and said, "I shall have to ask her about that."

Kade closed his eyes briefly, not sure he could stand any more of the woman's advice, but then his eyes popped open again as Averill said, "Husband?"

"Aye?" he asked warily.

"Is Stewart nice?"

He grimaced at the question. His family home had once been one of the finest castles around, but that was before his father had taken to the drink and left the care and well-being of the castle and its inhabitants to Kade's mother.

Not that she had not done a fine job, Kade thought with a frown. She had run it as well or better than any man, as had his sister after her, but when his father and brothers got into the whiskey, they could get violent. Things got broken, servants avoided the castle to avoid bearing the brunt of a whiskey-fueled temper, and the keep and people had suffered for it. The last time he'd been there, the castle had begun to show some small signs of neglect. But at the feast tonight, Kade had heard from Lord Mortagne's neighbor, one of the guests at the celebration, that Lord d'Aumesbury had finally claimed and wed his sister, Merry. That meant that his father and brothers had been left to tend to Stewart, and he very much feared what he would find when he arrived.

Had Kade known this beforehand, he probably would have delayed the wedding and ridden home to tend to matters before marrying Averill and bringing her back. However, he hadn't known, and the deed was done and well and truly consummated. He had no intention of leaving her behind for even a day while he took care of things at Stewart.

"Is it?" Averill prodded, absently tugging at the hairs on his chest.

"It was," he admitted quietly. "And will be again if it isna now."

Averill lifted her head to peer at him curiously, but before she could ask what he meant by that, he said, "Ye'll see soon enough. We leave for Stewart the day after tomorrow."

"What?" she squawked, levering herself up to gape at him.

"Me men have no returned from their chore," he said quietly. "I would find out why."

"Oh." She frowned, her gaze suddenly moving around the room.

No doubt thinking of all that she would need to pack and take with her, he thought, and— suspecting she would ask for at least three days to manage it all—he said, "I'd leave tomorrow, but would no' have ye suffer days in the saddle when yer tender. I'm givin' ye time to heal. Ye'll have to pack what ye need most. The rest can follow later."

"Oh." She blushed, but whispered, " 'Tis very thoughtful of you, husband. Thank you."

"Aye," Kade grunted. "Now sleep. Ye'll need yer strength for the packin' and journey ahead."

Averill smiled faintly, and laid her head back down on his chest. She then gave a little sigh and wiggled about against him, making herself comfortable before allowing her eyes to close.

Kade stared down at her until her breathing turned slow and steady, suggesting she was asleep. Only then did he risk a small smile curving his lips as he recalled her "pleasuring" him. His little wife might not have known what she was doing, but she'd tried, and that was enough to please him for the moment. He would teach her how to do it properly later . . . and figure out some way to get her to leave off with the compliments without hurting her feelings.

The largest and handsomest piffle in England?

Kade chuckled softly, then closed his eyes to sleep.

Chapter Nine

"Oh, this water is cold."

Averill smiled faintly at Bess's complaint but didn't comment. Instead, she concentrated on cleaning away the dust and grime from their travels that day. It was the first night of their journey to her new home, and she'd found it a long, exhausting one. Aside from the fact that she had spent most of her life at Mortagne and wasn't used to traveling, Averill also hadn't slept well or long last night. She had worked late into the evening, sorting and packing what to take with her and what to have sent later, and had only given it up when Kade had entered and ordered Bess out of the room.

When Bess had protested that she had to prepare Averill for bed, he'd growled that he'd take care of that and had ushered the older woman to the door. And then he had assisted her, stripping away her clothes with the ease of a longtime lady's maid. It had made her wonder where he'd got all the practice in undressing women. It wasn't until he'd finished the chore, and she was climbing into bed, that she'd realized he'd been affected by that simple act. He'd stripped his own clothes off then, revealing a manhood that had grown swollen and an angry red.

Averill had bit her lip as she watched him approach the bed. Recalling and appreciating his intention to let her heal before their journey, she'd shyly offered to pleasure him again. Kade's eyes had widened with what she imagined must have been surprise at the offer, but he'd quickly shaken his head, repeating that he would let her heal before they left for Stewart.

Averill wasn't sure how her pleasuring him could cause her discomfort, but then supposed he feared he'd want to make love to her afterward and wouldn't risk it. Deciding he was really the most considerate and kind husband a girl could have, Averill had let the matter rest. She'd cuddled up next to him to sleep, more than glad that she'd punched Cyril and put him off marrying her. She really had got lucky, Averill had thought, and continued to think so.

Kade was truly a caring husband. His words were sometimes lacking and his tone often gruff, but he had proven very solicitous of her well-being on the journey today: taking her up on his mount to ride in his lap when she began to flag in the saddle, ensuring she had enough to eat and drink when they'd interrupted their journey to have the nooning meal, ushering her away to tend to personal matters first thing each time they paused in their travels, then ushering her and Bess here to bathe when they'd stopped to make camp for the night. Averill didn't think she could have asked for a better husband.

A burst of male laughter made her glance curiously to the right. Will and Kade were bathing just around the bend. Unable to see them thanks to the curve in the river, but within shouting distance, Averill found it comforting to know they were there.

"I've had enough of this cold, my lady. I am getting out," Bess announced, heading for shore.

"I suppose I am ready to get out as well," Averill said reluctantly. She then quickly ducked under the water to rinse the soap from her hair and body. By the time she resurfaced, Bess was out of the water and using one of the linens she'd brought down to the water to dry herself off. Squeezing her hair to remove the worst of the water, Averill headed back onto shore, murmuring a thank-you when Bess handed her a fresh linen to dry herself. By the time she'd done so, Bess was clothed and collecting her chemise to help her dress.

They had finished and were just gathering the damp linens to take back to camp with them when Kade appeared at the edge of the clearing. His head poked out first and he peered around, but once he saw that they were both out and decent, he pushed the rest of the way into the clearing and approached, with Will on his heels.

With Kade's own men not yet returned from delivering their message, Will had insisted that he and a small army of Mortagne men accompany them to Stewart. At least, that was the excuse he and Kade had given Averill, but she knew it was more than that. The two had been foolish enough to discuss the state of Stewart and Kade's intention to ask his father to step down while seated at the trestle tables. It was not so much foolish to discuss it there, as it was to expect they would not be overheard and the information passed around. Bess had got hold of the gossip and brought it to her. She was not riding to her new home as ignorant as they'd hoped.

Averill knew her brother and husband were just trying not to burden her with worry, but really, it was insulting that they thought of her as a weak, swooning female who needed to be cosseted and protected from harsh reality. Had they even considered that she might be able to help in this situation? She doubted it . . . and fully intended to show them the error of their ways once they got there.

"Come, Bess, I shall see you back to camp," Will said, moving to take the woman's arm as Kade headed directly for Averill.

The maid cast a glance her way, but Averill could not seem to take her eyes off her husband. Something about the way he approached made her feel like a rabbit being stalked by a fox. Aware that Bess had allowed Will to lead her out of the clearing, she forced a smile for her husband but also took a nervous step back, coming up against a tree trunk.

The action made Kade frown and pause a step away. "Are ye afraid o' me, wife?"

"N-no," she said, then grimaced as her stammer gave lie to the word. Realizing how silly she was being, Averill forced herself to take a step forward, placing her a hairbreadth away from her husband so that did she breathe in too deeply, her breasts would surely brush his chest.

For some reason, that made Kade smile, and he asked, "How are ye feelin'?"

Averill blinked in confusion at the question, unsure why he would ask it. Did she look pale or peaked? Frowning at the possibility, she said politely, "Fine, husband. And you?"

Kade chuckled, but explained, "I mean did the journey today trouble ye? Yer no' still tender from the beddin'?"

"Oh! Nay," she said, flushing brightly.

"Good," he said, then bent his head and kissed her.

Despite her surprise, Averill responded at once, her arms slipping up around his head, her lips drifting open in invitation, and her body melting into his as his own arms gathered her close. Truly, it felt like forever since he'd last kissed her, though it had only been moments ago. Well, the last one had been. He'd actually kissed her several times today: on waking that morning, as he'd headed out the door after dressing, before he'd lifted her into the saddle at Mortagne, and again each time they'd stopped that day, sometimes several times. In fact, he'd kissed her most passionately before leaving her here with Bess to bathe. That being the case, it was only natural that she would expect this time to be more of the same, a deep, passionate kiss, after which he'd lead her back to camp. However, rather than end the kiss and take her arm to lead her back to camp, Kade began to touch her as well, his hands roaming over her back, then dropping to cup her bottom, before moving to her upper arms to urge her back until she came up against the tree behind her. The moment she rested there, his hands moved to her breasts, squeezing them through the cloth of her chemise and gown. Averill moaned at the caress, her back arching to thrust her eager breasts most wantonly into his palms.

Kade's response to that was to thrust his hips forward, grinding his hardness against her as he began to tug at the top of her gown and chemise. She felt cool air brush over her nipples, then his head ducked down to draw one into his mouth, and she heard a hiss thunk over her head.

Frowning, Averill tilted her head back to glance up, wincing as several strands of hair were torn from her scalp. She then gasped at the sight of the arrow protruding from the tree, still quivering in the air. Averill was vaguely aware of Kade also lifting his head, but was still completely unprepared when he suddenly dragged her to the ground, shouting out as he did.

At first, Averill feared he'd been injured by a second arrow or even grazed by the first, but then a sudden clamor of sound drew her head around as several Mortagne soldiers burst out of the bushes on every side.

"Where did it come from, my lord?" one of them asked.

Kade pointed silently across the river directly opposite, and several men immediately began to wade into the water, but he called them back.

" 'Tis no use harin' across the river. The archer will be long gone ere ye get to the other side," he pointed out.

The men hesitated, but reluctantly moved back toward them as Kade stood and helped Averill to her feet.

"Are ye all right?" he asked, shifting to block the men's view of her as he quickly helped her tuck herself back into her gown.

"A-aye, my l-lord, husband," Averill whispered, aware she was blushing.

Kade frowned and gave her a quick, but thorough, kiss. When he lifted his head, he said, "Do ye wish me to have one o' the men see ye back, or will ye wait a minute while I speak to them and allow me to accompany ye?"

"I will wait," she decided.

For some reason, her response brought a tiny smile to his lips, but it was gone quickly. He gave a nod and moved off to consult briefly with the soldiers. He was back after just a moment, taking her arm to lead her along the path into and through the woods to the larger clearing where they'd stopped to make camp. Averill glanced around as they walked, noting that while two of the men were following, the rest were spreading out and moving into the woods.

"Husband?" she asked. "Who do you think shot the arrow?"

He frowned, but then shrugged. " 'Twas probably a bandit."

"A bandit?" she asked doubtfully. "That makes little sense. What would a bandit gain from shooting us with his arrow from across the river?

Kade smiled faintly, and said, "I didna say 'twas a smart bandit."

"But—"

"I ken it makes little sense, wife," he interrupted. "But I've been away for three years and have no enemies I know of who would wish me dead. And since no one would have reason to kill you either"—he shrugged—"it was most like a bandit . . . or an arrow gone astray."

That seemed like perfectly sound reasoning to her, so Averill nodded and fell silent, but she couldn't help thinking there might be some other explanation. It had been a close call, and only luck and his ducking his head to suckle at her breast had saved him from an arrow in the back of the neck.

Actually, she realized, glancing at Kade, he was tall enough that it would have struck him between the shoulder blades. Aye, they had been very lucky.

Averill drew her horse in beside Kade's and peered up the hill toward the castle ahead. Her gaze slid over the solid stone outer curtain and the keep beyond. At this distance it looked a strong, well-built castle, a good place to call home. When the sun chose that moment to come out from behind the clouds it had been veiling itself in most of the day and shone a bright shaft of light on the edifice, Averill could only think it was a good omen.

She glanced to her husband, her eyebrows drawing together as she took in his expression. When he remained still and silent, she asked, "Stewart castle?"

Averill thought it must be, but there was just something about Kade's expression that made her uncertain. He looked stern and forbidding, a sharp contrast to the smiling, teasing Kade who had been in evidence since the wedding. He did not look like a man glad to be arriving home.

"Aye," Kade said grimly. " 'Tis Stewart."

"It does not appear to be falling down yet," Will commented, drawing her gaze his way as he drew up on her other side.

"Wife."

Averill turned attentively to her husband at that growl. The man had taken to calling her Avy since the wedding, so she knew whatever he wished to say was important. "Aye, husband?"

"Ye'll stay close to me or yer brother at all times until I say otherwise, and do as I order without question, ye ken?"

Though it was couched as a question, Averill didn't mistake it for anything but the order it was. She nodded solemnly in response, wondering for the first time just how much trouble he was expecting.

Satisfied by her nod, Kade grunted and urged his horse forward. Averill immediately followed suit, staying close as promised. Will stuck to her side like glue as well, so that they rode three abreast as they started up the slight hill. A glance over her shoulder showed that the soldiers who had accompanied them were also riding three abreast, their number trailing away into the woods, too many to count.

Averill grimaced and turned back in the saddle, thinking that the men on the wall could be forgiven for thinking them an invading army. But then, from what she understood, that was pretty much what they were, Averill acknowledged with a sigh. If Kade's father would not willingly step down and allow him to run the castle properly, Kade intended to force the issue, and her brother and father had supplied the army to do so.

* * *

Kade wasn't terribly surprised to find the gates closed and the drawbridge rising when they reached it. He was only surprised the drawbridge wasn't already fully up. The men on the wall had surely had the time to get it all the way up between spotting the approach of the English army riding with him and their arrival at the castle. However, judging by the drunken shouting on the parapet, and the calmer and much grimmer replies of someone who was not drunk, it seemed obvious his father had not wished the drawbridge lifted at all, but one of the soldiers had ignored his wishes and done the right thing. It sounded as if the soldier was now getting a drunken bollocking for doing so.

"Hail!" Kade shouted, drawing his mount as close to the edge of the moat as he could.

The shouting above stopped at once, and the sober voice called, "Who goes there?"

"Kade Stewart, son of Eachann," he shouted back. "And who are you?"

"Aidan Stewart, cousin and first to Laird Eachann Stewart," came the grim answer even as a drunken voice crowed, "See I told ye we werena bein' invaded, Aidan. 'Tis me brother. Lower the damned drawbridge, ye silly fool."

The drunk speaker wasn't his father then, but either Gawain or Brodie, Kade surmised. Both of his brothers were younger and had not enjoyed the opportunity to be trained away from Stewart. Unfortunately, that meant that all they'd been trained in was raising a mug of ale to their mouths. Not for the first time, Kade sent up a silent prayer of thanks to his mother for insisting he be sent to his uncle Simon the moment he was walking.

A head appeared at the top of the wall. "Yer wearin' English clothes and riding under an English flag."

Kade nodded. It was the man named Aidan who he knew was actually a second or third cousin to his father. The man had been a loyal soldier and Eachann Stewart's first for as long as he could remember. Noting that he sounded grim and calm despite the drunken slurs still being cast at him from above, Kade explained, "Aye. I've no clothes of me own at the moment. These are borrowed from Mortagne, as are the soldiers. He offered to accompany us to see his sister, my bride," Kade added, gesturing to Averill beside him, "safely to her new home."

Aidan considered that, then asked, "Where are Domnall, Angus, and Ian?"

"That's what I'd like to ken. They made it here then?"

"Aye, and left more than a week past."

"Only a week?" he asked with disbelief. "I sent them here more than three weeks ago."

Apparently convinced, Aidan shouted to the men to drop the drawbridge, then explained, "They arrived here in good time then, but had to await yer father's pleasure to speak to 'im. He was

. . . indisposed," the man finished dryly, then gave up talking as the drawbridge began to lower with a loud rumble.

'"Indisposed,'" Kade muttered with disgust, knowing it was a euphemism for drunk to the gills. He gave a start and glanced to the side when Averill's hand suddenly covered his own where it rested on his reins.

" 'Twill be all right, husband," Averill said quietly, offering him a reassuring smile.

Kade forced a smile in return and watched the drawbridge lower, his thoughts on the confrontation ahead. As it dropped the last few feet, he turned back to Averill. "Remember, stay close."

"I am your wife, my lord. My place is at your side," she said simply.

Kade nodded, but as he faced forward, it struck him that there was an air of determination about her that was rather disconcerting. It gave him the sneaking suspicion that she might be up to something. He turned back to eye her narrowly, but she merely smiled sweetly back, the same dear woman who had tended him through his illness and married him at Mortagne.

The deep thump of the drawbridge slamming to the earth distracted him. Shaking off this worry for now, Kade caught up his reins and started across the bridge to his childhood home. Some would think poorly of him for what he intended to do, but this had been his mother's intention from the moment she began to natter at his father to send him to Simon for training. Maighread Stewart had loved her husband, but she had not been blind to his faults. She had known he was in the grip of drink and that it would one day have him so firmly in its clutches that all at Stewart would suffer. Every time she had visited with Kade, she had drummed it into him that the day would come when he would have to take over the running of Stewart from his father—by force if necessary—for the good of their people.

Today is the day, Kade thought grimly, as they rode across the bailey and straight up to the keep stairs.

As he stopped and dismounted, Kade could hear the drunken calls of whichever brother had been on the wall. The man was crossing the bailey to greet them, but Kade had no interest in stopping to talk to someone in the shape his brother was. Ignoring his calls, Kade lifted Averill down from her mount and immediately urged her up the stairs into the keep, aware that Will was directly behind them with his sergeant at arms at his side.

He moved so quickly in his effort to avoid his brother that Kade didn't take note of the shape of the bailey. It was impossible not to note the state of the keep itself, however. He entered the great hall and stopped abruptly, mouth tightening and nose twitching at the scent that filled the air.

From what he'd been told, it had only been seven months or so since his sister, Merry, had married and moved to England. It seemed obvious that little, if anything, had been done in the great hall in that time, and it wasn't hard to figure out why when overloud laughter drew his gaze to the trestle tables, and he saw his father and another man seated there. Obviously, the brother on the wall had been Brodie, for Gawain was the second man at the table, or rather, under it, Kade thought grimacing as he watched the younger man laugh his way right off his seat and onto the rushes.

His gaze swept the rest of the hall, taking in the smoke-stained walls that were in need of a good whitewashing, as well as the dirty tapestries that hung there. Some of them were attached by only one hook and hung like sad, windless flags. He turned his attention to the room itself, taking in the lack of furniture except for a couple of trestle tables, then he glanced at the floor, noting the beyond-filthy rushes littered with food and other things he didn't care to identify. There were also broken bits of wood about that he suspected at one time had been furniture.

What seemed worse to him was the complete lack of bodies in the room. The great hall was the heart of the castle, and at both his uncle Simon's home as well as Mortagne, it had always been full of people—soldiers coming and going, maids bustling about, and people just sitting to speak or eat. But here there was no one but his father and brother. The heart of this castle was broken, and no one wished to enter.

"Bess, I will need my bag from the cart."

Averill's whispered words drew his attention to the fact that the cart had apparently reached the bailey, and his wife's maid had entered in search of her. Kade turned to see that the maid had not entered alone. There were several Mortagne soldiers behind her, holding up his now apparently unconscious brother, Brodie, with his arms drawn over their shoulders.

"He took a tumble on the stairs," one of the men explained in hushed tones, avoiding his eyes as he spoke. All the men were avoiding his gaze, Kade noted, and felt shame rise up within him for the showing his kin were making.

"Take him to his room, and I shall tend to him there," Averill ordered quietly.

"Aye, my lady," the man who had explained their presence said. Then he cleared his throat, and asked, "How do we sort out where that is exactly?"

Kade saw Averill blink twice, then she turned to him to whisper, "Do you know where his room is?"

When he shook his head, she glanced toward the two men at the table and bit her lip. Gawain was flat out on the floor, snoring, and his father wasn't far behind. The laird's eyes were closed, his head hanging down on his chest, and he was sliding from his seat to join his son in the filthy rushes.

Kade was grinding his teeth together at the shameful sight when Averill suddenly called out, "You there! Boy!"

It was only then he saw the small head poking through the door to the kitchens. It was a lad of no more than six or seven, with huge eyes presently locked on the duo now napping under the table.

"Hello!" Averill called again, moving forward.

Apparently satisfied that his laird and the laird's son were unconscious and, therefore, no threat, the boy turned his attention to her. His eyes grew even wider, though Kade wouldn't have thought it possible, then he stuck a thumb at his own chest, eyebrows rising in question.

"Aye, you," Averill said with a touch of exasperation. "Come here."

He hesitated briefly but then slid through the door and moved reluctantly forward.

Kade couldn't help noticing he gave the table and its two snoring men a wide berth and suspected that was due to the violence he'd heard accompanied the drink his kin enjoyed so much. Noting a couple of fading bruises on the lad, Kade deduced that he didn't always move cautiously enough.

"What is your name?" his wife asked gently, once the boy paused before her.

"L-Laddie," he stammered anxiously.

Averill stiffened, but simply said, "Good day to you, Laddie."

"G-good d-day to you, me l-lady," Laddie murmured back.

His wife's face softened at his stuttering. She dropped to her haunches before the boy so that their faces were at the same level, then leaned forward to whisper to him. Kade was very curious and wanted to move closer to hear what she said, but restrained himself and merely waited.

As Averill whispered, the boy nodded and nodded, acknowledging every word she said, and when she finished, he beamed a wide smile and nodded once more. Apparently satisfied, Averill straightened and led the boy back to him.

"Laddie, here, is willing to direct the men as to which rooms are your father's and brothers'," she announced. "But 'twould be faster were they all taken up at once."

When Kade hesitated, Will said, "My men are at your disposal,"

" 'Tis no necessary," a voice called out, and the soldiers shifted aside, dragging their burden with them to reveal seven burly Scots standing just inside the door. Kade hadn't heard them enter, but supposed they'd done so while he was distracted watching his wife talk to Laddie. Now they moved forward as one. The speaker was tall and beefy with red hair and a ruddy complexion. He paused before Kade and eyed him up and down before nodding with apparent satisfaction that he was who he'd claimed to be. "Me laird."

"Aidan?" Kade asked, recognizing the voice that had questioned him from the wall.

"Aye," the warrior answered, then gestured to the men who had entered with him. They all immediately began to disperse. Two moved to relieve the English soldiers of their burden, and the other four collected Kade's father and other brother.

Kade watched long enough to note that while the men's faces were grim, they were careful with their burdens as they lifted the men and carried them to the stairs.

"So ye've come to kick yer da out of the laird's chair, have ye?" Aidan asked.

Kade turned his gaze back to the man, eyes narrowing. He sensed Averill moving closer, and while he'd ordered her to stay close, he now wished she'd move away rather than nearer. If he had to fight, he'd rather not risk her getting in the way. Glancing to the side, he caught her hand and urged her behind him, then scowled, and growled, "Aye."

Aidan's response was to scowl back, and growl, "'Tis about bloody time."

Kade allowed himself to relax. He almost even smiled, but managed to restrain the urge and merely nodded instead.

"Stewart needs ye," Aidan said, then added solemnly, "that's no' to say I won't ha'e to fight ye does yer father order it. He's me laird."

It was all Aidan had to say. The soldier was loyal to the oath he'd given to Kade's father. He wouldn't expect any less. This was his battle, and while the people might wish him to win, they would fight him if their laird ordered it. He respected that and could only hope they gave him the same loyalty should he succeed, so said seriously, "Then I'll try to see he doesna order it."

Aidan nodded. "Angus said ye took a blow to the head when yer ship broke up on rocks."

"Aye. Fortunately, I have good friends, and they saw me home and well," Kade said. He turned to his right, gesturing to Averill's brother. "This is one of them. Lord William Mortagne."

He waited as Aidan nodded in greeting, then turned to his left expecting Averill to be there, only to have to turn again as he recalled he'd pushed her behind his back. He found her kneeling behind him, whispering back and forth with Laddie. It was only then he realized that the boy still remained close by, his directions unneeded since the Stewart men had known where to take his father and brothers.

"Avy?" he said quietly.

She glanced up, then patted Laddie and straightened. "Aye, husband?"

"Come." He caught her hand, tugged her to his side, and turned to face Aidan again as he said, "Me wife."

Averill seemed somewhat dismayed by the terse introduction, but he saw no reason for further explanations. He'd said outside the wall that Will and his soldiers were there to escort him and his wife, Will's sister, to Stewart. There was no need to explain again.

Aidan smiled at Averill and nodded politely. "Me lady."

"G-good d-day, sir," Avy murmured.

Kade frowned at her stuttering and the way she ducked her head. She did not do it around the Mortagne soldiers, but then she knew and was comfortable with them, he supposed. Her doing so now reminded him of his intention to work on her self-esteem, and he promised himself he would just as soon as he could . . . but not now. It was a matter for another day, he decided, and gave her a reassuring squeeze of the behind that made her gasp and jump a bit. He sensed her turning a sharp gaze on him but had already turned his attention to Aidan.

"As me father's *indisposed*," Kade said dryly, using the word this man had used earlier, "mayhap ye could give me an accountin' o' what has been happenin' while I was away."

"Aye," Aidan said agreeably.

Kade nodded and started to lead the party to the trestle tables, but paused when Averill tugged on his hand. Frowning, he glanced back and raised an eyebrow in question.

Averill hesitated, then drew him away from the others to whisper, "While you are busy with Aidan, I thought mayhap I would go above stairs and see if there are any rooms suitable for sleeping in. They may need to be cleaned or—"

"Aye," Kade interrupted with a sigh. He had not considered that, but if the bedchambers upstairs were in as poor repair as the hall, there was definitely some work to do before the sun set. He was not sleeping on the hall floor and wouldn't allow Will or Averill to do so either. He'd rather take them out and set up camp in the bailey. The thought was not a happy one for Kade. While he had left Averill alone after their wedding night, first to allow her to heal, then on the journey here simply because there had been no privacy and he hadn't been willing to toss up his wife's skirts in front of a hundred men, he had sustained himself the entire journey with the reassurance that once they reached Stewart and the privacy of a chamber, he would have her again. The possibility that there might be no inhabitable chamber had never occurred to him.

"Go ahead," he said now. "But take the boy with you, and if there is trouble, just shout, and I will come running."

He waited just long enough for Averill to nod, then bent to press a kiss to her lips before turning away to continue to the table.

Chapter Ten

"This one is Merry's room," Laddie announced as he opened the door.

Averill stepped into the room but came to an abrupt halt. This was the fourth room he had shown her. The three before it had been in good shape except for a few cobwebs and dust. It seemed obvious to Averill that Lord Stewart and his sons never bothered to enter the other bedchambers. However, it was now equally obvious that the same could not be said for this room.

" 'Tis a m-mess," Laddie stated the obvious with a grimace, following as Averill finally continued into the room.

Taking note of the returning stammer, Averill murmured, "I thought we had agreed that you need not be nervous with me?"

Laddie flushed and glanced away, admitting, "I f-feared ye m-may be angry w-when ye saw all th-this."

"Well, I am not," she assured him. "And even if I were, I would not be angry with you."

Laddie nodded, the stiffness in his stance easing. He even managed a small smile.

Averill smiled in return, then turned to peer over the room. While the rushes on the floor were not fresh, they were not filthy like those below. She suspected they had not been changed since Kade's sister, Merry, had left. Other than that, though, this room more resembled the great hall than the other chambers. It looked as if someone had attacked it in a fit of temper. While a solid oak chair sat before the fire, a small table that had once stood beside it was a mass of broken wood in the rushes. The bed was in one piece, but all of its linens and furs had been torn off and lay in a heap in the corner, and someone had managed to rip one of the shutters from the window. She had no idea where it was, but the remaining shutter was askew, hanging by only one fitting.

A sound drew her gaze around to the door, and Averill spotted Bess in the doorway. The maid held the medicinal bag she'd been sent for, forgotten in her hand, and her eyes were wide and horrified as she peered around the room.

" 'Tis a mess," Bess said with a shake of the head.

"Aye," Laddie lamented, then announced, "The laird did it."

"What?" Averill and Bess asked as one, turning to the boy.

He nodded solemnly. "Comes in here all the time, he does. Usually can't walk straight and bumps into things and such. He and the boys break a lot of things in the castle that way, but the laird is the only one comes in here," he assured them. And then the boy grimaced, and added, "He cries."

Averill straightened a bit at this news, feeling a bit of hope. A father who missed his daughter so much it made him cry could not be all bad, she thought, then wondered if her own father missed her as well. She believed he might a little, but didn't think he'd cry. At least, she hoped not and was fretting over the possibility when Laddie added, "I heard him." The earnest tone in his voice suggested to her that he suspected they might not believe such a thing. When she nodded solemnly to assure him she did, he relaxed a little, and added, " 'Twas a shameful sight, I'll tell ye. I was embarrassed for him. He was cryin' and moanin' and stumblin' over things. Then he fell on his arse and just sat there blubberin' on about who was goin' to run the keep now Merry was gone."

Bess clucked with disgust, but Averill sighed with disappointment that it wasn't his daughter he missed but her running of the house. Really, she was finding it hard to like the man, and she had not even met him yet.

Shaking her head, Averill walked to the door and held out her hand, "My medicinals please, Bess."

The maid handed them over almost reluctantly, and as Averill began to dig through the contents, asked anxiously, "Are you sure you're wanting to do this, my lady?"

"Aye," Averill said firmly.

"But . . ."

Averill held up her hand to silence the maid, then glanced to the boy to say, "Laddie, could you go below and fetch me some mead or cider?"

"Aye, my l-lady," he said eagerly, and Averill smiled faintly as he burst into a run to do her bidding. He was such a sweet boy.

"My lady, about this plan of yours," Bess said anxiously as soon as Laddie was out the door.

Averill sighed and turned to face her maid.

"'Tis a sound plan, Bess," she insisted firmly. "Nothing discourages a behavior like an unpleasant result."

"If that were the case, the hangovers Lord Stewart and his sons surely suffer after they drink would have put them off of it decades ago," her maid said grimly.

"There is a vast difference between a sore head that passes once you have started drinking again and the inability to keep anything, including the drink itself, in your stomach," Averill assured her. "Trust me, if Laird Stewart and his sons are violently ill every time they drink, they will stop drinking. 'Tis plain common sense."

"Aye, but what if they realize you are dosing them?" she asked worriedly.

"They will not know," Averill assured her. "We will give them this first dose while they are unconscious, dribble it down their throats while they sleep just like we fed Kade the broth when he was unconscious."

"You got little of that down his throat, and surely won't be able to get much down theirs," Bess muttered darkly.

Averill frowned as she realized this was true. Perhaps she had to rethink diluting the tincture in mead and should just drop a few drops of the concentrate straight down their throats. Aye, she decided, that would work nicely.

"Come," she said, and led the way out of the room.

"Where are we going?" Bess asked in a hiss, as they moved up the hall.

"To give the tincture to Kade's father and brothers."

"I thought we needed mead for that?" Bess asked with dismay.

" 'Twill be easier if we just slip a few drops of the tincture down their throats," Averill explained. "And if we are quick, we can have it all done before Laddie returns."

"Oh, dear Lord," Bess muttered, but then followed silently as Averill sought out and found Kade's father's room.

"God's breath, how does he stand it?" Averill murmured, gazing over the Stewart laird's bedchamber. While there were no lit candles or fire to light the room, it was still only midday and enough sunlight was coming through the open shutters that the room and its occupant were more than visible. Which she could only think was a good thing. This room was as bad as the great hall, the floor littered with discarded clothes and food, broken furniture, and torn-down tapestries. On top of that, it smelled as if someone had died there.

Grimacing, she turned to Bess, only to find her missing. Frowning, she moved back to the door to see her cowering in the hall.

"What are you doing?" Averill asked in a hiss.

"I'll wait out here and stand watch," Bess said quickly.

"Nay, I need your help. You need to hold his mouth open while I pour the tincture in."

"Oh, please, my lady," Bess begged, shaking her head. "I cannot—"

"You can," Averill insisted, catching her hand and dragging her into the room.

"We really shouldn't be doing this. I think you need to—"

"Hush, you will wake him," Averill whispered with exasperation as she retrieved her tincture and opened the vial.

"The second coming wouldn't wake him," Bess

said with disgust, peering down at the insensate man.

"Then what are you afraid of?" Averill asked dryly. "Open his mouth."

Bess snapped her mouth closed and bent to open Lord Stewart's. The moment she'd grasped his chin and forehead and pulled his lips apart, Averill leaned over and tipped the tincture to drip a mouthful in.

As soon as she straightened again, Bess released his mouth and hurried for the door. Averill clucked with exasperation at the woman's cowardice, but otherwise ignored her and watched Eachann Stewart's face as she put the lid back on her vial. A relieved breath slipped from her when Lord Stewart began to smack his lips and work his mouth, automatically swallowing the liquid inside. Satisfied, she took a moment to examine him, noting that he looked very similar to Kade except that he was older and had a red and bulbous nose. That would be from the drink, she supposed with a little shake of the head.

"My lady," Bess hissed from the safety of the hall.

Sighing, Averill turned and moved to join her.

"Can we not go below now and—"

"Nay," Averill interrupted firmly. "We have to do the brothers now. Gawain first, I think. His room is closest."

"Surely dosing the father is enough. There's really no need to—"

Ignoring her words, Averill simply caught Bess's

hand and dragged her to the next room. Fortunately, after several steps, Bess, blessedly, gave up protesting. It made things go much more quickly, and within moments they were done and slipping out of his room as well.

"This is the last one," Averill said encouragingly as she led Bess to the last door in the hall.

"Thank God," the maid muttered. "Your mother must be rolling in her grave at the business you get up to."

Ignoring her, Averill led the way into the room. Of the three, it was in the worst shape. It seemed obvious that the three men had no care for their possessions. Each room sported broken furniture and other items that had been destroyed, but here even Brodie's bed was broken, one of the newel posts having been snapped, leaving the draperies hanging down at one corner.

Shaking her head, she moved to the bed and waited for Bess to pry his mouth open. Averill then bent to pour in her tincture.

"There," she said as she straightened. A little sigh of relief slipped from Averill's lips as she closed the small vial and slid it back into her bag of medicinals. " 'Tis done. All we can do now is wait and see what comes of it."

"Thank God," Bess breathed, releasing her hold on Brodie's mouth. "Please, my lady. Let us get out of here now."

"Aye," Averill said with exasperation and decided she'd never again take the maid along with her on such excursions. Bess had whined and carped the entire time, fretting like an old woman.

Well, all right, Averill acknowledged to herself, at more than forty summers Bess *was* an old woman. Still, that was no reason to be as timid and nervous as a mouse. 'Twas no wonder the maid had been so scandalized by what Sally and Old Ellie had been telling her about pleasing a man—the woman wouldn't have the heart to try any of them. She'd probably lain quivering in bed, eyes squeezed shut every time her husband had tried to mount her . . . and wouldn't that have been a pleasant experience for both of them? she thought with disgust.

"My lady," Bess hissed.

"I am coming," Averill muttered. "I just—"

She paused abruptly and gave a startled shriek as Brodie's hand suddenly fastened itself around her wrist. Eyes widening and shooting up the bed, she found herself staring into his bleary gaze.

"Here, lovey, how about a kiss?" he slurred, giving her arm a tug.

"Yer da may no put up much o' a fuss," Aidan said quietly. "He's no a stupid man and, despite the drink, kens things are slippin' away here. Another family takes to its heels every day, moving to greener pastures, and those that remain behind are only awaiting their chance. Half the castle staff is gone, and of those that remain behind—" He shook his head. "Cook is gone, the maids'll no even enter the great hall anymore, and the men avoid it, too . . . Aye, yer father may be glad to pass the title and responsibility on to ye."

Kade fervently hoped so. While he hadn't spent much time around Eachann Stewart, the man was still his father, and Kade had no wish to commit patricide. But after all he'd learned from Aidan about the state of affairs here, he couldn't simply walk away this time and leave his father in charge either. Stewart was in a bad way.

"Did you say the cook is gone?" Will asked, and the dismay in his voice drew the first smile Kade had managed since sitting down to talk with Aidan. After three years of rotten food and near starvation in that hellish prison, Will had an insatiable appetite. Kade had been amazed at the food he'd seen the man put away since rising from his own sickbed. He'd been even more amazed to find himself matching him bite for bite and was slightly upset to hear there was no cook, himself. But not nearly as forlorn as Will appeared to be.

"Aye," Aidan said, and grinned at Will's expression. "But I ken where he is and suspect he could be convinced to return does the situation change."

"Mayhap ye could—" Kade paused abruptly, eyes shooting upward as a great shrieking and wailing sounded overhead. Before the end of the first shriek, he was on his feet and running, his heart slamming against his chest as a litany of possible reasons for the sounds ran through his mind. The women might have stumbled upon a mouse or some other vermin while preparing the rooms above stairs, or one of them might have had an accident and hurt herself grievously. He was hoping for the former.

Kade reached the top step in time to see young Laddie charging up the far end of the hall with a trio of maids on his heels. As he started after him, the lad came to a skittering halt at one of the bed-chamber doors near the end of the corridor and thrust it open. The hallway immediately resounded with loud, panicked, and completely unintelligible screeches that were now joined by the loud slur-ring voice he'd heard heckling Aidan at the gate.

"Come on, lass, just a quick tumble. I promise I'll make ye like it."

Brodie! Cursing, Kade rushed forward and burst in on a scene he would not soon forget. Averill appeared to be in a wrestling match with Brodie. He was sitting up, struggling to pull her onto the bed from the far side, while she did everything she could to resist. Meantime, Bess, the source of the shrieking and wailing, was on the near side of the bed, pounding on his head and back trying to make him release her mistress.

Laddie and the three maids had apparently come to an abrupt halt inside the door at the sight as well, but even as Kade took everything in, the boy spurted across the room, snatching up a shield that lay discarded on the floor as he went. Leaping onto the head of the bed with the heavy metal item, he swung it up, then brought it back down with a horrible gong as Kade started across the room. The action didn't knock Brodie out as the boy had probably hoped, but it certainly got his attention. Releasing Averill, he swung around toward the boy, emitting a furious roar as he did.

Laddie's eyes became great holes of horror in his head, then he slammed the shield down again, putting every bit of weight and strength he had behind it. That time it worked. Brodie's eyes rolled up in his head, and he collapsed in a heap on the bed. Laddie immediately tossed the shield aside and scrambled across the bed to leap off on the other side and crouch beside Averill.

"Are ye all right, me lady?" Laddie asked anxiously, catching at her arm and tugging at it in an effort to help her up even as Bess finally stopped her shrieking and rushed around the bed to help as well.

"Oh, my," Averill said breathlessly as she sat up from where she'd fallen when Brodie had released her. "Aye, I am well, thank you, Laddie. That was very brave of you."

"Aye, 'twas," Kade growled, as Bess and Laddie helped his wife to her feet. The maids by the door had noted his entrance as he'd passed them and begun to sidle out of the room at once. Though he noticed that while they'd taken themselves out of striking distance, they had not left completely but were peering in around the edges of the door, trying to see past Will and Aidan, who had followed him.

Bess, Averill, and Laddie, however, had not noted his entrance and did so finally with wide eyes and surprised gasps.

"Oh h-husband," Averill said breathlessly. Forcing a smile, she avoided his gaze by brushing down her skirt as she murmured, "We . . . er . . . I was j-just ch-checking to be sure your br-brother did not do himself an injury when he fell. Unfortunately, he woke up and . . . er . . . seemed to think I was . . . w-well, he th-thought . . ."

"I ken what he thought," Kade growled, catching her arm and urging her toward the door. In his drunken state, Brodie had obviously thought her one of the maids and had intended to have at her. And, apparently, he hadn't cared if she was willing or not. That infuriated him. It seemed obvious he'd have to have a stern talk with the man when he woke up. In the meantime, he had a wayward wife to deal with.

"I told ye to stay close unless I said otherwise, did I no'?" he asked grimly as he led her past Will and Aidan and into the hall.

"Aye, and I d-did," she said swiftly. "Y-you said I c-could c-come above stairs and—"

"And check to see what shape the rooms are in," Kade interrupted grimly. "I didna say ye could check on Brodie."

Much to his surprise, she nodded. "Aye. Y-you are right. I should n-not have—"

"Nay, ye shouldna," he said grimly, then paused in the hall to ask, "Which o' the rooms did ye settle on fer us?"

She hesitated, then said, "The three at the end of the hall need only an airing, dusting, and a change of linens. The rushes are old but clean and will do for tonight."

Nodding, he started forward again, urging her toward the last room at the opposite end of the hall, as far away from his brother's room as possible. He ushered her in, turned to close the door, and then scowled when he saw that everyone was following . . . everyone except for Laddie. There was no sign of the boy.

"Where's the lad?" he growled with a frown, worried he was still in the room with Brodie and that if his brother woke up, he might be in trouble.

They all peered around rather blankly at his question, and Aidan said, "I'll find him."

"Thank ye," Kade muttered. "Send him here when ye do."

Nodding, Aidan turned away to head back up the hall, and Kade glanced to Will. "I'll be down in a minute."

Will hesitated, his gaze sliding from his stern face to Averill, who was now biting her lip, but he nodded and turned to head for the stairs. Glad he wasn't going to interfere, Kade ignored the women, closed the door, and swung around to face his wife.

"I w-was . . ." Averill's eyes darted around as if seeking an escape, then she gasped with surprise when he caught her hand and tugged her up against his chest. "Husband?"

Kade kissed her: a deep, wet one that spoke of his hunger for her and was propelled partially by the fear he'd suffered at the shrieking that had brought him running. Just as quickly as he tugged her into his arms, he broke the kiss to glare down at her. "Stay away from Brodie."

"Aye, husband," she breathed, her voice dreamy, and she tugged his face down for another kiss.

The bold action startled a smile from Kade that turned into a frown when a knock at the door sounded before he could even begin to kiss her in return. Sighing, he lifted his head and set her away to answer the summons. But a small smile formed on his lips when he heard her sigh of disappointment as he reached for the door handle. Promising himself he would ease that disappointment tonight, he pulled the door open and scowled out at Aidan, then dropped his gaze to the boy he held by the collar. Kade took in Laddie's wide eyes and pale face, then glanced to the women now gathered around Bess, twittering nervously a few feet away.

Stepping into the hall to join Aidan and Laddie, he pushed the door open wider, and said to the women, "Get yerselves inside and help me wife ready the room."

It was all he had to say. The women bustled forward and hurried into the room at once, seeming eager to escape his presence. Laddie was equally eager and tried to follow them in, but Aidan still had him by the collar and tugged him back.

The boy's shoulders sagged, and a defeated sigh slipped from his lips when Kade pulled the door closed. He then raised sad, resigned eyes, opened his mouth to speak, found he had no voice, and swallowed a lump that had apparently lodged itself in his throat, to ask, "Are ye gonna k-kill me now?"

"Kill ye?" Kade asked with shock. His eyes shifted to Aidan, who looked just as startled as he was, then he glanced back to the boy, and asked, "Why the devil would I do that?"

" 'Tis ag-against the laws for a p-peasant to hit a noble," Laddie said in quavering tones, then, just in case Kade had forgotten, he added, "And I hit yer b-brother."

"Aye, he did," Aidan pointed out solemnly.

Kade grimaced but kept his eyes on Laddie, and said, "But ye did it to save me wife, did ye no'?"

"Aye," he admitted, shoulders straightening and mouth setting rebelliously. "And I'd d-do it again even if ye will k-kill me for it. Lady Averill is nice and p-pretty, and he's a nasty mean c-cur even if he might be me d-da."

Kade stiffened. "Yer da? Brodie's yer father?"

All of the stuffing went out of the lad, and he shrugged unhappily. "Me ma s-said he w-was."

Kade stared at the boy, now seeing the family resemblance. He had the Stewart features, and the same red hair as Brodie and Gawain, though his was darker. His eyes were also the same deep green as Kade's sister, Merry's, and his own. Mouth tightening, he asked, "Who's yer ma'?"

"B-belle," he answered sullenly.

"She was a chambermaid here," Aidan said quietly.

" 'Was'?" Kade asked with a frown.

"Died last month," Aidan said, face grim. "When the laundress took to her heels, the maids started trying to do the washing. She lost her balance and tumbled in the vat while stirring the clothes over the fire. Burnt something awful she was, died a week later."

After days of pain and suffering, Kade thought grimly. His gaze slid over the boy's ratty clothes and dirty face. "Who tends ye now?"

Laddie shrugged dully.

"The maids look after him some," Aidan answered. "Keep him out of harm's way when they can."

Judging by the bruises the boy sported, that wasn't often, and Kade wondered if his brother even knew the lad was his spawn . . . or cared. Sighing, he shook his head and straightened. "I'm no' killin' ye."

Laddie glanced up hopefully.

"In fact, I sent fer ye to commend ye fer defendin' me wife," he said solemnly. " 'Twas verra brave. Ye'll make a good soldier one day, and I'll see ye squired in a year or two."

Laddie sucked in a long breath at this news, his eyes starting to shine.

"Until then, though," Kade added firmly, "I'd have ye stay close to me wife. She'll teach ye manners and other things a knight needs to ken, and ye can guard her for me as ye did today."

"With me life, me laird," the boy vowed, the shine in his eyes becoming tears of gratitude.

Kade shifted uncomfortably under the adoration beaming from the boy's eyes, then nodded sternly.

"Go on, then, keep an eye on me lady wife," he ordered, turning to open the door for him. The women in the room paused in their nattering to glance toward the door as Laddie rushed inside beaming, and Kade added, "Make sure she doesna leave this room without me say-so."

"Aye, me laird," Laddie said importantly, then ruined it by smiling so wide Kade feared he'd split his face.

"B-but, husband," Averill protested, rushing across the room.

The moment she stopped before him, Kade bent and gave her a kiss. It was quick, but thorough, and her eyes were closed, a little sigh slipping from her lips as he lifted his head.

"Aye?" he asked.

Her eyes blinked open, confusion in their depths for a moment, then she seemed to recall her protest and frowned. "I cannot stay here. I need to see to a room for Will as well."

Kade nodded slowly, but his mind was on the fact that her stammering had not continued after the kiss. It was not the first time he'd noted that a simple kiss from him seemed to make her forget to be self-conscious and stutter. It seemed he'd just have to kiss his wife a lot to distract her from herself. A terrible duty that, but he was man enough to tend to it, he thought with a grin.

"Husband?" she prodded, scowling now.

Forcing himself to the matter at hand, Kade cleared his throat, and said, "Fine." He glanced over her shoulder to Laddie. "She may travel betwixt this room and the one she's chosen for Lord Mortagne, but nowhere else without me permission."

Averill gave a gusty sigh of disgust, but Kade merely kissed her forehead, pulled the door closed, and headed for the stairs with Aidan.

Chapter Eleven

Averill scowled at the door her husband had just closed, then turned to survey Laddie and the women in the room. She'd just been getting acquainted with them when Kade had interrupted to let the boy in and give his ridiculous order. Aside from Bess, there was a thin young maid named Lily, with lank mousey blond hair and dull eyes. Morag, a middle-aged woman with dark hair and a face that looked as if it had not smiled in a very long time, and an old crone with wiry grey hair and the sweetest smile she'd ever seen. Her name was Annie.

Averill smiled wryly to herself. She'd sent Laddie for mead or cider, and he'd returned with the last three maids left in the keep to explain why there was none. It seemed Laird Stewart saw no need for mead or cider now that his daughter was gone. Ale and whiskey were all that were on offer in the castle. That was something she would need to see to quickly, Averill decided, but it would mean a trip to one of their neighbors, for she'd already been told there was very little in the village. Since their laird never bought any, no extra was made, and the remaining villagers at Stewart made enough only for their own consumption.

Sighing at all the problems quickly becoming apparent, Averill took a moment to feel sorry for herself. But then her usual positive spirit reasserted itself, telling her it was better to be Kade's wife with a heap of trouble to sort out, than Cyril's wife and with probably a whole different set of worries—ones that couldn't be fixed with a bit of time and elbow grease.

"Right!" She straightened her shoulders. "Let us set this room to rights and move on to my brother's so that the men can bring up our belongings."

The women nodded and burst into activity. With her, Bess, the three maids, and even little Laddie helping out, it went very quickly. Although it might have gone quicker still had Laddie not constantly tried to help her. Every time she picked up something or began to dust an item, he was there trying to aid her. In truth, while she found it sweet, it was a bit exasperating, too. The boy was constantly underfoot, staring up at her with adoring eyes, his chest puffed out from pride like a rooster's. His stammering had halted, however. It only occurred a time or two as they worked, and only when he addressed Morag. He seemed to find her intimidating.

"There," Averill said, as she and Bess finished making the bed in Will's room sometime later. "I think we are finished."

"Aye, 'twill do for now." Bess straightened and glanced around the room with satisfaction, but then scowled as her gaze moved down to the floor. She toed the rushes they stood on, and added, "Though I wish we could do something about these rushes."

"We can tend them tomorrow . . . or perhaps the next day," Averill murmured, thinking they could wait until after she got in some mead and cider.

"Will ye need us anymore, me lady?" Annie asked, moving toward the bed at a pained shuffle. The woman suffered terrible arthritis, but she hadn't let it slow her down. She'd worked just as hard as the rest of them.

"Nay, Annie. Thank you," Averill answered. "With just the three of you, I know there must be duties you are neglecting while here. Go on and tend them."

Nodding, the maid turned and led the other two women to the door. Averill watched them pensively, then glanced to Bess when the maid commented, "Annie seems a nice one, but the other two are a grim pair."

"Aye," she agreed. "Mayhap you could try to catch Annie away from Morag and Lily at some point in the next day or so and find out why."

"I can tell ye why," Laddie said eagerly.

Averill glanced to him, one eyebrow raised. "Can you?"

"Aye. Me ma and Annie used to fret over it." He paused, his expression turning serious as he tried to recall what he'd heard, then said, "Lily was to marry the blacksmith's son, ye ken. She loved him somethin' fierce. But then me d—Laird Brodie," he corrected himself. "He took a shine to her one night while in his cups and wouldna take no for an answer. When the blacksmith's son, Robbie, found out, he called off the wedding. She cried and begged, but he said as how she knew better than to be caught by the goat when he was drinkin' and—"

"The goat?" Averill interrupted uncertainly.

Laddie flushed, but admitted in a mutter, "That's what they call me d—Laird Brodie. The randy, red goat."

"I see," Averill murmured. "Pray, continue."

"Well." He frowned, trying to regather the threads of his story, then shrugged. "He just said as how she must ha'e wanted to be caught, and he'd no raise the goat's bastard."

"She's with child?" Bess asked, eyebrows rising.

"Nay." Laddie shook his head, but then added, "She was but lost the bairn ere it was grown in her. Lily ain't been right in the head since."

"I see," Averill murmured, and sighed unhappily. She was really beginning to dislike Brodie Stewart. "And why is Morag—?"

"Morag is Lily's ma," Laddie said, as if that explained it all, and Averill supposed it did.

Shaking her head, she straightened her shoulders. "Well, thank you for telling me, Laddie. It explains a good deal, I shall—"

A sudden curse in the hall made her pause. Averill glanced toward the door the maids had left open just as a group of men were struggling past. Her eyes widened on the unconscious man they carried, then she rushed forward. "Husband!"

Her cry made the men pause at once, and without further ado they changed direction and carried him inside.

"One of the maids said yours was the room at the end of the hall," Will complained as they moved past her.

Averill didn't bother to explain that this was supposed to be his room. They were much alike anyway, and she was too desperate to find out what was wrong with Kade to wait while they carried him back out and to the next room.

"What happened?" she asked, moving up beside the bed to peer down at her husband as the men laid him down and shifted out of the way.

"One of the stones fell from the curtain wall and caught him unawares as we were surveying the bailey," Will answered grimly, moving up on the opposite side of the bed to peer down at Kade.

"Fortunately, he had just turned and started to move away, and it merely sheered the side of his head and hit his shoulder. Had he not moved when he did . . ."

Will left the consequences unspoken and merely shook his head, but Averill didn't need him telling her what might have happened. The stones used to build the curtain wall and castle were huge and heavy; one hitting him square would have killed him. As it was, there was a nasty, long, bloody gash just behind his ear, she saw, turning his head for a better look, then removing his tunic to see what damage had been done.

"I need water and my medicinals," Averill murmured. She was vaguely aware of Bess moving to fetch her medicinals while one of the men moved out to the hall to bellow down the stairs for one of the maids to bring water, but most of her attention was on Kade as she brushed his hair out of the way the better to see his injury.

"How bad is it?" Will asked quietly.

Averill was silent as she bent to better examine the head wound. It was bleeding quite freely, but she didn't think the damage was as bad as she'd first feared. There was a large bump, and some skin and hair had been sheared away by the boulder, but it would not need stitching. However, while it didn't look bad, that didn't mean all would be well. Head wounds were infamously tricky to deal with.

Sighing, she straightened to accept the small bag

Bess was holding out, "Was he knocked unconscious at once, or did he swoon after?"

"I doona swoon. That's a woman's trick."

Averill glanced down with a start at that growl from Kade, relief pouring through her as she saw his eyes were open. Eyes softening, she asked, "How do you feel?"

"Me head is achin' like a son o' a bi—" He paused abruptly, then sighed and muttered, "Well, 'tis achin'."

Averill bit her lip to keep from grinning at his editing his own words. She was so relieved that he was awake and complaining, she could have sung. Instead, she nodded solemnly and turned to take the water as Lily appeared beside her, a bowl of it in hand.

"Here is a clean linen, my lady," Bess appeared again, having thought of what Averill hadn't.

"Thank you," Averill murmured, and quickly dampened the cloth in the water before turning back to Kade, only to find he'd sat up in the bed and was sitting sideways on it, his feet on the floor. She almost reprimanded him, but then decided it would make things easier for her this way, so simply stepped between his knees and set to work.

"What happened?" he asked Will in a growl, as she began to clean the wound. "One minute we were walkin' along, and the next I'm here."

"A stone fell from the curtain wall as we were turning to head back inside," he explained. "It caught you on the side of the head."

"And the shoulder," Averill muttered, noting the scraping and bruising there.

"A stone *fell*?" Kade asked with disbelief, then scowled and shook his head. "The wall did no' look to be in such poor repair. I shall ha'e to inspect it, and—"

"Sit still," Averill interrupted firmly. "I am trying to clean the wound, and you are shaking your head and wiggling about on the bed like a child."

Kade turned a scowl her way. "I am no wigglin'."

When Averill merely snorted at that and bent back to her work, Aidan cleared his throat, and said, "The wall isna in poor repair. I inspect it twice weekly. 'Tis in fine shape."

Averill scowled again as Kade immediately turned his head slightly to look at the man, then back the other way when Will quietly pointed out, "Not so fine if bits of it are falling away."

Aidan frowned, but nodded with a sigh. "I shall go see to that section right now. Mayhap I missed something."

"My brother will go with you," Averill announced firmly, when Kade turned his head yet again.

"Me?" Will asked with amusement.

"You may as well," she said sweetly. "For I want everyone out of the room while I finish this and 'twill give you something to do besides hang about in the hall."

When Will raised an eyebrow and glanced to Kade, he hesitated, but surprised her by nodding.

Averill did not know if it was because he did not trust Aidan or because he had realized that the distraction was making her task more difficult, but she was grateful either way.

The room quickly cleared out, everyone leaving, including Bess, and Averill sighed and bent back to her task. Without his constantly shifting about, she was able to clean both the wound on his head and that on his shoulder much more quickly. Once done, she slathered some cream on each. Averill then paused to debate whether to try to bandage either injury. Both were in awkward spots. Trying to bandage the one on his head meant wrapping it around his face or risking its falling off, and the other was so high on his shoulder that a bandage could not be tied around his arm.

"Are ye done?" Kade asked after a moment.

Averill sighed and shook her head. "I would put bandages on but worry they would just annoy you."

"Aye, they would," he agreed.

"Well then, I suppose I am done," she said wryly, and added. "Lie down, and I shall mix up a potion to ease the aching and help you sleep." She started to step away, only to find herself caught between his legs when they suddenly closed around hers. She became aware that their position put him at eye level with her breasts when he suddenly slid his arms around her bottom and leaned forward to nuzzle her through the cloth of her gown.

"Husband, you need to rest after your injury," she protested, the tingling his attention was caus-

ing in the nipple he was teasing making her voice
a little too breathless to be effective.

"I'm fine," Kade growled against her, his teeth
scraping her erect nipple through the cloth. "Me
head doesna even hurt anymore."

Averill was pretty sure that was a lie, but couldn't
seem to find her voice to say so as his hands slid
under her skirt and trailed up the outer sides of her
legs. When he reached her hips, he slid his hands
around to cup her behind, then urged her closer as
he continued to nuzzle her.

"Undo yer laces," he growled, releasing the hold
he had on one cheek of her behind to slip it around
front to urge her legs farther apart.

"Wh-what?" Averill asked uncertainly, biting
her lip and rising up on tiptoe as his fingers trailed
lazily up an inner thigh.

"Undo yer gown. Bare yer breasts for me," he
said.

Averill swallowed nervously but did as he asked,
reaching behind to tug the laces loose. She paused
then, however, shy of taking the next step.

"Do it." It was a quiet order, punctuated by his
hand's reaching the apex of her thighs and running lightly over the tender flesh there before drifting down again.

Swallowing, Averill slowly slid the gown off
her shoulders. It seemed she hadn't loosened all
the laces, and while the top of her gown dropped
away, the waist held, so that the skirt of the gown
remained caught above her hips.

When she paused then, Kade growled, "Yer chemise."

Sighing, she slid that off her arms as well, struggling a bit to manage it, but then it dropped away, too. Averill couldn't stop herself from catching at the garment and holding it to her breasts.

Rather than order her to let it go, Kade allowed his fingers to slide back up her leg until he found the soft, wet core of her again.

Gasping, Averill grabbed for his shoulders to keep her balance as her legs suddenly went weak. It allowed the cloth of her chemise to drop away as the top of her gown had, leaving her breasts bare. Kade immediately took advantage and leaned forward to take one naked nipple into his mouth.

"Husband," she moaned, as excitement exploded within her.

Kade let her breast slip from his mouth and raised his head to growl, "Kiss me."

Averill lowered her head at once to do as requested, kissing him fervently as he continued to caress her. She welcomed his tongue into her mouth, moaning as it rasped across hers, then broke the kiss and threw her head back on a gasp as he slid one finger inside her.

Bereft of her mouth, Kade immediately turned his attention to her breasts again, lathing and suckling them as he continued to excite her. Tension was growing inside her with every passing moment, and her legs began to tremble so much she feared they would give out, but then he sped up the rhythm, his caresses becoming firmer, almost demanding a response.

Averill gave it. The excitement bubbling within her suddenly boiled over, and she cried out, clutching at his head and shoulders as her body hummed with release. Kade stilled briefly, merely holding her close, then he withdrew his hands from beneath her skirts, tugged it off her hips, turned, and lowered her to the bed.

As she settled back on the bed, Averill watched through half-closed eyes as he stood and reached for the laces of his braies. He tugged them undone, let the pants drop away, and crawled onto the bed to settle between her legs; and then a knock sounded at the door.

They both froze and turned their heads toward it, then turned back to each other.

Kade hesitated, but then barked, "What?"

"We're returned with a report on the state o' the wall," Aidan announced.

Kade's gaze shifted to the door and back to Averill, and he shouted, "I'll come below in a while. I'll hear it then."

"You will want to hear it now," Will said in the serious voice that Averill recognized meant trouble.

Kade apparently recognized it, too. Cursing, he pressed a quick kiss to her forehead, then climbed off her and got up to dress, shouting toward the door, "Wait for me below. I'll be right there."

An "aye" came back, then the sound of heavy

footfalls told them that the pair were moving away. Once assured that they weren't going to try to enter, Averill immediately leapt off the bed and snatched up her discarded clothes to dress. The chemise was still inside the gown, and she merely had to pull both over her head and tug them into place, but the lacings were a bit of a struggle. Still, she managed them and was all ready when Kade finished donning his own clothes and headed to the door.

He had pulled it open, stepped out and glanced back, mouth opening to say something when he realized she was following. Frowning, he asked, "Where diya think yer goin'?"

"I am thirsty," she said, and it wasn't a lie. Averill was very thirsty, but she also wanted to hear what the men had to say about the wall.

Kade narrowed his eyes. "Stay here. I'll send a maid up with—"

A sudden loud, violent retching sounded from the room at the other end of the hall, and he paused, glancing that way with a frown.

"It sounds as if your father is awake," Averill murmured, managing not to smile at the fact that her tincture was working so well. When a second round of retching started from the vicinity of Gawain's room, she tilted her head. "And your brother, too. Perhaps I should look in on them. Neither sounds as if he feels very well."

Cursing, Kade caught her hand and tugged her behind him out of the room.

"Yer no' to go near me father or brothers without me being present," he lectured.

"Aye, my lord husband," she said sweetly. When he turned to scowl at her as if suspecting she was up to something, Averill simply added a little more sweetness to her smile.

Shaking his head, he led her down the stairs and straight to the table, shouting for drinks to be brought as he saw her seated.

"Tell me," Kade snapped the moment he was seated beside her . . . on the bench rather than taking the laird's chair, she noted. While he intended to take over as laird, he apparently would not do so until he spoke to his father. She thought that very fine of him.

"The wall is sound," Aidan announced at once.

Kade frowned. "It canna be sound if bits o' it are fallin' down."

"That is just it," Will said grimly. "There are no stones missing from the wall by where you were felled. The wall is intact."

Kade sat back at this news, a stricken look claiming his features. That seemed to suggest this meant something to him, Averill noted, but shook her head. "How can that be? If it did not come from the wall, where could it have come from?"

"That is the question," Will said dryly. "The stone must have come from elsewhere and been carried there."

Her eyes widened incredulously. "Are you saying someone dropped it on his head deliberately?"

"That is how it appears," Aidan said grimly.

"But . . ." She glanced to Kade. "After that arrow in the woods on the way here, you said you had no enemies, husband. Who would do this?"

"Arrow in the woods?" Aidan asked with interest.

Kade sighed and quickly gave him an edited version of what had happened in the clearing, leaving out exactly what he'd been doing when the arrow had pierced the tree.

"So ye ducked yer head and just missed takin' an arrow in the back?" Aidan muttered. He then shook his head. "I ha'e to say yer one lucky bugger, me laird. First ye survive the arrow, and now this?" He shook his head again. "Aye, ye've got angels on yer side, ye do."

"Aye, he does," Will assured him. "And then there is the boat journey."

Kade grunted absently, his thoughts apparently on how the stone could have fallen. Averill slipped her hand into his, drawing his attention. She asked quietly, "Who would wish you harm?"

He squeezed her hand but shook his head.

"No one. At least not yet," Kade added dryly, and she knew he was thinking of his father and the fact that he intended to ask him to step down.

"But—" she began, only to have him interrupt her.

" 'Twas probably an accident," he said soothingly. "No doubt one o' the men put the stone up there for some purpose or other, leaned against it all unthinking, and sent it tumbling off the wall."

Averill stared at him, not bothering to hide her disbelief, but he ignored her expression and turned his attention to Morag as the woman appeared before them with several mugs of ale.

"Thank ye," Kade said, as she set them down.

The maid glanced to him with obvious surprise and actually almost smiled. Apparently, Laird Stewart and his other sons were not given to such courtesies, Averill thought, and glanced toward the stairs, wondering how they were faring. She turned her attention to the maid, however, when the older woman paused at her side.

"Aye, Morag?"

"I was wondering what ye were wantin' us to do about the sup," she explained, looking uncomfortable, and added, "as Cook fled a week past."

Averill's eyes widened with dismay at this news. "What has Laird Stewart been doing about meals?"

Her mouth turned down with disgust, but her tone was emotionless as she admitted, "He and the boys ride down to the inn in the village when they're hungry. Or they make do with whatever they can find around here."

Averill hesitated, then asked, "Is there any food here at all?"

Morag shook her head. "If there were, I'd be cookin' something fer ye as we speak. I'm a fair cook if I say so meself, and Lily's got a knack with pastries."

Averill filed that information away, then glanced

to her husband as he turned to join the conversation.

"'Tis all right, Morag. We shall make our way down to the inn to sup," he said quietly, then asked, "What do you and the other servants do about meals?"

Morag seemed surprised he would ask, but shrugged. "There's only Annie, me daughter, Lily, and me in the keep anymore. We go down to me sister's to eat in the evenin's. Her husband's a fine hunter and kind enough to have been providin' fer us since Lady Merewen left and all went to hell."

Averill glanced at Kade, worried about how he would take the bitter words, but he merely nodded solemnly, and said, "I am glad to hear it, and glad yer family hasna fled like the rest."

Morag hesitated, but then glanced to Aidan, and apparently thinking he'd tell anyway, turned back to admit, "We probably would ha'e were me mother no' so old the move would kill her; but she is, so we've stayed in the hopes things would get better."

"Well, I'm grateful fer it," Kade rumbled, then dismissed her with a quiet, "Thank ye."

Kade waited until she'd moved away and was out of hearing distance before turning to Aidan to ask, "How the devil did things get so bad, so quickly?"

"It hasna been that quickly. Merry has been gone more than seven months now," Aidan pointed out quietly. "Besides, the seeds were sown long before

Merry left. Most were ready to leave once yer lady mother died and only stayed fer Merry. Once she was gone . . ." He shrugged.

Kade nodded grimly and stood, catching Averill's arm to help her to her feet. "We may as well head to the village now and see if they can scrape together something to feed us. Yer welcome to join us, Aidan." He waited to see the man nod before sliding his glance to Bess, who stood hovering behind Averill. He added, "Ye'd best come, too, Bess. There's nothing here fer ye to eat."

The maid nodded, and they all moved toward the doors. Kade opened them, and led Averill out, only to come to an abrupt halt as his gaze slid over the English army set up in his bailey.

"They have stores to last them several days," Will said quietly when Kade dropped Averill's arm and turned to him. "Enough even to last a while do they do a bit of hunting. I will just have a word with my first before we go."

Averill slid her hand silently into her husband's as they waited. His face was expressionless, but she knew he had found the news Aidan had imparted depressing. She did, too, but was more concerned by the business of the falling stone. She didn't believe for a moment that it was an accident. Why would anyone place a great boulder on top of the wall? And how could anyone accidentally knock it *off* the wall? She didn't think Kade believed that either. She suspected he was trying to protect her from worry and knew there was no use asking him his thoughts on the matter. He would just repeat that it was probably an accident and change the subject. It left her to worry about it on her own. Obviously, not everyone was happy to have him home. She would have to keep her eyes open and watch for trouble. *I am quite happy with my husband and have no intention of losing him,* Averill thought grimly as Will finished his talk and Kade urged her down the stairs to meet him.

The inn in the village was a sad affair, small and dim with little to no business from what she could tell. Certainly there was no one there when they arrived, and no one entered before they finished their meal and left again. Their own entrance caused something of a stir, and they found themselves hovered over and feted by the owner and his wife. It seemed obvious they were glad to see Kade returned.

That or they were just glad of customers, Averill supposed, as Bess helped her prepare for bed once they returned. It was really rather early to be going to bed, but it had been a long journey there, and the days to come promised to be just as long. *There is much to do to set my new home to rights*, Averill thought, and glanced to Bess to say, "'Twas quiet when we came up. Are the laird and his sons recovering? Did any of them come below after you returned?"

While Averill had stayed behind with Kade and Will, who had wished to speak to the innkeeper after their meal, Aidan hadn't wished to tarry, and Bess, weary after their journey, had opted to return to the keep with him.

"I don't know about that," Bess said with amusement. "A chorus of retching comes from their rooms, then there's silence for a while ere the retching starts up again. I suspect they are sleeping between each bout."

Averill nodded. "They have not called for help or whiskey?"

"Oh, aye, they've called," she said dryly. "But Morag, Lily, and Annie must have left for Morag's sister's right after we headed for the inn. They were not here to answer their bellows, and I certainly wasn't going to."

"Nay, of course not," Averill agreed solemnly.

"There we are," Bess said, turning her toward the bed. "Now to bed with you. We've had a long day and will no doubt have another on the morrow."

"Aye," Averill agreed, climbing into the bed. "Thank you, Bess."

"You're welcome, my lady," Bess said, heading for the door. "Good sleep."

"And to you," Averill murmured, then glanced toward the door as it opened before Bess could reach it.

Kade appeared, spotted Bess, stepped aside for her to leave, and entered. He pushed the door closed behind him with a yawn as he headed for the bed.

Averill watched silently as he tugged his tunic off over his head, her eyes gliding over his strong, wide chest. Kade smiled a completely male smile when he caught her looking and paused to stretch in a way that showed off his muscles. Averill bit back the amused smile that tried to claim her lips then, but thought it adorable that he would show off for her. When he turned his attention to untying the string at the waist of his braies, she watched curiously, eyebrows rising when he appeared to have trouble. At first, she thought he was teasing, but then he cursed and began to tug at it with irritation and she realized he had somehow knotted it in his hurry to dress earlier. Pushing the linens and furs aside, she rose up on the bed and shifted to her knees to move to the side of the bed.

"You will break the tie like that, husband. Let me see if I can free it," she said quietly.

Kade hesitated, but then released his hold on the material and moved forward for her to have a go. He truly had snarled it up somehow, Averill noted as she began to unravel the tight knot. It took some doing, and she spent several minutes working at it before the knot came loose. Breathing out her relief then, she raised her head to offer him a smile of triumph that froze when she saw the expression on his face. It was hungry and hot, and she blinked in surprise and glanced back to where she had been working, only then noting that his manhood had grown while she labored and was pressing against the front of his braies.

Recalling the pleasure he'd given her that afternoon, and that they'd been interrupted before he'd found any himself, she thought briefly and slipped off the bed and tried to move around him, but he caught her arm.

"Where are ye goin'?" Kade asked, a frown replacing the desire of a moment ago.

"Just to get my bag," she assured him, managing to tug her arm free.

"Yer medicinal bag?" he asked with surprise. "What for?"

"'Tis a surprise. Get in bed, I shall be right back."

When he sighed and shook his head, but did move toward the bed, she headed for the chest that held her bag. It lay inside on the top. She took it out and quickly searched its contents, squinting in the poor light available. Bess had left only one candle lit in the room, and that was on a table beside the bed, so only the barest hint of light was managing to reach the corner where she knelt by the chest. Finding the ointment she wanted, she opened it quickly and began to slather it on her right hand.

"What are ye doin'?" Kade called from the bed, sounding rather suspicious. "Come to bed."

"I will. Just one moment," she said with exasperation as she closed the ointment with her ungreased hand and dropped the bag on top of the chest. Keeping her hand behind her, she then returned to the bed.

Kade eyed Averill suspiciously as she crossed back to him. There was a look in her eyes that suggested she did indeed have a surprise, one he wasn't sure he would enjoy. He watched narrowly as she climbed onto the bed, then noted that she was keeping one hand behind her back.

"What ha'e ye got there?" Kade asked, then instinctively grabbed for the linens and furs he'd pulled up to cover himself with when she suddenly dragged them down. He wasn't quick enough, and found himself lying there, bare from the knees up, his erection waving forward and back as if greeting her. Kade was on the verge of demanding to know what she was about when Averill suddenly brought her hand back around and clasped his waving penis.

Kade snapped his mouth shut and sucked air in through his gritted teeth as he stared at her wide-eyed.

"Old Ellie told me how to please a man as you pleased me this afternoon," she explained, beginning to move her hand.

"Old Ellie?" he asked, horrified to hear that his voice had come out several octaves higher than his usual baritone.

"A maid at Mortagne. She's very old and very wise, and she said to grease my hand up and pump you like I am milking a cow," Averill explained cheerfully and as he sagged back onto the bed, eyes closing with dismay she proceeded to do just that, closing her finger and thumb just under the head of his penis, then closing each succeeding finger around it, one after another, as if urging milk out of a cow's teat.

Unfortunately, she had it the wrong way around. Were his manhood an udder, she would be forcing the milk back up inside him rather than out. However, he wasn't a cow, what she was holding wasn't an udder, and what she was doing wasn't likely to bring anything squirting out of him. In fact, Kade could feel his erection dwindling away as she continued to work at him . . . then he couldn't feel anything at all.

Frowning, he opened his eyes and lifted his head to peer down. His manhood was there, hanging sadly over the top of her hand like an empty drinking skin, but he couldn't feel it. His eyes were just widening with the horror that she had somehow unmanned him, when Averill stopped what she was doing, released him, and frowned down at her hand.

"How odd, my hand seems to have gone numb," she said with bewilderment.

Kade felt hope stir within his heart and cleared his throat before asking in even tones, "What is it ye used to grease yer hand?"

She turned to him with surprise. "Just an ointment from my medicinals."

"Is it one to numb pain?" he asked carefully, then frowned with worry when Averill shook her head.

"Nay. This one is just to—" She paused suddenly and raised her hand to her face to give it a sniff.

Kade narrowed his eyes and waited.

"Oh d-dear," Averill breathed, eyes widening.

"Oh dear what?" he asked, biting his tongue to keep from shouting the question. Dear God, one did not sniff the ointment she had just greased her husband's pole with, then say "Oh dear" like that.

"I f-fear I m-may have g-got the ointments m-mixed up," she admitted, looking forlorn. "'*Tis* one to numb pain. 'Twill not harm you, but—"

Sighing with exasperation, Kade brought her explanation to a halt by catching her arm and dragging her down to lie half on top of him.

"'Tis all right," Kade muttered.

"B-but I w-wanted to p-please you," Averill cried, trying to rise back up.

"'Tis all right," Kade repeated, unsure whether to weep with relief that she hadn't permanently unmanned him or howl with frustration that the third attempt to tumble his wife since their wedding night had gone awry. At least, he'd intended to tumble her when he'd entered. Sighing, he rubbed her back soothingly, and said, "Ye do please me, wife . . . Verra much."

"Truly?" she asked on a sniffle.

"Aye," he growled, and glanced down, catching her dashing a tear away from her cheek. Kade sighed at her upset. The woman was trying, 'twas just a shame she had been given poor advice . . . well, and that she'd got her ointments mixed up in the dark corner, Kade thought with a grimace as he glanced down at his poor, numb manhood. The sad thing was lying flopped on his leg as if in a swoon, and he wondered unhappily how long that would last.

"Thank you, husband," Averill murmured. "You please me, too."

"Good," he muttered, then cleared his throat and asked, "Wife? How long do the effects o' this ointment last?"

Averill was silent for a moment, a small frown gracing her lips as she thought, then said, "I believe it lasts for a couple of hours."

"Oh." Kade sighed again, miserably this time. He'd been looking forward to bedding his wife again after their long journey, but it looked as if he was going to have to wait another night.

"I am sorry, husband," she said miserably. "I just wanted to please you as you did me."

"And ye do," he assured her once again, hugging her closer. And it was true, Kade realized as he continued to rub her back soothingly until she drifted off to sleep. Despite everything, he was very pleased with his wife. She was clever, sweet, passionate, and, in his eyes, quite lovely. She was also willing to try things she didn't have a clue how to do. That spoke well for the future. He could see them being very happy together once everything was settled . . . if he could just stop her from getting advice on the marriage bed from the maids, he thought dryly.

Chapter Twelve

"My lady!" That whispered hiss gave Averill a start. She whirled guiltily away from the door she'd just eased closed to find Bess storming up the hall, a scowl on her face.

"Your husband ordered you not to get anywhere near his father and brothers without him. What are you thinking, going in there by yourself?"

Averill grabbed the woman's arm to hurry her away from the door. Bess had continued to whisper, and she didn't fear the low sound's waking anyone in the rooms at that end of the hall, but she also didn't want Kade to catch her there.

"I merely slipped in to each man's room to leave a pitcher of ale for him," she explained, keeping her voice low. "They will be dehydrated after being sick all night and will want a drink when they wake."

"Ale dosed with that weed of yours," Bess guessed grimly. When Averill grimaced, but didn't deny it, she sighed, and said, "What if Brodie had woken up and attacked you again?"

"I did not get near enough he could have grabbed me," Averill reassured her quickly. "And he didn't wake up and try anything, so all is well. Now"—she straightened and urged Bess toward the stairs—"let us go below. Kade wishes to head out today in search of mead and food for the castle and will be displeased do I tarry."

Bess peered at her narrowly as they started down the stairs into the great hall. "How did you manage to get three pitchers of ale up here without anyone noticing?"

"My husband is outside with Will, preparing our horses, and Laddie and the maids are in such a flutter cleaning the kitchens in preparation for the food and drink we hope to bring back, they hardly noticed my coming and going." Kade had re-assigned the boy to helping the maids because she was not going to be there today for him to guard, but Averill suspected he would be back at her side when they returned.

"And I was straightening your room," Bess finished dryly and shook her head as they reached the bottom of the stairs and crossed the great hall. "You're proving to be a sneaky one, my lady."

"Thank you, Bess," Averill said cheerfully, and the maid shook her head again.

"Is there anything you want done while you are

gone?" Bess asked, as they stepped out onto the keep's front stairs and peered down at the bailey filled with Mortagne soldiers milling about aimlessly.

"Aye," Averill said grimly. "I would have the rushes and detritus cleared out of the great hall."

"And how do you expect me to do that with no servants?" Bess asked dryly, and frowned as she noted the way Averill was eyeing the English soldiers. "Oh nay! Surely you don't think they will listen to me and set their hand to cleaning?"

"They will if Will orders them to," Averill responded, then, spotting her brother crossing the bailey toward the keep, started down the steps, calling his name.

"I cannot believe you have my men acting like ladies' maids."

Kade smiled with amusement at Will's repeated complaint. He glanced to the man who rode on his left, then to his wife on the right when she gave an annoyed cluck.

"I do not have your men acting like ladies' maids," she said firmly, and pointed out, "Ladies' maids do not remove nasty old rushes from a great hall."

"Neither do soldiers," Will shot back.

"Mayhap, but 'tis not as if they had anything else to do," she pointed out with exasperation. " 'Twill keep them busy and help pass the time."

Kade shook his head and let them go at it. It was

obvious the pair were siblings. They had been bickering about Averill's request that Will have the men help clean out the great hall since leaving Stewart. Although, "request" was not exactly the proper description, he supposed. His wife had made the request sweetly and, when Will had steadfastly refused, had then browbeat him just as sweetly into agreeing. Kade had been impressed with her perseverance. She could be a stubborn lass when she got the bit between her teeth.

"This is all beside the point anyway, Will," Averill said now. "You agreed. The men are helping, and I appreciate it very much. 'Tis no sense carping about it now."

"Aye," Will agreed morosely. "And 'twill be all your fault do they never speak to me again. They were less than pleased at the order."

Averill shrugged, unconcerned. "They will get over it. There are many things in life that one would rather not do, but must . . . Which reminds me," she added, turning a small frown to Kade, "are you sure we should go to Donnachaidh for supplies? Surely we have other neighbors we could approach?"

"Aye," he acknowledged.

"Then might it not be better to go to one of them?" she asked hopefully.

"Why do ye so dislike the idea o' going to Donnachaidh fer it?" Kade asked patiently.

"Because he is a devil," Averill said at once.

"Ha'e ye met him?" he asked curiously.

"Nay," she admitted.

"Then how can ye ken he's a devil?" Kade asked, reasonably enough he thought.

"Because they call him the *Devil* of Donnachaidh, husband," Averill said with exasperation, then added, "I doubt he was given the name for his kindness."

"Nay, he wasna," he acknowledged, then added, "he gained the name because he is fierce in battle."

"Aye, but—"

"And," Kade interrupted her, "we are going to him because Donnachaidh is no' far to journey and his wife is sister to the husband of *my* sister. As such, of all our neighbors, he is the one most likely to give us the aid we need."

"Oh," Averill murmured, seeming soothed by this news. "I had not realized there was a family connection."

Kade merely shrugged. He was a little annoyed at having to explain himself. He was not used to that and did not think he would like to make it a habit. However, they were newly married, and Averill was still getting to know him. Hopefully, in the future, she would trust his judgment and not question his decisions.

They crested the hill then and found themselves looking down on a forested valley that surrounded another hill. Crouching on top of it stood Donnachaidh castle. Kade eyed the intimidating edifice for a moment and turned in the saddle to peer back and be sure the cart and the dozen soldiers they'd brought along to guard the hoped-for goods on their way back were keeping pace. Finding them virtually on their heels, he nodded his satisfaction and started down the hill.

Despite their English dress, they did not find the gates closed and drawbridge down when they reached Donnachaidh. Instead, they were greeted by a party of three men who rode down to meet them halfway up the hill. The lead man was a fellow named Tavis, a fair-haired, bonnie man whom Kade had run into before in battle. Fortunately, they had been on the same side as the Donnachaidh warriors for that excursion, and Kade knew this man to be the cousin of Cullen Duncan, or the Devil of Donnachaidh, as they called him.

The last time he'd met Tavis, the man had been full of smiles and had managed to charm his way under every skirt they'd encountered . . . which was a surprising number considering the circumstances. This time, however, he was quiet and almost stern. He also hardly looked at Averill, which seemed terribly out of character as Kade knew Tavis had a weakness for redheads. Wondering about the change in the man, he explained his presence and followed him up the hill into the bailey at a leisurely pace while the other two men rode ahead to warn the lord and lady of their arrival.

By the time they halted at the foot of the steps, Cullen Duncan and his wife, Evelinde, were starting down the stairs. Kade eyed the smiling, petite blonde briefly, but then turned his gaze to the taller, dark-haired man and offered a nod of greeting before swinging out of the saddle and moving to lift Averill off her mount. By the time he set her on the ground and turned, Will was at his side and the Devil of Donnachaidh and his wife were stepping off the stairs and moving toward them.

"Stewart," Cullen greeted with a nod.

"Duncan," Kade said, nodding back.

A moment passed, then Kade's eye was drawn to the petite blonde as she poked an elbow into the man's side.

"Me wife," Cullen introduced with a grimace, hauling the woman up to his side with an arm around her waist.

Kade nodded at the woman and caught Averill's hand and tugged her to his side to announce, "Me wife." Nodding to Will, he added, "And her brother."

The introduction was purely for Lady Duncan's sake. Will had told him when he'd first mentioned coming here that he'd met Cullen Duncan at court some years ago and liked him.

"Oh, for pity's sake, you shall be beating your chests next," Evelinde muttered with exasperation, then smiled at Averill, and announced, "I am Evelinde."

"You are English," Averill said with surprise.

"Aye. As are you."

They beamed at each other, then his wife recalled herself, and said, "I am Averill."

"Good morn, Averill," Evelinde said politely, and gestured to the man at her side. "This is my husband, Cullen."

Averill turned to peer up at the man, bit her lip, then nodded, and said, "M-my l-lord." She winced at her own stuttering, but then turned back to Evelinde and forged on saying, "Th-this is m-my br-rother W-will, and—"

She glanced up with surprise when Kade drew her around to face him. He then ducked his head and kissed her. He was quick, but thorough in the doing, gathering her close and thrusting his tongue into her mouth quickly a time or two before lifting his head and letting her go.

Averill stood before him, eyes closed and expression soft, until he murmured, "Wife."

"Aye, husband?" she asked dreamily, eyes slowly opening.

"Finish the introductions."

"Oh, aye," she breathed, then, still peering up at him, said almost absently, "Evelinde, this is my husband, Kade."

"I am glad to hear he is your husband," Evelinde said, and he heard the amusement in her voice but didn't care. He was nodding with satisfaction that his kiss had sufficiently distracted his wife that her stammering had subsided again. He had thought it might.

Bending, he gave her a kiss on the forehead, then turned her toward Evelinde. "Go visit with Lady Duncan while I speak to her husband."

"Aye, husband," Averill murmured, moving forward to join the other woman.

Smiling widely, Evelinde drew her arm through her own, and the two women put their heads together, chatting and laughing like old friends as they made their way up the keep stairs.

"I see you like yer wife well enough," Cullen said with amusement, as they watched the door close on the two women.

Kade shrugged, and explained, "Kissing her stops her stammering."

"I see," Cullen said slowly, then, face solemn, suggested, "So ye kiss her for medicinal purposes."

"Aye. Ye could say that." He felt his lips twitch with amusement.

Will snorted at the claim, and the three men started laughing as they turned to walk across the bailey.

"Nay!"

"Aye. Numb as a dead hen," Averill assured her hostess wryly, and while she could feel herself blushing, she was also grinning at her new friend's horrified amusement over the tale of last night's debacle.

"Oh dear!" Evelinde gasped. "And he was, too?"

"Aye," she said on a forlorn sigh. "And he shriveled up like an old man in a cold bath."

"Oh no!" Evelinde squealed, and burst out laughing.

Averill immediately joined in, seeing the humor of the situation now that it was a day past. She wasn't sure how they had got onto the topic. They had started out talking about Cullen's reputation as the Devil of Donnachaidh. Averill had curiously asked Evelinde what her reaction had been to learning she was to marry the man. After a hesitation, Evelinde had blushed and told her about her first meeting with the man, a rather risqué tale that had set Averill laughing, and she had suddenly found herself blurting out her own calamity last night.

She supposed it was surprising that they were revealing such intimate details of their married lives to each other so soon after meeting, but Averill had felt comfortable with Evelinde from the start, and after several hours of chatting over cider, felt as if they were old friends.

"What has the two o' ye cackling like a pair o' old witches?"

Averill and Evelinde stopped laughing abruptly at that question from Cullen Duncan, exchanged a wide-eyed glance, then turned those same wide, guilty eyes toward the men now approaching the trestle table where they sat.

"H-husband," Averill gasped, leaping to her feet with alarm at the possibility that he might have overheard.

The curiosity on Kade's face and the way he raised an eyebrow as he, Cullen, and Will crossed the last of the distance to join them reassured her he hadn't; but she still fluttered nervously where she stood.

"Well?" Cullen prompted as he paused behind Evelinde and bent to press a kiss to the petite blonde's forehead. "What is it ye find so funny?"

Averill's panicked gaze sought out Evelinde, but she needn't have worried. Her new friend merely smiled sweetly, and said, "Oh, 'twas just a silly old wife's tale."

That answer made Averill eye her new friend with some respect. The woman had told the truth. It was a wife's tale, hers, and yet the way Evelinde said it made it sound like something else entirely. The men immediately lost interest in hearing about it.

"Is something amiss?" Averill asked uncertainly, wondering why they were already returned.

"Nay," Cullen assured her. "We merely came in for the nooning meal."

"Oh!" It was Evelinde's turn to jump up with alarm. "I did not—Oh," she breathed with relief as the door to the kitchens opened and maids started out, food and drink in hand. "Bless Biddy. She, at least, is thinking."

Averill smiled faintly, knowing her new friend was speaking of Cullen's aunt Elizabeth, whom everyone called Biddy. She'd met the woman briefly after Evelinde had led her inside, but then Biddy had disappeared to the kitchens, and Evelinde had explained that Cullen's aunt loved cooking and spent a good deal of time in the kitchens doing it.

The maids reached the tables, and they all settled down to eat. The men were quick about it, then up and gone back to the business of bartering for and packing supplies. Averill and Evelinde got up to take a walk around the gardens behind the kitchens but were back sitting at the tables talking away when the men returned the second time.

Averill smiled at her husband as he approached, but her smile turned down when he raised an eyebrow, and asked, "Are ye ready to go?"

"Already?" she asked with dismay. The time had flown by so that it seemed they'd only just arrived.

Kade's expression softened as he took in her disappointment, and he slid an arm around her waist as he growled, "We'll visit again another day . . . if 'tis all right with Cullen and his lady wife?"

When Kade glanced to their host and hostess, Evelinde launched to her feet, nodding eagerly. "'Tis definitely all right, is it not, husband?" She didn't wait for him to respond, but added, "And we shall ride over to visit you as well once things settle down at Stewart."

"Oh, aye, you must," Averill said at once. "We would like that."

"Then 'tis settled," Kade said abruptly. "Let's go."

He used the arm around her waist to turn her to start across the great hall.

Averill frowned at what she considered a rudeness and craned her neck around, scowling at Will when she found him directly behind her, blocking her view.

Her brother shook his head with amusement, but promptly moved aside so that she could see Evelinde and Cullen trailing them to the doors.

"Thank you so much for everything," Averill said then. "Lunch was lovely, and I enjoyed our visit."

"As did I," Evelinde assured her, smiling. "I must write to Merry and tell her how lovely you are. Mayhap she and Alexander will visit once the babe is born, and we could all get together."

"That would be lovely," Averill agreed. Evelinde had assured her that Merry, Kade's sister and sister-in-law to both her and Evelinde, was as nice as pie and not at all deserving of the title the Stewart Shrew. Averill had been relieved to learn this though she'd never heard the woman called that. After hearing this and meeting Cullen Duncan, the supposed Devil of Donnachaidh, and seeing how sweet and gentle and considerate he was with his wife, it did seem to her that the Scots were fond of giving people inaccurate nicknames. It made her wonder if Kade had a nickname she did not know about. She pondered the matter as they said their final good-byes and mounted. They were headed out of the bailey before she even noticed that the wagon was now piled high with goods Kade had purchased from Donnachaidh, then merely paid it passing attention.

* * *

"What has ye lookin' so pensive, wife?" Kade asked, breaking the silence that had fallen between them all as they'd left Donnachaidh territory. Before that, Averill had been as chatty as a child, twittering on about how nice Lady Duncan was, and how much she liked her, and how she had enjoyed the visit. Every second word had been Evelinde this and Evelinde that for some miles after leaving Donnachaidh.

"Nothing," she said at once, then asked curiously, "Do you have a special name too, husband?"

"A special name?" he asked with surprise.

"Aye, like Cullen is called the Devil of Donnachaidh and your sister, Merry, is the Stewart Shrew," Averill explained.

Kade grimaced at the title his sister had been saddled with. He knew she'd gained it purely from trying to keep their father and brothers from drinking themselves to death . . . and it was probably their father and brothers who had given it to her, he'd guess. But she didn't deserve it.

"Nay," he said at last.

"Why not?" She looked terribly disappointed he noted as she staunchly argued, "From all Will has told me, you are as fierce a warrior as Cullen. So why has no one given you a special name, too? Mayhap we should think of one ourselves."

Kade shook his head with amusement at the suggestion but then glanced around with surprise when Will spoke up.

"I have a name for him."

"Do you?" Averill asked eagerly and leaned forward in the saddle to peer past Kade to her brother in question. "What is it?"

"The Stewart Saint," Will responded at once.

"The Stewart Saint?" Averill echoed uncertainly.

"Aye, for surely he's a saint for marrying you," Will explained.

Kade grinned at his teasing, but Averill scowled, sniffed, then turned to face forward, her cute little nose rising snootily in the air and lips pursing with displeasure . . . Kade watched her for a moment, a smile on his face. She was flushed with color after her visit with Evelinde. Several tendrils of her fine, fiery hair had fallen from where they'd been swept up on top of her head and were framing her face. And her eyes were sparkling like two emeralds. His wife was beautiful, he thought with pleasure, and felt blood rush to his groin, making him hard. After the incident with the ointment, it was a relief to know he could still get hard, Kade thought wryly, then glanced around to see that they'd reached the edge of Stewart land.

"Will?" he growled abruptly.

"Aye?" The man raised an eyebrow in question.

"Yer sister and I are stopping here a while. We'll catch ye up."

One eyebrow flew up on Will's face, but he nodded and continued on when Kade urged his horse to the side, forcing Averill's mare off the trail as well.

"Why are we stopping, husband?" she asked

curiously, as they watched the cart and soldiers ride by.

"I've a mind to show ye a spot I quite liked as a child," he said, then added, "Me mother used to take Merry and me there for picnics when I visited."

"Oh." She smiled, seeming pleased at the idea, and urged her mare to follow as the last of the soldiers rode past, and he headed his own mount across the trail and into the trees. It had been a long time since Kade's mother had taken him to the clearing he was thinking of, and Kade had a little trouble finding it. In the end, he simply followed the river along until the clearing suddenly opened up before them.

"Oh, this is lovely," Averill breathed. An enchanted smile graced her lips as her eyes slid first over the surrounding trees, then to the river and small waterfall before them. "I can see why your mother brought you here."

Kade merely grunted his agreement as he dismounted. He then turned and lifted her off her mount.

"Are we far from Stewart?" she asked, as he tended to the horses.

"Nay." Kade turned back to see that Averill had moved to the edge of the clearing by the waterfall. With one hand braced on the sturdy trunk of a tree there, she leaned out and used her other hand to catch some of the cold, clear liquid pouring down and scoop it to her mouth. Thinking it was no wonder she was thirsty after the way she'd chattered away on leaving Donnachaidh, Kade moved over beside her. He waited patiently until she'd satisfied her thirst, but the moment she paused and turned to him with a smile, he lowered his head and kissed her gently. A little sigh from her lips at the contact made him smile, and when her arms slipped around him and Averill opened her mouth, Kade let his tongue slide out to explore. Her mouth was cold from the water, but he soon warmed it, his hands roving over her body to warm it, too.

When she began to gasp and wiggle in his arms, he began to tug at the neck of her gown, but Averill immediately caught at his hands and broke their kiss.

Eyebrows rising in question, he lifted his head to peer down at her, but she was slipping from between him and the tree.

"What—?" The word had barely left his lips when he stumbled in surprise and fell back against the tree as Averill suddenly turned him. Regaining his balance, Kade straightened and asked with confusion, "What are ye—?"

The question died in his throat when she suddenly knelt before him and began to work at his braies. Recalling the last time she'd got near his manhood, Kade immediately reached down to stop her, but she pushed his hands away, muttering, "I would please you . . . With my mouth."

That did not encourage him any. The last time she'd "pleased" him with her mouth, she'd licked at his erection like a cat cleaning its paw, causing him no end of frustration and—

"Yeow!" Kade gasped, rising up on his toes in shock when, having difficulty with the tie that held up his braies, she simply tugged him out of his pants and took him in her mouth.

"What—?" He'd been going to ask what she thought she was doing, but that was pretty obvious. It also seemed obvious that she'd got some proper advice from someone, because she was doing a damned fine job of "pleasing" him . . . with her mouth. Kade closed his eyes and leaned his head back against the rough bark of the tree. His hips automatically thrust into her strokes as she caressed him with her lips, drawing them down its length and back up. When she began to work her tongue over the tip at the same time, though, Kade couldn't bear it anymore. He'd brought her here to make love to her, and if he didn't stop her soon, he was going to be as useless as he'd been last night after the ointment had numbed him . . . but for a different reason.

Growling under his breath, Kade forced her head back until he slipped from her mouth and caught her arms to draw her to her feet.

"Was I doing it wrong?" Averill asked with worry. "Evelinde said—"

Kade almost stopped to ask her what the devil she was doing talking to Lady Duncan about things like this, but he had noted while they were there that the two women had bonded quickly . . .

and really, he was grateful for the advice Averill had received this time. Letting the matter go, he switched places with her, forcing her back against the tree and kissing her passionately.

Averill didn't kiss him back, and when he lifted his head to see what was wrong, immediately repeated, "Was I doing it wrong?"

A small frown of combined worry and disappointment was drawing her eyebrows together, and he quickly shook his head.

"Nay. Ye were doing it right," Kade assured her. "But I've a mind to love ye."

"Oh." She managed a smile and relaxed then, and Kade quickly bent to claim her mouth once more. This time she kissed back and allowed her arms to creep around his neck, and Kade grunted his satisfaction. He was hot and hard and eager to get her as excited as he so that he could sink himself into her warm, wet depths, but her gown was in the way. When he began to tug at the neck blindly, she released him to help, reaching behind herself to tug free the laces holding it in place. It dropped away then, and Kade sighed his relief as the chemise followed. He broke their kiss at that point to glance down at the bounty revealed, his hands moving greedily to close over both breasts at once.

Averill moaned as he began to knead and squeeze them, then began to tug fretfully at his tunic, drawing it up his body. Kade regretfully released her breasts to tug the top off over his head.

Tossing it aside, he peered down as she began to run her hands over his now-bare chest. Much to his surprise, when Averill paused to tweak at his nipples, he liked it, and he allowed it for a moment, busying himself drawing her skirt up her legs. Once it was high enough that he could slip his hands beneath, however, he moved in closer to kiss her again, forcing her hands still on his chest.

Averill moaned, then gasped as he clasped her bottom with one hand and found the core of her with the other. Much to his relief, he found her wet for him already, but he continued to touch and caress her when he felt her hands at his braies again. This time she was able to undo them and Kade felt the cloth slide away down his legs to pool around his ankles. He broke their kiss then, and ducked his head to catch one nipple in his mouth, the hand between her legs caressing more urgently.

When Averill began to pant and gasped his name, Kade finally lifted his head and shifted his hands to her hips, intending to lift her up and impale her on his manhood there against the tree. But before he could, a terrible pain exploded in his back, propelling him forward.

Averill grunted as he fell against her, then grabbed instinctively to hold him up as he started to slide to his knees. She managed to keep him on his feet, and asked with concern, "What is wrong, husband?"

"Me back," Kade groaned, shaking his head to try to clear his vision.

Averill frowned and leaned around him, trying to see what the problem was. He heard her gasp, and she said with some panic, "There's an arrow in your back."

"That explains it," he muttered grimly. Pain was screaming through his back, streaking outward from a point somewhere between his shoulder blades.

"Husband?" Averill's voice was growing shrill with worry as she asked, "Have you swooned?"

"I'm a warrior, wife. Warriors do no' swoon," Kade growled, forcing away the faintness trying to lay claim to him.

"Oh," she said, sounding doubtful. "It's just that your eyes were closed."

"I was resting them," he snapped.

"I see," she murmured, and for some reason that irritated the hell out of him.

"I am still on me feet, am I no'?" Kade asked, and he *was* on his feet, but just barely. Damn, it felt like someone had swept the legs out from under him. He was hard-pressed not to let them buckle and drop him to the ground. The only thing keeping him upright was the knowledge that if he did, he was most likely a dead man . . . and he would be leaving his wife to fend for herself.

That last thought made Kade's mouth thin and his determination swell. He had to get Averill on her mount and on her way out of the clearing. Now. Before he was shot again or they were otherwise attacked.

Kade's jaw tightened at that very real possibility, and he forced himself upright. The small action
was enough to double the pain in his back. It left
him slightly breathless for a moment, but also
forced out the dizziness that had been threatening
him. Grinding his teeth against the pain, he caught
Averill by the arm and began to urge her across the
clearing to their mounts.

She was dragging her feet, however, and he
wasn't surprised when she protested, "Husband,
should we not tend your back?" Averill fretted,
digging in her heels and trying to tug her arm
free. When Kade paused to scowl down at her,
she quickly added, "We should at least remove the
arrow."

Kade opened his mouth to respond, but paused
as a hiss and thud sounded directly behind them.
They both turned back to see an arrow quivering in
the tree they'd just passed. His mouth tightened.

"Nay," he said firmly, urging her forward again.
Kade didn't have to drag a reluctant wife this time,
however; she was now moving almost faster than
he. It seemed she'd gathered the gravity of the situation. Had they not moved when they had, he'd
probably have a second arrow in his back.

The knowledge made his stomach turn over.
Whoever had shot him had not loosed the arrow
and fled but was sticking around to ensure he
completed his task. *Bad news for us*, Kade acknowledged as he urged Averill quickly to her mount.

It was a relief when they reached the beast.

Aside from the fact that they could now use the horses as cover, a strange numbness seemed to be descending on his extremities, and his vision was dimming at the edges, Kade feared he wouldn't be able to remain conscious much longer.

"Husband, shall I help you mount? I can—"

Kade ignored Averill's twittering, drew on the last of his strength, caught her by the waist, and proceeded to toss her up into the saddle. She gasped in surprise at the precipitous action, but managed to stay in the saddle rather than tumble off the other side of the beast. That was a relief since he didn't think he could have done it again.

"What—?" Averill began.

"To the castle," Kade ordered. He slapped her horse on the hindquarters as he did, and the mare immediately shot forward, carrying her mistress away. He watched them ride out of the clearing and stumbled the few feet to his own mount. He grabbed for the saddle when he reached his mount's side, but that was as far as he got. It seemed as if his strength had ridden off with his wife. It took an inordinate amount of strength just to place his hand on the saddle; pulling himself up onto it was beyond him at that moment.

He would just rest for a moment, he decided, leaning against his mount. He would regather his strength, then mount up and ride out. Kade knew those were lies even as they ran through his head. There was no strength to regather, and resting would do him little good. He was fading fast and pretty much done for.

But at least he'd seen his wife safely away. That thought had barely floated through his mind when the pounding of hooves made him stir from the lassitude laying claim to him. The bastard who had shot the arrow into him was coming to finish the job, he thought, and automatically reached down to clasp the hilt of his sword, wondering even as he did if he had the strength to even unsheathe the sword.

"Husband, are you not coming?"

Kade stiffened and lifted his head to peer blankly at Averill. She had reined in next to him and peered down at him from her mount with concern.

"Husband?" she prompted.

"What are ye doing back here?" he snapped, anger bringing his shoulders back and making him stand up straight. "Ye were to ride to the safety of the castle."

Averill's eyes widened with surprise, but then her expression turned stubborn, and she shook her head. "What kind of wife would just ride off and leave you here alone and wounded?"

"An obedient one," he growled, anger giving him the strength to raise his foot and jam it in the stirrup. *Good God, did I really think her too sweet and biddable to survive in Scotland?* Kade wondered with disgust.

"Aye well, I shall be as obedient as you wish once

we are back at the castle, and I have tended your wound," she announced firmly. "But for now we need to get away from here, and you need to get on your horse so that we may do it. Do you need help with the task? Shall I dismount and—?"

"Nay," Kade snapped, the offer sending his anger up a couple more degrees and giving him the strength he needed to propel himself upward into the saddle. His behind had barely settled on the leather when he felt a sharp punch in the side.

"Husband!" Averill's horrified shout came to Kade as if from far away as he slumped forward on his horse and darkness began to crowd his vision.

Chapter Thirteen

"Husband!" The cry was half panic and half shock as the second arrow suddenly appeared in Kade's side . . . and that was how it seemed; one moment there was just the one arrow protruding from his back, then another suddenly appeared in his side.

Averill quickly urged her mare closer to his mount, noting with some concern that while he had been pale after the first arrow, he was now almost grey. His eyelids were at half-mast, and sweat had broken out on his forehead. Biting her lip, she glanced to the woods opposite them, searching briefly for the archer who had loosed the arrow, but she saw nothing. That did not mean he was not there, however. He might even now be creeping closer to get in another shot. The very thought made her heart fill with more panic and the determination not to allow it. She was not losing her husband. Averill very much feared she had fallen in love with the man.

In truth, she suspected she'd been half in love with Kade before he'd even come out of his deep sleep and opened his eyes. It was all those stories her brother had told her . . . that and the fact that she found him very attractive. But after experiencing the pleasure he gave her, and the kindness and consideration with which he treated her, there was no hope for it. Averill loved him, and that was that. Fortunately, she was a practical girl and didn't expect him to love her in return. She was just grateful he had found her or her dower worthy enough for marriage.

Her gaze slid over the woods one more time. Birdsong filled the air, and all there was to see were trees, bushes, the waterfall, and the river. The idyllic scene was a sharp contrast to the fear and anxiety she was suffering, and it didn't fool her for a minute. They had to get out of there and quickly. The archer could already be aiming another arrow at Kade.

That thought at the forefront of her mind, Averill glanced back to her husband. Kade's eyes were closed, and he was slumped forward in his saddle. For one moment she feared him dead, but then she saw his chest move and released a small sigh of relief. Averill took a second to think what to do, but there seemed little choice. She could not ride her mare and lead his mount for fear he might slide off. She also couldn't take the time to try to remove the arrows or tend him in any way until she had him somewhere safe.

Cursing, she quickly dismounted, grabbed up both reins in her hands and struggled to mount her husband's horse behind him without jostling him too much. In the end, Averill jostled him a lot in her struggle to accomplish the awkward maneuver, but at least she did not accidentally nudge either the arrow in his back or the one in his side, she thought as she finally settled astride the horse behind Kade. He lay across the saddle, leaving her to sit on the animal's haunches. She had never ridden astride, but it was the best she could do at the moment.

Averill clucked her tongue and urged the horse to move, relieved when the beast listened and started forward . . . and then she realized her next problem. She had no real idea where they were or how to find her way back to Stewart.

"You are awake."

Kade had just blinked his eyes open when he heard that relieved comment. Shifting his eyes farther along the bed, he found himself peering at Will, seated in a chair watching him, and for one moment thought himself back at Mortagne, still recovering from the head wound he'd taken when the boat had broken apart. However, he was on his side, his back paining him, and a quick glance over the room beyond Will told him he was at Stewart.

"Some bugger shot me with an arrow while I was tryin' to tup me wife," he said with disbelief as his memories flooded back to him.

"I suspected that was what you were about when you asked me to ride on with the cart," Will said dryly.

Recalling it was his wife's brother he was talking to, Kade frowned, and muttered, "Sorry."

Will shrugged that away, and asked, "How are you feeling?"

"Sore. Where's Averill?"

"I sent her below to have something to eat and drink once she finished tending to you," Will said quietly. "She was quite shaken by the whole incident, and I thought a meal would help settle her nerves a little."

"I am surprised she managed to get me back here on her own," Kade murmured. The last thing he recalled was pain tearing through him as he surged up to mount his horse, then nothing. He wasn't at all sure he'd managed to get himself on the beast ere losing consciousness.

"She had some trouble finding Stewart on her own," Will said quietly. "It was nearly the sup and raining by the time she rode into the bailey. Amusement tipping the corners of his mouth, he added, "She caused something of a stir."

"Aye, well, ridin' in with me across me horse's back, an arrow stickin' out o' me would do that."

"Oh, no one noticed you at first, they were too

taken with the sight of Averill to pay you any attention," Will said with dry amusement, and when Kade looked startled, he explained, "After riding around for a while trying to find her way back to Stewart, Averill decided she could not wait any longer to tend your wound and stopped to take care of it. She tended you right there on the horse. Managed to get the arrows out, then tore up her gown and somehow managed to get it under your chest and across your back as a makeshift bandage, and then continued to search for Stewart. She said she was never so glad of a sight as when she crested the hill and saw Stewart."

"So 'twas the sight of me wife in her chemise that distracted everyone from me?" he asked.

"Aye." Will grimaced, and added, "And, as I said, by the time she rode into the bailey, it was raining."

"Raining?" Kade asked, eyes widening as he considered how that would affect the thin linen of Averill's chemise.

"She might as well ha'e been naked," Aidan said dryly from behind him. When Kade instinctively started to turn to see the man, a hand lodged itself at his hip to stop him. "Ye'll no' want to be doin' that, me laird. Best to stay on yer side for a day or two until the worst o' the healin' be over."

When Kade stilled, the hand was removed, and Aidan moved around the bed, dragging with him the chair he'd been seated in on the other side of

the bed. He set it down next to Will's and settled in
it to eye Kade, and announced, "Yer wee wife was
a damned fine sight."

Kade scowled at the comment, but the soldier
just grinned, and added, "Yer a lucky man."

"She did look rather magnificent," Will commented, sounding surprised. "Her hair was soaked,
and slick to her head, the chemise plastered to her
figure." He frowned and muttered, "I am not sure
when she grew up, but she obviously has."

Despite the pain plaguing him, Kade couldn't
help but smile with amusement at his words. He
supposed it was an uncomfortable realization for
a man to have regarding a sister. She had always
just been little Avy to him, and today he'd had his
blinders removed and seen her for the beautiful
woman she was.

"She couldna tell us who shot ye though," Aidan
said, shifting the conversation onto a more important subject. "She said as how she didna think ye
would ken either."

"Nay." Kade sighed, closing his eyes briefly. "He
must ha'e been in the woods behind me. I ne'er saw
a thing. I felt it, though," he added with a grimace.

"So," Aidan said grimly, "ye had an arrow loosed
on ye on the journey here, a boulder dropped on
yer head, and now two more arrows shot into ye . . .
I'm thinkin' someone's tryin' to kill ye, me laird."

"Aye," Kade said grimly. "The question is who?"

"You have been away for almost three and a half
years," Will pointed out. "Surely you would re-

member someone you have offended so much that he would hold a grudge this long?"

"Ye'd think so, wouldna ye?" he asked dryly, and took a moment to search his mind. As far as he knew, he had no enemies at all.

When Kade finally shook his head in bewilderment, Will cleared his throat, and asked, "You do not think your father or one of your brothers could be behind these attacks, do you?"

"Why the devil would they want to kill me?" he asked with amazement. While he planned to take over as laird, they didn't know that yet . . . and wouldn't until they sobered up long enough for him to speak to his father.

"They may have heard of your return and plans to take over as laird here," Will pointed out. "Ian, Angus, and Domnall may have discussed it and been overheard."

Kade was frowning over that when Aidan shook his head, and said, "They havena left the keep in months. They couldna ha'e been the one to shoot the arrow on yer journey here or even today."

"Hmm." Will frowned, looking disappointed that Kade's own kin couldn't be who was trying to kill him, but then straightened, and asked, "You do not have secret passageways here like we have at Mortagne, do you?"

"Nay," Aidan said at the same time that Kade answered, "Aye."

"Which is it?" Will asked with amusement.

"Aye, we do," Kade said, noting Aidan's shock.

His mother had told him it was a secret among the family, but he would have thought Aidan should know.

"Well then, one of them could have slipped out using the secret passage to drop the rock on you," Will said with apparent satisfaction.

"But they couldna ha'e traveled down to England to shoot the arrow at him and come back without me noticing," Aidan said firmly. "'Twould take days, and none of them have been out o' me sight for more than a few hours or a night while sleeping."

"They could have hired someone," Will pointed out.

Silence fell in the room as they all considered the possibility that his own family might wish him dead after all.

Averill had eaten the fine meal Morag prepared and was bringing a tray of the delicious stew upstairs for Kade when she heard a shuffle along the hall. Pausing at the top of the stairs, she glanced in the direction of the rooms belonging to Kade's father and brothers, her eyes widening slightly when she saw the Stewart laird, standing in the doorway to his room, holding himself upright by clutching at the door and the frame.

She hesitated, her gaze slipping to the tray she held, but then turned her feet and headed in the man's direction.

"Good eve, my lord," Averill said quietly as she

paused before him. "'Tis good to see you up and about. How are you feeling?"

The Stewart raised his head slowly, as if afraid it might fall off did he move too quickly. He eyed her blankly. Eachann Stewart looked atrocious, Averill noted with interest. His eyes were red and bloodshot, his skin grey beneath the wild salted red hair that sprang out of his head. He sported a beard and mustache as wild as the hair on his head.

"Who the devil are you?" he asked in a growl, one that was rather reminiscent of his son's when he was grumpy, she noted.

Averill offered him a blinding smile, and answered, "Kade's wife, Averill."

"Kade has a wife?" Eachann Stewart asked with obvious surprise, then frowned. "The lad went and got hisself married without me there?"

"Aye," she said simply.

"Oh." He lowered his head, his eyes landing on the tray she held. He immediately turned green at the sight of the food, but when he spotted the mug, he grabbed it up and gulped it down, only to sputter with disgust. "This is no' whiskey."

"Nay," Averill said dryly, as he dropped the empty mug back on the tray. "'Tis honey mead, and 'twas not for you, but your son."

"Oh." Eachann Stewart looked miserable and even a little lost. He was also swaying in the doorway unsteadily.

"You do not look well, my lord," she said quietly. "Mayhap you should go lie down."

"I am thirsty," he said plaintively.

"I shall bring you some mead and food," Averill assured him, setting the tray down on the hallway floor so that she could take his arm and usher him back inside.

"I doona drink mead. I prefer whiskey," he said grimly as she urged him into bed. "Bring me some whiskey and food."

Averill sighed as she straightened, but merely asked, "Are you sure you would not rather have mead? You don't appear to be handling the whiskey well, and I worry it will make you sick again."

"Nay. 'Tis no' the whiskey causin' that. 'Tis a sickness. I would ha'e whiskey. 'Twill fix me right up."

"Very well, I shall bring you whiskey. But you cannot blame me does it make you ill. I did warn you," she said, turning to move back to the door.

"Ha! Whiskey make me ill," he muttered, as she left the room. "Whiskey is the water of life, lass."

Averill closed the door without comment, stooped to pick up the tray again, and hurried along the hall to the room she and Kade shared. She had just shifted the tray to open the door when it was suddenly opened for her. She glanced up and blinked at Will in surprise.

"I was about to fetch Kade a drink. He is awake and thirsty," he explained almost absently, his attention on the tray she carried. He noted the empty mug with a frown, but then glanced to the stew. "That smells good."

"Morag made it, and 'tis very good, but 'tis for

Kade," Averill said firmly, and added, "I can bring you some, though, if you wish. I need to go back for more mead anyway."

"More mead?" Will asked with amusement. "What happened to the first of it?"

Averill hesitated, but then decided it might be best not to mention Kade's father, and simply said, "I fetched the mug for it, but forgot to put the mead in ere coming above stairs."

Will chuckled and took the tray. "If you would bring me some stew on your return, I would appreciate it. I will feed Kade while you are away and finish our conversation."

Averill nodded and decided she would bring Aidan some, too. She plucked the empty mug off the tray, then waved him away. "Go on. I will get the door for you."

Nodding, Will turned to head back toward the bed, and the moment he did, she stepped in and reached out to pluck her bag of medicinals off the chest a few feet from the door. She then stepped out, pulled the door closed, and hurried for the stairs.

The maids and Laddie were all bustling around the kitchens when she entered, still putting away and organizing the supplies they had purchased from Donnachaidh. One would have thought it was Christmas the way they all hurried about, flushed with pleasure and smiling as they worked. Well, all except Bess, she acknowledged. Not that the maid looked unhappy to be helping, but she

had not been without as the others had for so long,
and while the occasional indulgent smile curved
her lips as the others exclaimed over the things
they unpacked, she was not quite as enthusiastic.

Fortunately, distracted as they were, they left her
to it when Averill explained she was fetching more
mead for Kade and stew and mead for Aidan and
Will, and she was able to load three mugs of whiskey on the tray as well without anyone's noticing.
She then carried them out to the trestle tables, set
the tray down, retrieved her tincture, and quickly
dumped some into each mug of whiskey.

Releasing a little satisfied sigh then, Averill
picked up the tray and headed above stairs, heading first to take the food and mead to her own
room, where the men waited. She was about to
open the door when she realized she couldn't
carry the whiskey into the room without drawing questions. Grimacing, Averill set down the
tray, started to remove the whiskeys to set them
on the floor, but then paused and straightened
with them instead. Once she entered the room,
she might have difficulty leaving again and worried Kade's father would make his way down-
stairs and drink untainted whiskey were that to
happen. She would just deliver one mug of whiskey to him and leave the others on the bedside
tables as she had with the doctored ale that morning, then take the tray in to Will and Aidan and
see how her husband fared.

Averill was passing Brodie's room when the

door suddenly opened beside her. She swung her head around with surprised alarm, but he didn't even look at her. His eyes were focused on the whiskey she held as if it were screaming his name. Before she could even say a wary, "Good eve," he snatched the mug from the hand nearest him and slammed the door closed.

"Enjoy," Averill murmured dryly, and continued on to the laird's room, with the two still clutched in her other hand.

Averill almost carried both into the room, but then thought better of it and set one on the floor outside the door before carrying the other in.

"Oh, there ye are." Kade's father sat up in bed with relief when she entered.

"Aye, and I have brought you your whiskey. Howbeit, I really do not think you should drink this," Averill said as she crossed the room. "I have seen this before and fear it will not go well."

"Seen what?" he asked, licking his lips and reaching for the mug when she paused beside the bed, but Averill held it just out of reach.

"This reaction to drink," she explained calmly. "Some can drink all the days of their lives without effect, but a very few grow a distaste for it in body and can no longer handle it after indulging for a long time. Judging by how ill you have been, I fear it is that way with you."

"Doona be ridiculous, lass," he scoffed. "Gi'e me the whiskey."

"Very well. I did warn you," Averill said, and

handed it over. She then turned to head back across the room, eager to get the food to Will and Aidan before it grew cold. Even so, at the door she paused and glanced back. "Are you sure you would not like some stew, too?"

The Stewart did not even lower the mug pressed to his mouth, but shook his head, mug and all in response.

Shaking her own head, Averill stepped out of the room and pulled the door closed. She then grabbed up the last mug of whiskey and moved on to the next room.

She had expected to find Gawain asleep, or at least that was what she'd hoped for. However, when Averill eased the door open and crept inside, it was to find him flat in bed, wide-awake, and staring at the ceiling. His unguarded expression was a mask of misery before he became aware of her presence and jerked his head in her direction.

"Who are you?" Gawain asked with a small frown.

Recalling her tussle with Brodie, Averill hesitated, but then moved cautiously forward. "Kade's wife."

"Kade is back?" The man sat up at once, revealing his bare chest, and Averill paused a good six feet from the bed, eyeing him warily as she nodded.

"Aye."

"An' yer his wife?" he asked, looking her over curiously.

"A-aye," Averill answered, suddenly self-conscious.

He smiled faintly. "He's lucky, yer pretty."

Averill blinked in surprise at the compliment, then noted his eyes shifting to the mug she held.

"Is that fer me?"

"Aye." She stiffened her spine a bit, and moved slowly forward. "Your father requested whiskey, and I brought some for you as well in case you wanted it."

"Nay." Gawain grimaced with distaste and turned his head away as if he could not even bear to look at it, but then remembered his manners, and added, "Thank ye though."

Averill tilted her head and eyed him curiously. He was an attractive man, or would be were he not looking so rough. Like his father's, his long hair was a tangled mess, and he sported several days' growth on his face, but his hair was a little darker than Brodie's, and he had eyes as fine as Kade's. She was pretty sure he must be an attractive man when cleaned up. He also wasn't gasping for the drink like his father and brother appeared to be on first awaking.

"Are you sure you do not wish the whiskey?" she asked at last, testing him.

He shook his head grimly. "I am sick unto death of the stuff."

Averill nodded, but after a hesitation, set it on the table. If he was truly over it after vomiting for two days, well and good. If not, and this was just a hiccup in his desire for it, a third day would probably seal the deal.

"In case you change your mind," she explained when she saw him watching her.

Gawain grimaced again, but merely asked, "Where is Kade?"

"He was struck by two arrows this afternoon on our way back from Donnachaidh," she admitted unhappily. "He is abed for now, mending."

"Struck by arrows?" Gawain asked with alarm, then tossed his linens aside to stand. "Will he recover? Which room is he in?"

Relieved to see he had braies on, Averill moved forward to catch his arm and steady him when he stood and swayed weakly.

"Why am I so weak?" he asked, sounding frustrated.

"I would imagine that is due to consuming little more than whiskey for several days and spending the last two retching that back up," she said, not unsympathetically.

"Aye," Gawain said with self-disgust. "I need food, but there is none in this miserable, forsaken place."

"No place is forsaken," Averill said quietly. "And there is food. We collected it from Donnachaidh today. I shall bring you some if you wish it?"

"Aye. Thank ye."

Averill nodded. When he pulled free of her hold and crossed the room on shaky legs to kneel before a chest and open it, she found herself watching him curiously. She knew none of them very well, but Gawain seemed different than his father and

Brodie. He also had kind eyes, and she wondered how much of the drinking he had done was from a true desire for it and how much was simply to be included with his brother and father.

"Why do you drink?" she asked suddenly.

Gawain glanced at her with surprise, then smiled wryly. "All Stewart men drink."

"Kade does not," she pointed out.

"Aye. He was the lucky one," Gawain murmured distractedly as he sorted through the clothes in the chest. "Sent away as a lad . . . I ha'e often wished I had been, too." Longing flashed briefly across his face, and he shook his head. "But I wasna. Only Kade."

Averill was silent, wondering if Gawain resented Kade for that, and if so, was it enough to make him try to kill him? She doubted it. Gawain seemed like a good man who had merely lost his way, and she had heard no tales of cruelty about him.

On the other hand, Brodie was one to keep an eye on, she thought. There was a cold indifference and cruelty about Brodie that made her naturally wary, and that would have been the case even without the stories she'd heard about him.

"There." Gawain sighed with relief once having chosen a tunic and donned it, then turned to Averill. "Will you take me to Kade?"

"Aye," she murmured, and ushered him to the door. Gawain seemed a little steadier on his feet as he walked up the hall beside her, but she noticed he held one hand out toward the wall as if in preparation for catching himself should he fall, and Averill knew he did not feel as well as he appeared.

She was aware that Gawain watched curiously as she stopped and bent to retrieve the tray of food she'd left by the door to the room she and Kade shared, but didn't comment, and he opened the door for her to enter once she was upright again.

Murmuring a thank-you, Averill slid past him into the room and led the way to the bed as the men stopped talking and took note of their entrance.

Will and Aidan both noted Gawain's presence at her side with narrowing eyes, but Kade actually scowled and, uncaring of how his brother might take it, barked, "I told ye to stay away from me father and brothers unless I was with ye!"

"Aye, but he wished to come see you," she said simply, as Will stood to take the tray from her. The moment he had, she ushered Gawain into the chair her brother had vacated, worried the man might fall down if left standing.

Will scowled at her for it but merely settled on the side of the bed with the tray, his eager eyes moving over the offerings.

"One is for Aidan, and I brought you both some mead," Averill announced as she moved around the chair Gawain now sat in to step up close to the bed by her husband's head. She bent to press a kiss to his frowning forehead, and said, "I am glad to see you awake, scowling or not. How are you feeling?"

Kade grimaced as she pressed the back of her

hand to his forehead to feel for fever, and grumbled, "Heartily sick o' findin' meself in bed is how I feel."

Averill smiled faintly and straightened. There was no sign of fever, and if he was well enough to complain, he would soon be up and about. As far as she could tell, both arrows had lodged in muscle and missed hitting any organs or bone. He'd been very lucky. Her gaze slid to the empty bowl, and she asked, "Have you had enough to eat, or shall I bring you more?"

"I wouldna trouble ye," he muttered.

"'Twould be no trouble," Averill assured him. "I am fetching Gawain some, and 'tis little effort to fetch two rather than one."

That just made him glare. "Yer no a servant. Ha'e one o' them bring it up."

"The servants are busy," she said with exasperation. "Do you wish for more, or not?"

When Kade grimaced but nodded, she smiled, and said, "Then I shall be right back."

Averill heard retching coming from up the hall the moment she stepped into it. Frowning, she quickly pulled the door closed behind her and peered in that direction. The sound was coming from both Brodie's and his father's rooms, but the reaction had come on much more quickly than she'd expected. It made Averill wonder if, in her rush to dose the whiskeys before anyone caught her, she might have put more than she'd intended in each. She bit her lip briefly at the possibility, but then shrugged and headed for the stairs. The men would either quit drinking, or they would spend the rest of their days hanging over their chamber pots. It was better than begetting bastards on unwilling maids, and then beating them. Not that she knew whether Laddie's mother had been willing or not, but Lily apparently hadn't been. Sighing, Averill descended the stairs for her third trip to the kitchens.

Chapter Fourteen

"Wife?"

Averill blinked her eyes open at that soft query and found herself staring into the darkness over the bed. She had been lying there, trying to go to sleep for some time, but was finding it difficult. Her mind was awhirl with worries. Stewart was a desperate mess, but she had no servants to fix it. The three men who had survived captivity with her husband and Will were missing, something she knew weighed heavily on his mind and which in turn troubled her as well, and someone was trying to kill her husband. All in all, Averill thought she had more than her fair share of troubles at the moment.

A rustle and sigh sounded next to her, remind-ing her of another worry. She was in bed with her husband and afraid to move for fear of jostling him and causing pain. Averill had offered to sleep in another room, but he had insisted she sleep with him "as a wife should." Now she was too worried about moving in her sleep to manage dropping off and escaping her troubles for a bit.

"Aye?" Averill said at last on a sigh.

"I just wondered if ye were asleep," Kade responded.

Averill shifted carefully in the bed to face him even though she couldn't see him. "Can you not sleep?"

"Nay," he said on a sigh.

"Do you wish to talk?"

"Talk?" he asked as if he didn't understand the word.

Averill suspected he didn't do much of that. He seemed more prone to grunts and one-word comments than to actually holding conversations. She did not mind. Her father and brother could be much the same in certain moods.

"Aye," she said now. "Did you have a good visit with your brother, Gawain?"

"Aye," Kade answered.

Averill waited for him to add more. When he didn't, she commented, "He seems much more like you than like Brodie and your father."

"Aye," Kade agreed.

Averill rolled her eyes, but prompted, "Did you tell him you intend to take over for your father?"

"Aye."

It seemed obvious to Averill that she had to stop asking "aye" and "nay" questions. Clearing her throat, she asked, "What did he say?"

A pause followed her question, and Averill was just wondering with a little frustration why he had cared to know if she was awake when he did not wish to speak, when he said, "Gawain thinks Father'll be glad to be relieved o' the burden."

Averill was congratulating herself on managing to get him to say more than "aye" when he added, "So does Aidan."

"Well that is good, is it not?" she asked.

"Aye."

Averill bit her lip and pressed on, asking, "Have you figured out who might wish you dead, husband?"

She heard a chuckle from his side of the bed, then he said dryly, "Ye ask that like yer askin' do I prefer mead or cider to drink."

Averill was grimacing over that when he added, "Nay. I've no figured it out. I've no figured out a lot of things."

Frowning over his fretful tone, she asked, "What else have you not figured out, my lord husband?"

After a short pause, he burst out with, "Where the devil are me men? We should ha'e passed them on the way here, and even did we miss them, they should have arrived at Mortagne, learned we'd headed here, and arrived by now."

"I am sure they shall show up soon," Averill said soothingly, though his question got her wondering

where they had got to. As he'd said, they really
should have arrived here by now. They had been
three men on horseback, able to travel much more
quickly than their own party of soldiers and carts
had traveled to Stewart from Mortagne.

"They had best show up soon," Kade said grimly.
"I am counting on them."

"For what, husband?" she asked curiously.

He was silent, then muttered, "Ne'er mind. Ye
should sleep, wife. 'Tis late."

Averill frowned at the words. Her curiosity was
piqued, and she'd really rather have him tell her
what he was counting on the men for but doubted
he would. Sighing, she laid her head back on the
bed and closed her eyes, though she knew she
would not sleep a wink.

"Good morn, my lord," Averill said cheerfully as
she entered Kade's father's room. It had been three
days since Kade had been felled by the arrow, and
each day she provided his father and Brodie with
her dosed whiskey, then waited to see if they would
drink . . . and each day they drank, then spent the
rest of the day retching.

Averill was beginning to worry that they would
damage themselves with their retching did they
not soon break and stop drinking, but now that the
plan was in motion, she saw no alternative but to
continue it. The only good thing was that Gawain
had given up the drink. He was even staying away
from ale and had switched to mead or cider with

his meals and when thirsty. The man had also cleaned himself up, and begun to eat properly, growing more handsome every day. She was starting to think he would make someone a fine husband. Her husband had noticed the difference in him as well, and the two were developing a bond. Gawain could often be found in the room she and Kade shared, playing chess or just talking with his older brother as he recovered from his wound.

"I have brought you more whiskey, my lord," she announced and held the mug out as she reached the bed.

Laird Stewart took one look at the mug she held and grabbed for his chamber pot as he began to retch violently.

Averill bit her lip and set the mug on the table beside the bed.

"Perhaps some food would settle your stomach," she said quietly. "Certainly the whiskey does not appear to agree with it."

"Nay, no food," he groaned, then added, "I'm dying, lass. Me days are numbered, and I'm soon to meet me maker."

"Hmm," Averill said dryly. "I am sure you are not dying, my lord. I really think 'tis just your body announcin' it's had enough whiskey."

"Nay, I'm dying," Eachann Stewart assured her in a pitiful moan.

Averill rolled her eyes. "You cannot die, my lord. Who would tend to your people?"

"Bah." He waved a hand in disgusted dismissal.

"I'm sick o' it. All those servants and soldiers carpin' on about needin' this and wantin' that. I'll no' spend me dyin' days bein' tugged at by one and all." He shook his head. "Kade can do it. He is next in line and can take on the burden."

"I'm glad to hear ye say so," Kade said suddenly. "I was goin' to force ye to step down anyway."

Averill spun around at that announcement to find her husband in the doorway with Will, Aidan, and Gawain at his back. He was a touch pale, and was leaning against the doorframe, but he was up and dressed and in a plaid of all things, Averill noted, and found herself staring with fascination at his naked knees and calves.

"Are ye serious?" Kade asked now, moving slowly into the room. "Are ye ready to cede the title?"

Averill noted the stiff way he held his shoulders and knew his back and side were still troubling him. She would have preferred he stay abed for a few more days at least, but now that they were married, he was a much more troublesome patient and had refused to listen. She'd left him that morning in a huff over his being up and getting dressed.

"Aye. Ye can ha'e the title and job and good luck to ye," Eachann Stewart said grimly. "I ha'e had enough."

Kade eyed him for a moment, then glanced over his shoulder to Gawain, Will, and Aidan. "Ye heard. He's abdicated. I am laird now.

When they both nodded solemnly, he turned

back to his father to say firmly, "There'll be no changin' yer mind, now."

"I ken," his father said wearily, and dropped the chamber pot to lie back on the bed with a sigh, "Now come tell me about yer time away ere this illness takes me and I'm gone."

Averill shook her head with amusement at his dramatics and slid past the three men in the door to make her escape before Kade remembered he'd ordered her to stay away from his father and brothers and had just caught her in his father's room.

She was pulling the door closed behind her when she saw Morag moving up the hall, a mug in hand, and a look as grim as death on her face.

Frowning, Averill moved to intercept her. "Is that for Brodie?"

"Aye," the woman said grimly. "He caught Laddie loiterin' in the hall, cuffed him, and said to get that little maid Lily to bring him some whiskey. I told the lad I'd be bringin' it up."

Averill sighed at this news, knowing Laddie had been loitering in the hall waiting for her to make an appearance. He had taken his chore of guarding her very seriously once the supplies were all put away and the kitchen set to rights. Averill had been forced to rise early to make her morning deliveries of whiskey to the two remaining drinking Stewart men, slipping in at the crack of dawn to set the whiskey on their bedside tables. She was usually out and at the trestle table below before Laddie came looking for her. This morning, however, she had been held up by her argument with Kade over his getting out of bed, and the boy had paid for it.

"I shall take the whiskey," Averill said quietly.

"Nay, me lady, he—"

"I shall take it," she said firmly, unwilling to have untainted whiskey given to the man. It might ruin any progress that her dosing the drinks he received had made. The fact that Kade's father had turned up his nose at the drink this morning gave her hope that Brodie would soon give up the drink as well.

Morag scowled but could do little but hand over the whiskey. She could not disobey a direct order from her lady.

Trying to ease the moment, Averill announced, "You may tell the others that Laird Stewart has ceded the title to my husband. Things shall be different around here from now on."

"Thank the sweet Lord," Morag murmured, a smile tugging briefly at her normally stiff lips. "Aye, I shall go tell Lily and the others right now."

Averill watched her go, waiting until she had moved out of sight down the stairs, then retrieved the vial of tincture from the small bag hanging from her skirt. She had taken to carrying it with her always for just such a reason. Now she dumped the last of the tincture in and grimaced. She had brought three vials of the stuff on leaving Mortagne, assuming that would be enough. But if this drink did not work, she would need to make more today.

Shaking her head at being burdened with such

a task when she had so much else to do, Averill slipped the empty vial back into her bag and
moved to the door to Brodie's room.

She found him sitting on the side of the bed,
head bowed in misery, but he lifted his head as she
crossed the room, and she felt a moment's guilt at
the sight of him. After five days of the tainted whiskey, the man looked even worse than his father.
He had lost weight and was trembling, but still he
held his hand out for the whiskey as if it were food
and he a starving man.

Averill handed it over silently, making sure not
to get close enough for him to grab her, then turned
to start across the room, pausing abruptly when
she saw her husband filling the doorway ahead.

"H-husband," she said nervously. "I-I w-was
j-just—"

"Come here," Kade interrupted gruffly.

Averill hesitated, but then hurried forward. The
moment she stopped before him, he took her arm
and turned to drag her from the room. He didn't
bother to close the door behind them but simply
led her up the hall to their own room and urged
her inside.

Averill bit her lip worriedly as she turned to
face him. She was expecting him to give her hell
for going against his order to stay away from his
brother and father. Instead, he shocked her by
barking, "What did ye put in it?"

Averill's eyes widened in horror as she realized
he must have seen her in the hall.

Licking her lips, she stuttered. "I-I w-was—"

"Doona start stammering to try to soften me up," Kade said firmly, and she gaped at him with amazement.

"I d-do n-not—" she began.

"Wife," he snapped.

She sighed, then got out anxiously, "A t-tincture t-to make them s-sick and s-stop th-them w-wanting to drink."

His eyes widened incredulously. "Ye've been the one making them sick, no' the whiskey?"

"Aye," she admitted shamefaced, and waited for him to explode, and he did, but not with anger as she'd expected, but laughter.

"Why ye clever little wench," Kade said with admiration as his laughter faded.

Averill eyed him with uncertainty. "You are not angry?"

"Nay. I'm verra grateful. Gawain has no' drank in days and is becomin' the man he was meant to be. And it certainly made things easier with me da. He's sure he's dying and handin' over the title without a drunken argument," he pointed out, then added, "And he's still had naught to drink o' the whiskey ye left him by the time I recalled I should gi'e ye hell fer ignorin' me orders, so I followed to see ye dosing Brodie's whiskey."

Averill grimaced, but cautioned, "I suspect Gawain would have stopped on his own once he knew you were here. I do not think he drank as heavily or for the same reasons as your father and brother did. As for your father and Brodie, your father may slip again and drink the whiskey I left, and Brodie is well in the whiskey's clutches and still asking for it."

Kade shrugged. "If they drink, they drink. But if they're sick every time they do, they'll soon stop."

"Aye, well, I am all out of the tincture and am not sure I can find the weed I used to make it around here," Averill admitted regretfully.

Kade frowned at this news. "Where does it grow?"

"In damp areas," she said.

He considered the problem, then nodded. "Mayhap 'twill be by the river. We will take a ride out this afternoon."

"Nay," she said at once, shoulders stiffening in preparation for a battle. He had won the argument about getting up that morning, but Averill was determined he would not win this one. "You are not going outside the bailey. I will ride out with Will and a couple of his men, but I will not have you injured again. You are only just starting to recover from your wound."

Kade shrugged that worry away. " 'Twill be fine. We will take the soldiers."

"*You* may take the soldiers," she said grimly. "But I am not going through another day like that one, thank you very much. You may find the weed on your own are you so determined to go."

He frowned. "But I doona ken what weed it is."

"Then stay here and let me go out with the men to find it," Averill bartered.

He scowled at her, anger on his face, but there was admiration, too. "Ye're turnin' out to be a tricky lass, wife."

"Aye." Averill smiled, knowing she had won.

Kade shook his head, but then said, "Verra well. I'll stay here. I've much to set into action now I'm officially laird anyway. But yer to stick close to Will and no' wander off from yer guard."

"Aye, husband," she said at once, giving him a sweet and dutiful smile.

Kade's lips twitched, and he shook his head. "In all the things he told me about ye, Will never once mentioned this streak o' cleverness ye ha'e."

"I am not clever," she said at once, then repeated her mother's often-spoken warning. "Cleverness is unappealing in a woman."

"Neither is hair like fire supposed to be, and yet I find both verra appealin'," Kade assured her, slipping an arm about her waist and drawing her up against his chest, only to wince as the damaged muscles of his back complained.

"You must be careful," Averill said solemnly, raising a hand to caress his cheek.

"Aye." He sighed, then gave her a crooked smile, and said, "Someday I will get to bed ye again, wife."

"I look forward to it," she whispered, and rose on her tiptoes to kiss him. It was a quick brushing of lips only. Averill had no desire to start something they could not presently finish.

A knock at the door sounded as she lowered her heels back to the floor, and when Kade let his arm slip from around her waist, she slid away to open it and found Will on the other side. He smiled at her, then glanced over her shoulder to Kade.

"Your father is wondering if you will return."

"Aye," Kade said, moving up behind Averill. "But first I've a favor to ask o' ye."

"Anything, my friend," Will assured him.

"Averill has run out o' one o' her healing weeds and must take a little jaunt down by the river."

"I will accompany her," Will said at once, and added, "as you have much to do here."

"Aye. Thank ye," Kade muttered, and his expression told Averill he was not fooled at all by the words. She suspected that he, too, had noted the worry that had flashed over Will's face and the alacrity with which he'd offered to accompany her and also concluded that her brother was as eager to keep Kade from going out and making himself a target as she was. "I'd suggest ye take at least a dozen men with ye, just in case. Two would be better, but—"

"I shall take three dozen," Will said with a grin, then added, "as they will be glad to be doing something."

"Well," Averill said brightly, "you had best go speak to your father, husband. We will head out at once and return quickly."

"Aye," he growled, and started to bend as if to kiss her, but paused and winced as it triggered pain in his back.

Averill quickly rose to brush her lips across his again, and whispered, "Do not strain yourself today. Give orders only and leave the labor to others, and if you grow weary, rest. There is no shame in it; you are healing from a dangerous wound."

"Aye, aye," Kade muttered, pushing her gently toward Will. "Now get ye gone so I can start settin' this keep to rights."

Nodding, Averill stepped past her brother into the hall and headed for the stairs, with Will on her heels.

"Take a dozen men with ye, Will," Kade called, then added, "Nay, two dozen. And doona let her out o' yer sight. She can be a tricky lass."

"Aye," Will answered, as they started down the stairs. And then he snorted. "Tricky? Where the devil did he get that idea?"

"I do not know," Averill said, offering him a sweet smile.

Will shook his head. When they reached the bottom of the stairs, he said, "I shall arrange everything while you break your fast."

"Have you eaten already, then?" she asked absently as she noted Laddie's head poking out of the kitchen door. Even as she spotted him, he turned to say something to the women in the kitchens, then slid through the door to approach her. *My little guard dog,* she thought with amusement. Presumably, he had decided 'twas safer to watch for her from there than to loiter in the hall and risk Brodie's unpleasantness.

"Aye. I have been up for hours," Will said, drawing her attention back to him. "You and Kade slept late. Was his wound troubling him?"

"Nay. At least he did not complain, but we both had trouble sleeping. I was too busy fretting about the possibility of rolling over in my sleep and jostling him, and he, no doubt, was busy fretting about everything else."

"Aye. He's had much to fret about," Will said solemnly as he ushered her to the table. "But his father's giving up the title and position as laird eases one of those worries."

"And adds a hundred more," Averill said wryly.

"But even those hundred worries will not burden him as much as the possibility of having to fight his own father for the right to run Stewart," he assured her.

Averill nodded, knowing Kade hadn't worried over the possibility of losing in a battle with his father but over the very fact of having to fight him. It was hard to take arms against kin even if it was occasionally necessary. Fortunately, it wouldn't be necessary here.

"Good morn, little man," Will greeted Laddie, as the lad met them at the table. "Will you keep Lady Averill company while she breaks her fast?"

"Aye. I tol' the women she was about," Laddie announced importantly. "And Lily's bringin' her something."

"Good lad," Will praised, then glanced to Averill as she sat down. He said, "Do not rush. It will take me some time to arrange things."

Laddie climbed up on the bench beside her as Will left. He smiled at her brightly and wished her good morn, looking happy and cheerful despite the new bruise by his eye. Brodie had cuffed him well, Averill thought unhappily, but forced a smile, and said, "You seem very chipper this morning, Laddie. What has you smiling like that?"

"Ye'll see," he said with certainty, then explained, " 'Tis a surprise."

"A surprise?" she asked with interest and glanced toward the kitchens as the door opened and Lily trooped out with Morag, Annie, and Bess following. Lily was biting her lip and flushed with some excitement as she crossed to her, but the other three women were positively beaming with anticipation. Even the usually dour Morag.

"Somethin' to break yer fast with, me lady," Lily said with a pleased flush as she set the tray before her.

Averill peered down at the offerings, noting her customary morning cider, and her eyes widened at the sight of the flaky pastries. She raised her eyes back to Lily. "Did you make these?"

The girl nodded, looking fit to burst.

"Try one," Laddie demanded. "They fair melt in yer mouth and are so delicious Annie wept. Lily had to fight us off to keep us from eatin' 'em all up on ye."

"Did she?" Averill asked with amusement as she picked up one of the still-warm treats.

"Aye. And ye ken soon as the men ken about 'em, they'll gobble 'em up. So ye'd best be eatin' 'em while there are still some to eat."

Averill smiled at the claim, took a bite of the delicate pastry, and felt her eyes widen with amazement. Dear God the pastry did melt in her mouth, and the fruit center burst with flavor. She chewed slowly, sighing at the delicious flavor, then swallowed and turned adoring eyes to Lily.

"You are a goddess with pastries, Lily. This is quite the most delicious I have ever eaten. You obviously got your flair for cooking from your mother, for this is very fine. Even the Devil of Donnachaidh's aunt does not make them as fine, and she is renowned for them."

"Really?" Lily almost squealed the word, her face a wreath of awe and pleasure at the compliment, and, for the first time, Averill realized the girl was quite pretty when not looking the sad, miserable, pale girl she'd been since they arrived.

"Aye, really," she assured her.

"Thank ye, me lady." Lily grinned her relief and pleasure, and asked, "Shall I make more, then, diya think?"

"Oh, most definitely," Averill assured her. "For I fear Laddie is right. Once the men taste them, they will indeed gobble them up."

Beaming brightly, the girl nodded, curtsied, then turned to rush back to the kitchens, apparently eager to start at once.

"Thank ye, fer that, me lady," Morag said, watching with a fond smile as her daughter bustled away. Turning back to Averill once the girl disappeared into the kitchen, she added, "Ye've made her most happy with yer compliments."

"I spoke only the truth," Averill assured her. "You are both fine cooks, Morag, and I should be happy to leave the kitchens in your hands rather than have Aidan find the previous cook and bring him back if the two of you were willing?"

"Diya mean it?" she asked with amazement.

"Aye," Averill said solemnly.

Morag started to grin, but then paused as she peered around the great hall. Will's men had removed the rushes the day before, which had at least improved the smell in the room, but the filth caking the floor was more obvious.

"I would like it," Morag said on a small sigh. "And I ken Lily would, too, but it seems to me yer more in need o' a maid than a cook at the moment, me lady."

Bess moved to sit on Averill's other side, suggesting, "Mayhap you could make a trip down to the village and announce that your husband is now laird here, and the staff is welcome back."

Averill raised her eyebrows at the suggestion, and asked with surprise, "Do you mean they are all down in the village?"

"Nay, but Annie says the pub owner is the center of all the information about Stewart for those who left. His son will take the message around."

"But will the people return?" Averill asked solemnly.

"Aye," Annie said at once, settling with a wince on Laddie's other side. "They're Stewarts, and Stewarts would rather be at Stewart. All but the cook," she added with a grimace. "He was French and snooty as sin. All smiles and sighs when Lady Merewen an' her mother were around, but all snide and mean about the family the moment she was out o' earshot."

"Well then, I shall have to detour to the village when Will takes me out," Averill decided.

"Where's yer brother takin' us?" Laddie asked at once, and she smiled at the boy's determined expression.

"I have run out of a certain medicinal, and he is gathering some men to take me to look for more. I mean he is taking us to look for them," she corrected quickly when he began to scowl.

His expression relaxed then, and he nodded solemnly. "'Tis good to keep yer medicinals well stocked with the way the laird keeps gettin' hurt."

"Aye," Averill said dryly.

"How many men?" Annie then asked, looking thoughtful.

"I believe he said he was bringing three dozen with us," Averill admitted, then asked, "Why do you ask, Annie?"

"Well now, me lady, three dozen is a lot o' men. They could cut down and gather enough new rushes in a trice to bring back with ye," she pointed out.

"Aye, if she could get the men to do it," Morag said dryly. "They carped so much about gatherin' the dirty ones, I suspect they'll no' be pleased to have to collect fresh ones to replace 'em."

"Besides, the floor has to be cleaned ere fresh rushes are put down," Bess pointed out.

"The three o' us could do it," Annie said, and when the other two women gasped in horror, she shrugged. "A little hard work ne'er hurt a body yet. We could at least make a start on it, and if her ladyship does stop to talk to the inn owner and the word spreads, we may ha'e help with it by the noonin'."

The other two women grumbled but agreed.

"So?" Annie asked. "Will ye see if the men will gather some rushes while they're out there standin' around lookin' important?"

"Aye," Averill assured her, but thought she would do better than that. If they were taking only three dozen men with them, that left a lot of soldiers to mill around the bailey all afternoon doing nothing. It would not hurt them to scrape away the hard bits of dry filth on the floor so the women need only mop the stone after them. She would talk to Will, she decided, as the women all stood to move off toward the kitchens, leaving her and Laddie alone.

Glancing to the boy, Averill noted the way he was eyeing the pastries before her. Smiling, she took another one, then nudged the tray toward him. "Go ahead, help yourself. You will need your strength if you are going to be traipsing about cutting and gathering rushes."

"Me?" he asked with surprise.

"Well, aye. We cannot make the men do something we are not willing to do ourselves, can we?" Averill said reasonably.

He considered that, and asked, "Does that mean we have to help muck out the great hall when we get back?"

Averill grimaced, for it was a huge job, and she had no doubt the men and maids would still be working at it when they returned, which meant that they would indeed have to help out. Ah well, once started, quickly done, as her mother used to say when approaching unpleasant tasks.

Will was quick about arranging men to accompany them. He smiled when he saw her waiting at the top of the steps with Laddie beside her as he crossed the bailey, leading two horses and a pony as well as three dozen mounted men. That smile disappeared, however, when she asked him about having men aid in cleaning the great-hall floor.

"Avy," he groaned.

"I know," Averill said sympathetically. "But it

has to be done, and we are terribly short of staff at the moment. If they could just help out—"

"Aye," he interrupted, and reached out to practically toss her up in the saddle, before saying grimly, "I shall talk to my captain."

"Thank you," she murmured, watching him go.

Averill then glanced to Laddie, who stood uncertainly beside her mare, eyeing the pony Will had brought for him with a combination of longing and horror. She bit her lip at his expression, knowing he couldn't possibly have ever ridden a horse. She doubted he'd ever even left the keep except to make short excursions into the bailey, and while he was Brodie's son—legitimately or not—until they had arrived, he'd been treated like the maid's boy. She didn't know what her brother had been thinking, perhaps that this short jaunt to the river was an opportunity to teach the boy to ride, or perhaps because he'd been riding by Laddie's age, he'd unthinkingly assumed he knew how to as well; but she wasn't going to make the boy ride when he looked so terrified.

"Come along," she said abruptly, extending her hand and leaning down.

Laddie raised wide eyes to her. "Am I to ride with you, then?"

"Aye, since you have been ordered to remain at my side," she answered calmly.

"Aye." He looked relieved but did glance toward the pony once before taking her hand.

Laddie was heavier than he looked, and when

she struggled a bit to pull him up, several soldiers dismounted and were suddenly there to help.

"Thank you," Averill said with a laugh, as they got Laddie settled on the saddle before her.

"You're welcome, my lady."

"Pleasure to help, my lady."

"Happy to be of assistance, my lady."

Averill blinked as the men all smiled at her widely, bowing as they backed away. These were men she had grown up with and who had always treated her—as the daughter of their lord—with a sort of indifferent respect. Certainly they had never graced her with the flashing eyes and wide smiles they'd just bestowed on her, or even rushed so eagerly to her aid and with such alacrity. 'Twas odd, Averill thought, then shook her head slightly with bewilderment at their behavior as she turned her attention to ensuring Laddie was settled comfortably.

"Are you settled?" she asked, surprised to find him scowling at the men who had helped them. "What is wrong?"

"They shoudna look at ye like that," he said grimly. "Yer the laird's wife."

"Like what?" she asked with surprise.

"Like yer a lass they want to tup."

Averill was so shocked at the words, she could hardly catch her breath, then a short burst of laughter slipped from her lips.

"They were not," she said with disbelief, and then bent a frown on the boy, and asked, "And who has been teaching you to talk like that?"

"Oh, everyone says 'tup.'" He shrugged, then admitted, "I'm no' sure what tuppin' is exactly, except it's somethin' a man does to a woman he likes."

"Aye, well . . ." Averill cleared her throat, and said, "'Tis not chivalrous to use such speech in a woman's presence."

"Oh." He frowned. "But 'tis all right fer a lass to use it?"

"What lass did you hear use it?" she asked with amazement. Her mother would have forced her into a cold bath for hours had she caught her using such language.

"Annie and Morag use it. Just the other day, Annie was sayin' as how when she was takin' them some ale at the table, Lord Will and Aidan were laughin' and talkin' about the laird's disgust that every time he tried to tup ye, someone shot an arrow at him or some such thing."

Men! Averill thought and closed her eyes on a sigh.

"Besides, the soldiers use 'tup' all the time. They ha'e been goin' on about how lucky laird Kade is to get to tup ye." He frowned, and added, "I guess they havena heard that he's no gettin' to tup ye at all."

"The men think my husband is lucky?" Averill asked with amazement, for if she'd considered it at all, she would have worried they pitied the man. They all knew how many men had rejected her before he had accepted her to wife. Besides, none of them were blind and could surely see how plain and unattractive she was.

"Aye," Laddie nodded solemnly. "Ever since the laird was shot with the arrows and ye brought him home. They say ye came ridin' in all wet and nearly naked, sittin' at the laird's back like a conquerin' queen, and ye were a fine sight to see." He sighed. "I wish I'd seen it."

"I am glad you did not," Averill countered in a mutter, flushing as she recalled the day in question. She'd been more concerned with getting Kade to bed and tended than in her appearance. It wasn't until Bess had rushed up to drape a fur around her as she'd followed the men carrying Kade into their room that she'd even noticed her chemise was soaked, transparent, and plastered to her body.

Averill hadn't thought much of it at the time, for—in her experience—men never looked at her as anything but Will's plain little sister, or Lord Mortagne's ugly daughter. To hear what Laddie was saying was rather shocking to her. No one found her attractive. She did not even think that Kade could, though he acted as if he liked her well enough. She thought he was just being kind because he had grown to like her as she'd nursed him and because she was his friend's sister. Surely, those were the reasons he'd married her? That and for her dower, she had assumed. Now she was left to wonder about it all.

Chapter Fifteen

"My," Averill said with surprise, as the men set to work cutting rushes with wide smiles for her and some vigor put to the task. "See? They do not mind at all."

Will snorted at the suggestion. "They would not be smiling and working so diligently had *I* asked them to perform the task."

"I am sure they would," Averill murmured, turning to begin moving along the spongy earth in search of the plant she needed. While Will had agreed to detour into the village to speak briefly with the innkeeper and his wife, and had even agreed to allow the men to search for and gather rushes for her if they were willing, he had also refused to ask them himself, insisting she would have to be the one to do it.

Averill had felt a bit nervous as he'd called them

over to hear her, and she had stammered once or twice when she normally didn't when speaking to the Mortagne soldiers, but had been relieved and pleasantly surprised when they had all agreed to help. She didn't believe for a moment they would not have agreed had Will asked and not ordered it. In fact, Averill suspected they were all so bored to tears that they would have done nearly anything to end their ennui. And she was grateful for it. There was one more task off her list of things that needed tending at Stewart. They would have the keep in shape in no time at this rate, with or without the return of the servants.

Pausing as a familiar leaf caught her eye, Averill bent at the waist to lean down and brush the branches of a different plant aside to better see the one she wanted. She then nearly overbalanced as the soldier walking behind her didn't stop quickly enough and bumped into her, sending her lurching forward. Averill caught herself by planting one hand on the wet grass, and then stiffened in shock when she felt the soldier grab at her hips to keep her from falling. When he didn't immediately release her, she turned her head to peer wide-eyed along her back toward the guard. His own eyes widened in a sort of shocked horror as he took note of their stance, then he released her hips as if scalded and backed away.

"Sorry, my lady," he mumbled, but she couldn't help noticing his eyes were locked on her behind where it poked up in the air.

Completely flummoxed by it all, Averill pushed with her hand and straightened abruptly, managing a smile for Laddie when he hurried to her side, glaring at the hapless soldier like a small, mean dog.

"I do not think you need follow so closely, Dougie," Will said dryly, joining them from the woods where he'd disappeared to "water the bushes."

"Nay, my lord," the man said quickly, and took several steps back.

Nodding, Will glanced to Averill, and asked, "All's well?"

"Aye." She nodded and turned away to crouch by the plant she had been trying to get a look at.

"Is that it?" Will asked, squatting beside her.

"Aye," Averill murmured, quickly pulling out her knife to cut down the plant at the stalk.

"Is that enough?" Will asked as she straightened.

Averill smiled wryly and shook her head. "Several of these are needed to make one vial of the tincture."

"And how many vials are you wanting to make?" he asked with a frown.

Averill considered the matter, then decided, "At least two."

She was hoping to need only a couple of drops more before Brodie joined his father and brother in giving up the drink, but it was better to be safe than sorry.

Nodding, Will took the plant and turned to show

it to the men gathered behind them so that they could keep an eye out, too. There were six men altogether guarding them from harm. Averill thought it silly. Kade was the one someone was trying to kill. However, she supposed six was better than having thirty-six hounding their every step.

The thought made her eyes slide to the thirty men grimly hacking away at rushes. Several had already gathered a goodly sum of the plant stalks. They were holding them under one arm while trying to continue thrashing away at more while thusly hampered, and it made her frown and realize they should have brought a cart.

"Will?"

"Aye?" He turned back in question.

"We have no cart to carry back the rushes."

He clucked under his tongue with irritation, then turned and moved toward the working men, saying, "I shall send one of the men back to fetch a wagon."

Averill turned back to scouring the ground for more of the particular plant she wanted, then straightened and said, "Laddie, chase after my brother and ask him to have the other men keep an eye out for the plant as well. With so many of them watching for it, we may be done and back at the keep in no time."

The boy nodded and rushed after Will. Averill continued walking, but had only taken a couple more steps when she realized that she needed to water the bushes as well. Grimacing, she held off, preferring to wait until they returned to the castle and the privy, but by the time Will and Laddie returned, Averill was coming to the realization that she wasn't going to be able to wait.

Sighing, she straightened and gestured her brother over when he stopped to talk to the men guarding her.

"What is it?" Will asked, approaching.

Averill hesitated, then flushed and leaned up on her tiptoes to explain the situation.

"Ah," he said with a nod, then glanced around and gestured to the men before taking her arm to lead her into the woods. Laddie immediately began to follow, but Will glanced over his shoulder and shook his head. "You cannot stand guard this time, my little friend. She needs to empty the dragon."

Laddie's eyes widened incredulously. "She has a dragon?"

Will burst out laughing and merely waved him away. "I shall be right back and explain then."

When Laddie slowed but didn't stop, Averill glanced over her shoulder to give him a reassuring smile. " 'Tis lady things."

"Oh." He frowned but did not stop, and said, "Then why does he get to go?"

Averill rolled her eyes and sighed. "Fine. You may accompany Will."

Her gaze jerked to the men now moving forward as well, and she snapped, "But not you."

They stopped at once but glanced at each other as if wondering if they should disobey her.

"I have my two guards here and that is enough for this excursion. Why do you men not look for more weeds for me?"

They grimaced, but they also nodded and began to survey the ground. Though, she couldn't help noticing they seemed to be moving in the general direction she, Will, and Laddie were headed as they looked. Shaking her head, she muttered, "I shall thank Kade for this when we get back."

Will chuckled but merely steered her into the trees and along a little path for a way. He then paused, and asked, "How is this?"

Averill glanced around and then nodded. " 'Tis fine."

"Come along then, Laddie," Will said, releasing Averill to turn and catch the boy by the arm instead. "Let us move away so Avy can water the bushes in peace."

"Water the bushes?" Laddie asked, then clucked with disgust. "Well, why did ye no' say so?"

"Ladies do not discuss such things in public," Will said dryly.

"Hold on!" Laddie suddenly dug in his heels, forcing him to a halt. "I'm no suppose to let her out o' me sight. The laird said so."

"Aye, well you can hardly stay and watch, can you?" Will said dryly, catching him by the collar and forcing him on.

"Nay," he agreed, grabbing at a tree trunk to halt their progress again. "But how are we to ken does she need help?"

Laddie was a tenacious little fellow, Averill thought with irritation, wishing Will would just pick him up and carry him out of the small clearing so that she could tend business. She was fair to bursting to go.

"She will sing, will you not, Avy?" Will said.

"Nay, I will not," she said firmly. Averill couldn't carry a tune to save her soul . . . or even to get them to leave. "But I shall talk if you will both just please leave."

"There." Will glanced down at Laddie. "She will talk so we know she is well."

Much to her distress, Laddie took a moment to consider that before nodding solemnly and releasing the tree. "Well, all right then."

"Thank God," Averill muttered, barely waiting for them to step through some tall bushes and out of sight before yanking up her skirt. Honestly, 'twas sometimes such a trial to be a woman. Were she a man, she could have just turned her back to them and whipped it out. But nay. She was a woman who must drag up her skirts and chemise and squat without losing her balance, and—

"She's no talking," Laddie said with distress from the other side of the bushes. Those bushes then began to waggle as if he were coming back through them.

"I shall talk," Averill squeaked with alarm, and

thought really she had been, just not out loud. Sighing, she asked the thought uppermost in her mind, "What do you think Kade will do about his missing men do they not show up soon?"

Averill knew he was fretting about them. The worry hung on him like an old cape, and now that his father had abdicated, he could turn his attention to other worries. Domnall, Ian, and Angus, she knew, were at the top of the heap.

"If they are not here by nightfall, he is sending a riding party out to search for them tomorrow morn," Will answered.

"What?" Averill squawked.

"I said—" he began, but she interrupted.

"I heard you," she muttered grimly, and wondered why her husband hadn't mentioned that to her. Why was it men had no difficulty talking among themselves but seemed to find it impossible to discuss things with their wives? Her mother had always seemed to be the last one to know things at Mortagne, too.

"She's stopped talkin' again."

"Oh, for heaven's sake," Averill snapped with irritation. Really, all this fuss and bother was rather intimidating her body. It didn't seem to want to go in this situation. Clucking with exasperation, she said, "Can I not have a few moments of peace to—"

"Water the bushes?" Will suggested, seeming to assume she'd stopped because using the term would offend her sensibilities. But Averill had stopped because a rustling to her side had caught her ear. 'Twas a little ways off, but too loud to be a rabbit or some other woodland creature hopping about.

"What did ye mean when ye said she was emptyin' the dragon? She doesna really ha'e a dragon, does she?" Laddie asked suddenly.

"Nay, of course not," Will answered. "'Tis just another way to say she is watering the bushes."

"Oh," Laddie said, and then after a moment pointed out, "She isna talkin' again."

"Avy?" Will called.

"Aye?" she said absently, eyes scanning the woods nervously. She thought she heard a grunt, and was sure the rustling sounds were getting closer. Deciding she would have to wait until they returned to the keep, she dropped her skirts and chemise and started to stand. "Will, I think someone is—"

Her words ended on a shriek as a plaid-clad man stumbled out of the woods to her side. He turned his head to find her, raised a hand toward her, then collapsed at her feet even as Will and Laddie rushed into the clearing.

The man and boy paused to peer wide-eyed at the man lying unconscious on the ground. Laddie was the first to speak.

"What'd ye do to him?" he asked, the question drawing her startled gaze.

"Nothing," she said, even as Will knelt beside the man and turned him over.

"What is it?" Averill asked when he cursed. "Do you know who he—?" She stopped the words abruptly as she got a good look at his face. "Domnall?"

"Aye," Will muttered, tugging his plaid aside and raising the bloodstained shirt he wore beneath it to reveal the wound in his side.

"Let me see," Averill said at once, urging him out of the way so that she could examine the wound. She didn't glance up when the Mortagne soldiers charged into the small clearing in response to her shriek. They surrounded them, swords drawn and at the ready, but slid those swords away and murmured among themselves when they took in the situation. Domnall, Ian, and Angus had been at Mortagne for two weeks before Kade had awoken from his long sleep. The Scots were known to most, if not all of the English soldiers, and Averill heard Domnall's name murmured repeatedly as she examined the wound, then looked at the older and new bloodstains on his top.

"This wound is several days old and reopened," she announced grimly. "We need to get him to the castle."

Will nodded and moved opposite her to scoop the man up like a child. Averill watched worriedly, following when he carried him out of the woods and to where they'd tied up their horses. He handed Domnall to one of the soldiers to hold as he mounted, then took him up on his horse. As he waited for Averill and Laddie to scramble onto her mare, he glanced to the men now mounting. "Dougie, go tell the men to stop gathering the rushes and search the woods for Ian and Angus or anything out of the ordinary, and stay and help them."

The moment the man nodded and dropped back off his horse to hurry away toward the other men, Will turned his mount and set out for home at a gallop. Averill immediately urged her mare to follow and quickly wrapped her arm around Laddie when he nearly bounced his way out of the saddle. It was an automatic, almost absent action. Averill's mind was on Domnall and all she would have to do for him when they got him home . . . as well as the question of where Ian and Angus were.

"The men will ha'e to pledge their fealty to ye," Gawain pointed out as he followed Kade down the stairs.

"Aye," Kade muttered, but then paused abruptly and simply stared at the activity in his great hall. "What the devil?"

"It looks like yer lady wife has the English soldiers a-cleanin' again," Aidan commented with amusement, as Kade glanced over the mass of bodies in the room. They were not all Mortagne soldiers. There were also women dressed like peasants and even a few men in peasant garb working among them.

"Again?" Gawain asked, raising one eyebrow.

"Aye, she had 'em removin' the dirty old rushes the other day," he explained, then added with approval, "I notice she hasna set our men to the task. A sensible woman is yer wife. She kens what an Englishman is good fer but doesna make the mistake o' thinkin' a Scottish warrior is o' the same weak ilk."

Kade grinned at the comment but then stifled it, and said, "Will is a friend to me, and a damned fine warrior. His soldiers are capable men. Doona let them hear ye insultin' them so, no when they traveled all the way here to back me up."

"Aye, me laird, ye be right," Aidan said solemnly, then added on a sigh, "though 'twill be damned hard no' to tease 'em over this."

"Aye," Kade said, allowing his grin to escape as he continued down the stairs. After talking to his father since Averill and Will had left, he, Gawain, and Aidan had decided to have a drink at the trestle tables and discuss what he should do first now he was laird; but the idea was no longer appealing, what with the noise and bustle in the room, so he headed for the doors instead. "We'll take ourselves to the inn fer a drink rather than trouble the workers."

Aidan and Gawain murmured their agreement, and they had just reached the doors when one was tugged open, and a Scottish warrior started to hurry in. He paused abruptly when he saw Kade however, and announced, "I was sent to tell ye Lady Averill, her brother, and five o' his soldiers are chargin' up the hill at breakneck speed. Something is wrong. And it looks like Lord Mortagne has a wounded man on his mount with him."

Kade was moving right after the part about there only being five soldiers and their moving at full speed. He had watched them ride out from the window in his father's room and knew thirty-six men had ridden out. What the hell had happened to the others?

The party charged into the bailey as Kade was rushing down the stairs. He wanted to run to meet them but knew if they had some wounded with them, they would just charge past him, eager to get to the keep and tend them. So he waited at the foot of the stairs, straining his eyes to try to make out if Averill was all right. Much to his relief, she appeared healthy and well. She had Laddie before her on the mount, but there was color in her cheeks, and she didn't look to be in pain. He turned his gaze to Will then, his eyes automatically dropping to the body draped across his lap in the saddle. When he saw the plaid the man wore, he frowned, wondering who it could be.

Curious as he was, it was still Averill's mare he moved toward when she and Will pulled up before him at the base of the steps. He reached up to pluck Laddie from the saddle, set him down, then turned back just in time to catch Averill as she swung her leg over and dropped off her mount.

Kade kissed her quickly on the forehead for

being safe and well, then turned toward Will to find that Aidan and Gawain had already handled the matter and were carrying the man up the stairs between them.

"Who—?" he began.

"'Tis Domnall," Averill interrupted quietly and squeezed his hand in brief and silent sympathy before sliding past him to chase after the men.

"Domnall?" Kade echoed with amazement, staring after her.

"Aye." Will leapt to the ground beside him. "He has a sword wound in the side. 'Tis a few days old, but reopened. There is old blood on his tunic and new."

Cursing, Kade started forward. Will at his side, they hurried up the stairs even as Averill slipped through the doors and disappeared. "Did he say what happened?"

"Nay. He has not been able to tell us anything. I think he just stumbled up and passed out at Avy's feet."

"Ye think? Where were ye?" Kade demanded. "Ye were supposed to keep an eye on her."

"I was on the other side of the bush, waiting for her to finish relieving herself. I trust you did not expect me to hold her hand while she did that?" he asked dryly.

"We made her keep talkin' so's we kenned she was a'right, me laird," Laddie told him quickly, making his presence known as he chased them up the stairs. "She was a-talkin', then screamed, and we rushed around the bush to find Domnall lyin' there and her lookin' shocked."

Kade nodded at the boy's explanation as they reached the door, pulled it open, and hurried in to follow the procession across the hall and up the stairs. They caught up as they reached the large, empty room at the top of the stairs and watched silently as the men laid Domnall down and Averill immediately began bustling about, ordering water and linens to use as bandages, and her medicinal bag. Aidan and Gawain automatically responded to her requests, Aidan moving out to the hall to bellow below for water and linen to be brought. Gawain asked where her medicinals were, then rushed over to the chest to find them. Kade left them to it and moved up to the side of the bed and peered down at Domnall.

"Is it bad?" he asked, peering down at the pale man in the bed.

"Bad enough," she said carefully, applying pressure to the wound.

"Will he live?"

Averill bit her lip as she worked, then sighed and shook her head. "I do not know, husband. I will do what I can . . . and then we must pray he gets no fever and has not lost too much blood."

Knowing she could not do any better than that, Kade nodded and fell silent as Gawain rushed over with her medicinal bag. Moments later, Aidan was ushering in Bess and Lily with water and linens.

Both women took one look at the man in the bed and started to shoo the men out.

Kade could have countermanded them but did not. The women would do what they could, and the men's presence there would only distract them, so he merely headed for the door, saying, "Send for me if he wakes."

Will, Aidan, and Gawain were already in the hall waiting when he stepped out of the room. Their expressions were grim.

"It doesna look good, me laird," Aidan said grimly.

Kade glanced to Will. "Did ye search the area?"

"I set the men to it as we left. If Angus and Ian are out there, they will find them."

Kade nodded, but his hands curled at his sides. He wanted to be out there looking, too.

"Doona e'en think about it," Gawain said grimly, apparently knowing what he was thinking. "Ye're no' e'en healed from the last time ye sallied out of the bailey. Leave it to Lord Mortagne's men. If Angus and Ian are there, they'll find 'em."

"Aye," Will agreed. "Besides, I do not wish to be chasing after Averill when she hears you have gone out and chases after you."

Kade smiled faintly at the suggestion but reluctantly nodded. "I'll wait till they finish searchin' the woods, but do they no' find them, I'll no' wait till morn, as planned, to send the search party to check the way to England. They'll leave tonight."

The men all nodded and turned to head below.

* * *

The sound of a door opening drew Averill from the light doze she'd been enjoying in the chair beside Domnall's bed. Rubbing the weariness from her eyes, she sat up and glanced to the door nearest the bed, only to frown when she saw it was still closed.

Movement out of the corner of her eye drew her gaze to the second door to the hall just as Kade closed it. The door was at the opposite end of the room, and Averill had been told that the chamber had originally been two very tiny bedrooms but that the dividing wall had been damaged some years back by Gawain and Brodie, who had been drunk and wrestling. Rather than repair the wall, Merry had ordered the rest of the wall knocked down to make it one large guest chamber. So it was now the only room in the house with two entrances. That had been rather handy earlier today. While the men had clogged the one door as they slowly maneuvered the unconscious Domnall into the chamber, Averill had simply rushed to the second door and bustled inside to tend to readying the bed for the injured man.

"Wife." Kade paused at her side, bent to kiss her forehead, then straightened to peer at the pale man in the bed. "He's no' stirred?"

Averill shook her head, and said, "I heard a ruckus out in the hall earlier. What—?"

"Brodie," Kade answered grimly. "He was

wantin' to try more whiskey, sure he could keep it down now. The fool," he added dryly.

Averill frowned as she recalled she had no tincture for the whiskey. "What did you tell him?"

"I told him we were all out, then had Aidan fetch him up a tray o' food and said to tell him that I would see about gettin' more whiskey for him on the morrow."

"Did he eat it?" she asked curiously.

"Aye. The tray was empty when Aidan went to fetch it. He said he looked much better for havin' it, too. He was up and dressed and walkin' about without needin' to hold on to things. He hasna come below, though," Kade added. "The men brought back a bunch o' the weeds ye said ye were lookin' fer. Can ye make a batch o' yer tincture in the mornin'? I'll no' give him untainted drink."

"Aye. I will make it," Averill assured him.

Kade's voice was solemn when he said, "If this tincture o' yers doesna stop him drinkin', I'll ha'e to banish him. I'll no' ha'e him abusin' the servants and soldiers, and he can no' control himself when he drinks."

Averill nodded quietly, but merely asked, "How is your father?"

"He hasna touched a drop all day . . . but 'tis only one day, wife," Kade cautioned. "He could be back askin' fer it on the morrow."

"Aye." She sighed and wondered what it was about the drink that held them in such sway. Were their lives truly so retched they would rather drink themselves to unconsciousness than face it? Life was hard, but as nobles, theirs was better than most, and many would trade places with them in a heartbeat—men and women who quite literally worked their fingers to the bone, for little or no reward. The funny thing was those people were probably happier than Brodie and Kade's father, with all their advantages. It made no sense to her.

Kade's suddenly stiffening beside her drew Averill from her thoughts. She glanced at him curiously, then followed his gaze to Domnall to find his eyes open and peering around with confusion. Averill immediately stood to pick up the mug of mead on the bedside table. She'd had it brought up hours ago, and it was no doubt warm now, but she doubted if Domnall would care.

When she turned to the bed with the mead, Kade immediately moved around the bed to assist her in feeding it to him by slipping an arm under him to lift him upright.

Averill murmured a thank-you and pressed the mug to Domnall's lips, and said, "Drink."

The man looked as if he were about to protest, but then simply opened his mouth for her to tip some liquid in.

"Thank ye, me lady," the Scot whispered after the fourth sip.

Averill straightened and set the mug on the table again, then bent to feel his forehead. There was no sign of fever. She straightened and nodded at her husband.

"Can ye talk?" Kade immediately asked the man.

"Aye," Domnall said on a sigh.

"Where are Ian and Angus?"

"Dead," was the grim answer.

Averill's eyes shot to her husband with worry, noting that he looked as if the man had punched him in the gut. The blood had rushed out of his face, and he sank to sit on the side of the bed. Dismay and loss flashed across his face, then he schooled his features, and grimly asked, "How?"

" 'Twas after leavin' yer uncle's. We'd stopped to collect yer chest as ye asked—" Domnall paused to frown, then said, "Someone must ha'e kenned what was in it. We were attacked that night when we made camp. I woke to find a sword in me belly and a man standin' over me."

"Did ye recognize him?" Kade asked grimly and Averill didn't envy the man if Domnall did know who it was. Her husband looked cold and grim, and she had no doubt he would exact revenge. She was almost relieved when Domnall said, "Nay. He was a Scot though. At least, he wore the plaid."

He paused to lick his lips, and added, "I heard Ian and Angus screamin', then I blacked out. I am no' sure how much later it was when I woke up. 'Twas daylight, but it may ha'e been the next day, or the one after that. All I ken is the chest was gone, Ian and Angus were dead, and I felt sure I would soon be, too. Still, I bound mesel' up the best I could, buried them both, and rode for here."

"They left the horses?" Kade asked with surprise.

"I think they took the other two, but Ian's beast was there." He grimaced. "Contrary animal that he is, he probably threw whoever tried to ride him and returned to his master as Ian trained him to do. He was standing there eating grass when I woke up. I managed to mount him and head this way, but his left flank was troublin' him, and he wouldna travel at more than a walk." He sighed. "Still, 'twas better than me tryin' to make it on foot, but he threw me this mornin' as we reached Stewart land. It started me wound bleedin' again . . . and I thought I was fit to die when I heard voices. When I recognized that the voices were English, I at first feared I'd got mesel' turned around, had gone the wrong way and was back in England, but then I recognized Lady Averill's voice and . . ." He shrugged, not bothering to finish the rest.

Kade sighed and sat back slightly on the bed.

Averill hesitated, wanting to comfort him, but there was no comfort. She knew Kade had been quite fond of his cousin, Ian. So had Will been. Her brother had told her the three men had shared a cell while imprisoned. Thinking of her brother made her sigh. He would wish to hear this news.

"Shall I go fetch Will and Aidan?" she asked quietly.

When Kade nodded, she glanced to Domnall. "Are you hungry? Can you stomach food?"

"Aye," he said with a sigh. "I've had not but berries and whatever else I could find for days."

"Then I shall fetch you a meal," she said quietly, and turned to leave the room.

Aidan and Will were talking quietly at the trestle tables when she reached the great hall. Averill told them Domnall was awake, grateful when they asked no questions in their rush to get above stairs and see him for themselves. It may have been cowardly, but she had not wished to impart the news he'd had regarding Ian and Angus and would rather leave it to Kade or Domnall to tell them.

In her upset, Averill was nearly to the kitchen before she noted the clean, fresh rushes underfoot. Pausing, she turned to survey the great hall, noting that they covered the entire floor. It seemed that while the men had stopped gathering them once Domnall had appeared, they had gathered enough beforehand to do the job. She supposed she shouldn't be surprised. There had been thirty men working at it, and most diligently.

The room looked much better for it, though the walls were in need of a good whitewashing, she noted, glancing over them. And furniture was needed, and the tapestries needed cleaning, and . . .

Averill let her thoughts die there. The smell was gone and the floor clean. The rest could wait for another day.

Turning, she continued to the kitchens, pushing through the door, only to pause at the sight of a gaggle of men and women gathered around talking noisily.

"Oh, me lady!" Morag rushed over the moment she spotted her in the door. "Is there somethin' yer needin'? Would ye like yer sup now? 'Tis well past the dinner hour. Everyone else has eaten, and I asked the laird should I bring ye a tray. He said no to trouble mesel' to bring it above stairs, he'd send ye below for a break were ye hungry and sit with Domnall a bit himsel', but when ye didna come below, I thought mayhap ye'd fallen asleep and he hadna the heart to wake ye."

Averill blinked at the rush of words and managed a smile. "Aye. Nay. I came for—" She shook her head and tried again. "Who are all these people?"

"They are the first of the servants to return," Morag said with a smile as she glanced over the chattering crowd. Bess was among them, but none of them, not even she, had noticed Averill's arrival.

"Oh." Averill peered over the crowd curiously, then asked, "Why are they all in here?"

"Oh, well, they've been askin' about ye and the laird, and we've been reassurin' them all'd be well, and they should stay."

"And bribing them with Lily's pastries, I see," she said with amusement, as Lily set a tray of the delicious treats on the counter and people crowded in to get some.

"We've put some away fer ye and Domnall," Morag assured her, then added on a sigh, "If he wakes to eat them."

"Oh." Recalled to her reason for being there, she assured her, "He is awake. I came to fetch him food."

"Oh!" Morag positively beamed. "Awake and hungry. That's a good sign."

"Aye," Averill agreed. It was a very good sign. The man would be up and about in no time.

"I shall fix him a tray, then fix another and put it on the table fer you for when ye return," she said, bustling around and gathering meat and cheese and bread for Domnall. But suddenly she paused to glance at her, and asked, "Or would ye rather ha'e it in yer room? 'Twould be no trouble to run it up if yer weary from tendin' Domnall."

When Averill hesitated, tempted by the offer, she nodded and went back to work saying, "I shall run it up fer ye."

"Thank you, Morag," she said with real gratitude. "I appreciate the trouble."

"I tol' ye, 'tis no trouble," Morag assured her, then finished her task and presented her with Domnall's tray. "I'll bring yer own tray up in a jiffy."

"Thank you," Averill repeated, and moved to the door, only to thank the woman again when she appeared at her side to open it for her.

After the noise in the kitchen, the great hall seemed sadly silent, and Averill glanced around wondering why they were not out here talking, but then her gaze fell on the only two benches at the trestle tables that remained intact and realized there was nowhere for them to sit. Besides, while some of them had returned, they were probably leery of Brodie and his father drinking and coming down to cause a ruckus. She suspected it would be a while before any of them was comfortable enough to relax in the great hall again. Perhaps once Brodie was straightened out or banished, Averill thought as she mounted the stairs.

The men were talking quietly but fell silent when she entered. Suspecting they would wait for her to leave before continuing their conversation, she merely carried the tray over to set on the table beside Domnall and turned quietly to leave.

Her gaze slid up the hall to the rooms at the opposite end, and she listened for a moment, reassured when all she heard was silence. Hoping Kade's father and brother were sleeping and would not cause trouble tonight and scare off those servants who had returned today, Averill made her way to the room she shared with Kade and slid inside.

She was tired enough that she'd forgotten to grab one of the torches in the hall to light a candle, but a lit one sat on the chest by the door. She peered down at it with surprise, then whirled around when a rustle sounded behind her.

Averill stiffened, eyes going wide when she saw the man moving toward her.

Chapter Sixteen

"Br-Brodie!" Averill gasped with surprise, and instinctively began to back away when he started forward. "I-I . . . W-what are y-you d-doing here?"

"I came to see me brother's new bride," he growled, following her. "And to ask ye why ye've been poisonin' me."

Eyes widening with alarm, Averill glanced sharply to the door, but she'd already backed too far away for it to be a useful escape. Her next thought was to scream for Kade, and she opened her mouth to do so, but before even a peep of sound could leave her lips, Averill found Brodie's hand covering her mouth. His body immediately followed, pressing against hers as he forced her to continue backward, steering her toward the bed.

"I thought someone might be messin' with the whiskey when it started me barfin' every time I drank it," Brodie told her grimly, as they moved, "but I didna ken fer sure until tonight. Tonight, after I ate, I was feelin' much better, and used the secret passages to sneak out o' the keep and down to the inn fer a nip o' whiskey. And diya ken what happened?"

When she merely stared at him wide-eyed over his hand, he gave her a little shake. "Diya ken what happened?"

Averill quickly shook her head.

"Nothin'," he said silkily. "I didna toss up me meal all o'er the inn. I didna e'en feel a tetch queasy. I felt fine as rain. So I had another one, and sat to ponder who here at Stewart would want to make us all ill? And diya ken what?"

Averill quickly shook her head to prevent him shaking her again.

"I recalled 'twas always you bringin' the whiskey. Smilin' sweetly and offerin' it like some heaven-sent angel, all the while cautionin' me about how me body may no' be able to stand it anymore, and 'twas the drink makin' us sick." He shook her furiously. "But 'twas ye, wasna it?"

Averill swallowed, not sure how to answer that one. Did she shake her head and possibly infuriate him by lying, or did she nod and definitely infuriate him? Either way, the result wouldn't be good, so Averill merely stared at him, wishing she'd shrieked for Kade the moment she realized Brodie was in the room.

"Wasna it?" he repeated, full of fury. Brodie shook her so hard then that Averill saw stars, and for the first time, feared he meant to kill her.

Closing her eyes, she nodded.

"I kenned it, ye murderin' bitch," he spat, and threw her away like so much filth.

Averill gasped in panic as she felt herself falling, then grunted with surprise when she landed hard on the bed at an angle with one leg on and one leg off. She opened her mouth then to cry out for Kade, but Brodie was on her at once, knocking the wind from her and slamming one of his beefy fists into her head.

Groaning, Averill closed her eyes and shook her head, trying to get past the pain and fight off the darkness trying to claim her. If she lost consciousness now, she knew she was dead.

"I'm gonna kill ye," Brodie growled into her ear as he dragged her skirts up. "But first, I'm goin' have a little fun."

Panic ripping through her, Averill jerked her knee up. She caught him square in the bollocks. Brodie immediately reared upward, gasping for breath, and she suspected he was the one seeing stars now, then Morag suddenly appeared behind him, swinging an empty tray over head. Her face was a mask of fury as she brought it down, and she slammed it onto his skull with all the might of a woman who had worked hard every day of her life and the rage of a mother whose daughter had been done wrong.

It did not take two hits this time. Brodie's eyes rolled up in his head, and he slumped on Averill, out cold.

Morag immediately dropped the tray and began to drag at the unconscious man, trying to pull him off and free her.

"Me lady?" she gasped with her effort. "Are ye all right?"

"Aye," Averill said weakly, and raised her hands to help shift the man off her. They ended up rolling him into the middle of the bed, then Averill quickly scooted off the bed to stand. Morag steadied her with a hand on her elbow when she staggered a bit in her rush, peered at her with concern, then turned to look down at Brodie.

"He was always a bad seed, that one," she said grimly. "E'en as a lad. He ran around here, bullyin' everyone and gropin' the lasses."

Averill sighed. "Aye, well, I suspect he will not be a problem after tomorrow. Kade said he would talk to him, and did he not stop drinking, he would ban him from Stewart. I suspect Brodie will choose the banning."

"I suspect Laird Kade willna give him the choice once he sees yer face," Morag said grimly. "The bastard'll be lucky if he's only banned then. And once the laird learns he planned to rape and kill ye . . ." She shook her head. "I'd guess he's no' long for this world."

Averill grimaced. She had no liking for Brodie, but would not wish Kade to have to live with having killed his own brother over her.

"Mayhap we should keep this incident to ourselves," she suggested quietly.

"What?" Morag asked with amazement, then immediately began to shake her head. "Nay, me lady. He—"

"Was drunk and had a right to his anger. I *have* been dosing his whiskey," she pointed out.

"Oh, me lady. Doona do it," she said with sad disappointment.

"What?" Averill asked with surprise.

"Yer givin' him excuses like his own mother did. 'Twas ne'er that he was a bad child, 'twas that his da was a bad influence, or he was missin' Kade, Maighread said when he was younger, then when he was older, 'twas no' that he was an evil man, but that the drink had a hold o' him." Morag shook her head. "And now ye, too, will give him that excuse?" she asked with disappointment. "After what he tried to do to ye?"

"I—" Averill began, then paused helplessly to peer at the man.

"Has yer husband ever been angered at ye yet?" Morag asked quietly.

"Aye," Averill murmured, recalling his reaction when he'd caught her dosing the whiskey. He'd been furious because she had gone near his father and brother, and she'd been scared of that fury she'd seen in him.

"Did he lay a hand on ye in anger?" Morag asked.

Averill shook her head. He hadn't harmed a hair on her head.

"Just so. Kade is a good man, and good men doona take out their anger on others," she said firmly, then scowled toward Brodie, and added, "and that one is no' a good man. Doona give him excuses. Tell yer husband what he did. Or I will," she added grimly and turned to leave the room.

Averill stared after her, noting the spilled drink and food on the floor by the door. Morag had obviously just dumped everything the tray had held to use it as a weapon when she'd entered to see Brodie attacking Averill.

A grunt from the bed made Averill glance warily that way, but Brodie was still unconscious. However, she wasn't taking the chance that he would wake up. Averill ignored the mess, moved to the door, grabbed the candle, and stepped out to pull the door closed.

She had to talk to Kade, Averill thought, then stilled as Bess came rushing up.

"What happened? Morag just passed me on the stairs looking like thunder. Did she—?" The maid paused abruptly, as she reached Averill and saw her properly. "My lady! Your face!"

"Shush," Averill murmured, and caught her

arm to urge her up the hall. She led her past Will's room and urged her into the one between that and Domnall's. Closing the door softly behind her, she glanced around and sighed, then said, "We need to prepare this room for sleeping."

"Who's sleeping here?" Bess asked with a frown. "And what happened to your face? It looks like someone hit you."

"That would be because someone hit me," Averill said dryly.

"What?" Bess's eyes widened in horror. "Not your husband?"

"Nay. Of course not," Averill assured her, setting the candle down and beginning to strip the bed of the old linens still on it. With a bit of cleaning and dusting, the room would do fine for one night, she thought, then admitted, " 'Twas Brodie. He surprised me in my room. He had worked out that I have been dosing the whiskey."

"I *knew* that would come to trouble," Bess said grimly, moving around the bed to help her.

"Aye, well, it worked well enough for Gawain and his father," Averill pointed out. "And the two of them not drinking is better than all of them being stuck in a keg of whiskey the rest of their lives."

Bess just shook her head. "Your husband will knock him silly when he sees the bruise on your eye. 'Twas bad enough when he was beating on the servants, but now he's starting on you? Bah!" She shook her head.

"Aye, well . . ." Averill sighed and shook her head.

"You never said who we are making the bed up for," Bess pointed out, as they finished stripping it.

"For Kade and me."

Bess straightened with surprise. "What the devil is wrong with the room you have?"

"Brodie is lying in there unconscious."

Her eyes widened, but she set her shoulders, and said, "Well, we'll move the blackguard. We'll have the men take him and toss him back in his room, or the moat for all I care. There's no need to—"

"I would rather Kade not know Brodie is in there. I would rather he not get the chance to deal with him until the morn, when he has had a chance to get over the worst of his anger," Averill explained, sighing at the thought of Kade's anger when she told him what had happened.

"I see," Bess said dryly. "And how do you plan to explain why the two of you are not sleeping in your own bed tonight?"

"I shall tell him that Morag spilled the tray of food she'd brought up for me, and the bed is no longer fit for sleeping in, at least for tonight."

Bess nodded. "Lie you mean."

"'Tis not a lie," Averill said at once. "Morag did spill the tray . . . on the floor," she acknowledged, "but she did spill it, and the bed is not fit for us to sleep in with Brodie there."

Bess snorted. "More of your trickiness. I swear you never showed this tendency at Mortagne."

"I was not married at Mortagne," Averill muttered, then straightened. "We will need fresh linens and furs and—" She paused abruptly.

"What is it?" Bess asked, eyes narrowing.

"My linens are all in our room, and we will need the furs from there," she admitted unhappily, not eager to get anywhere near Brodie again.

Bess sighed. "Would it not be easier just to tell your husband—"

"Nay," Averill interrupted firmly, then sighed. "I shall go fetch them. You wait here."

"As if I would," Bess muttered, following on her heals.

Brodie was still dead to the world when they slipped into the room. Relieved, Bess and Averill scampered about, collecting linens, and clothes for her and Kade to don in the morning and carried them to the room they were to use that night. They then went to Brodie's room to fetch the furs on his bed. Averill had hoped they could use those and not bother with the ones Brodie was lying on, but one whiff of them killed that hope. Kade would know at once that something was amiss did she try to make him sleep under the odiferous furs.

Sending up a silent prayer that they could manage it without waking Brodie, Averill led the way back to the room. They took Brodie's furs with them, set them on the floor by the bed, then quickly and carefully rolled Brodie about to get the furs out from under him. Much to their relief, he didn't wake up. Averill then quickly threw his own furs over him on the bed, and they scampered away with the good ones.

Afraid Kade would head to bed before they could finish, they made the bed in record time and threw the fresh furs on. Bess then helped her prepare for bed before rushing off to fetch Kade.

Averill paced the room briefly as she awaited his arrival, practicing what she would say, then whirled to face the door when it opened.

"Bess said ye wished to speak—" Kade began, but then paused abruptly and closed the door when he realized she was wearing naught but a thin nightgown.

He stared at her for a moment, his eyes traveling her length in the flimsy gown. She wanted to raise a hand to cover her face, but forced herself not to. Averill was far enough away from the lone candle in the room that she knew she stood mostly in shadow, and he couldn't see her well enough to make out the bruise there. That was deliberate. Averill wanted to tell him what had happened before he saw what Brodie had done. She was sure it would soften the blow. At least she hoped it would.

"What're ye doing in here dressed like that?" Kade asked finally, his voice a low growl as he started forward.

"I am ready for b-bed." Averill paused to bite her lip as she noted the slight stammer, then forged on, "W-we are sl-sleeping here t-tonight."

Kade's eyes had narrowed at her stuttering, and he slowed his approach as he asked suspiciously, "What was wrong with the other room?"

"M-Morag spilled a tr-tray of food she br-brought for me, and the bed is not fit—"

The words died on her lips as he suddenly closed the distance between them and drew her into his arms for a kiss. It was a deep and sweet kiss that left her sighing.

"'Tis all right," Kade murmured, breaking the kiss to nuzzle her ear. "Accidents happen. I'm no' angry about it . . . so stop yer stammerin'."

"Aye, husband," Averill breathed, tilting her head to the side to give him better access.

"We can sleep here tonight, I'm sure the bed'll be dry for tomorrow," he continued, his hands roaming over her back.

"Aye," Averill moaned as the fingers of one hand found her breast and began to fondle it through the thin cloth. And then, recalling that she still had to speak to him, she gave her head a shake to clear her thoughts and covered the hand at her breast to still it as she blurted, "B-Brodie figured out I have been d-dosing the whiskey."

Kade stilled at once and slowly lifted his head to peer down into her shadowed face.

"He went down to the village to drink, and when the whiskey there stayed down, he put it all together. He th-thought I was trying to k-kill him and was very angry," Averill said quickly.

Kade released her at once and turned to head for

the door. "I shall go talk to 'im. I should ha'e done so ere this anyway."

"You cannot," Averill said quickly, giving chase and catching at his arm to stop him. "He is unconscious. Morag hit him over the head with the food tray."

He paused and swung back, but then froze, his eyes narrowing with rising fury as he saw her face. It was only then Averill realized she'd moved into the candlelight when she'd chased after him. She turned her head away quickly and tried to move back into the shadow, but it was too late. Kade caught her arm and drew her back into the light to examine her face grimly. When he spoke, his voice was cold and calm with a pure rage that was frightening.

"Did he do this?" Kade asked, brushing his fingers lightly over the skin by her eye. Even that light touch was enough to hurt, and Averill winced, but nodded wearily.

Kade released her arm at once and whirled to head for the door again.

"He is unconscious," she reminded him anxiously.

"Then I will beat him awake," Kade growled as he strode out of the room.

Averill followed as far as the door, watching worriedly, but relaxed a little when she realized he was headed for Brodie's room.

Her gaze slid the other way, toward their own room, where Brodie lay in unconscious bliss, then she backed into the room they were sleeping in that night. She eased the door closed and scampered to the bed to climb in.

Averill was settled in the bed and was lying waiting when Kade returned. His movements were jerky with anger as he crossed the room, stripping his weapons and plaid away as he moved.

"Is all well?" she asked quietly, eyeing him.

"Aye. The bastard isna in his room or below. He must ha'e regained consciousness and returned to the inn. He'll stay there for a week at least if he kens what's good for him, for he's in for a beating when he returns," Kade said furiously as he tugged off the shirt he wore under his plaid. The use of the damaged muscles in his back and side made him wince, and he sighed unhappily and forced himself to move more carefully as he crawled into bed beside her, arranging himself on his side, facing her.

Averill was biting her lip and worrying about the morning ahead, when Kade suddenly shifted himself closer to where she lay on her back. He then threw his arm around her waist and drew her side against his chest.

When Averill turned her eyes reluctantly to his, she saw by candlelight that his own eyes were open. He stared at her silently, his expression growing more rigid with every moment as he peered at the bruise by her eye.

"Did ye tend to that?" he asked in a low rumble. "Put something cold on it?"

No, she hadn't, Averill realized. In all her worry, she'd neglected to take care of it. But she was reluctant to admit that for fear that Kade would insist and head below to get something to place on it. With the way things were going, did he do that, Brodie would probably wake up and stumble out as he was passing, and all hell would break loose, Averill thought unhappily. She'd rather take her chances and risk not tending to it, she decided, and rather than answer the question, merely said, " 'Tis fine."

Before he could say anything else, she rose up on one arm to blow out the candle on the table beside the bed, immersing the room in darkness. The moment Averill reclined again, Kade pulled her back tight against his chest and sighed into her hair.

"I'll take care o' him in the mornin'. I'll hunt him down to do so do I need to. He'll ne'er hurt ye again, wife. I vow it."

"Aye, husband," Averill whispered, but his words had not eased her worry as he'd intended. She was now fretting about Morag and what the woman might say. While Averill had told Kade that Brodie had hit her, she hadn't told him that he'd intended to rape and kill her, and that he certainly would have had Morag not appeared. If the woman told Kade that as she'd threatened to do . . .

Averill bit her lip in the darkness and silently prayed that Kade did not kill his brother and have to live with the memory.

* * *

Kade eased from the bed, dressed quickly and silently, then crept from the room like a thief . . . all to keep from waking his wee wife. Averill was sleeping soundly finally after lying awake half the night. He knew because he'd lain there awake, too. He suspected she'd been fretting over what he intended to do to Brodie. It was what had kept him awake, that and grief at the loss of Ian. He and his cousin had always been close, but those three years sharing a cell with Will had brought them even closer. In that cell, they had spoken of things men didn't normally speak of, things like the hopelessness and frustration that had plagued them, and what sort of future they would have if and when they got out. For the man to have died just weeks after returning home was harder to accept than the rest of what had happened. Why let him suffer all that only to die the moment he was free?

God's plans made no sense to him at times, and Kade had lain awake fretting about that and the fact that in the morning he was going to tear his brother limb from limb. While they had been in that hellhole, the bastard had sat here on his arse, drinking himself silly, abusing the people of Stewart, and not doing a damned thing to keep the castle and lands from sliding into the horrid state they were both in. At least his father and Gawain had only neglected matters. Brodie had worsened them with his cruelty and vile behavior.

All that he'd learned about Brodie had enraged

Kade on his arrival at Stewart. So much so that he'd thought it best to give his temper time to cool before dealing with the man. Not to mention for the man to sober up before speaking to him, but now Brodie had gone too far. No one was going to raise a hand in violence to Averill. No one.

Kade's mouth tightened as he thought of what he'd seen once the sun had risen that morning. Averill's eye was black-and-blue and so swollen, he doubted she would be able to open it when she woke.

Brodie would pay for that . . . tenfold. His brother would never again make the mistake of thinking he could touch Averill in any way . . . or any of the servants. Kade was going to make that plain, then give him a choice: stop drinking or get the hell off Stewart land immediately and never return. . . . And he was going to do it before Averill woke up so that she could greet the day to the news that Brodie would never bother her again.

"Oh, good morn."

Kade blinked his thoughts away and glanced to the side to see that Will's door was open, and the man was standing in it as if he'd been about to step out as he passed.

"Morn," he rumbled.

"I was wondering if—"

"Not now," Kade said quietly to prevent waking anyone. "I ha'e to deal with me brother."

He caught a glimpse of Will's eyebrows rising, then he was past him, continuing up the hall.

"Which one?" Will asked in hushed tones, hurrying after him. "Gawain or Brodie?"

"Brodie."

"What has he done?" Will asked grimly.

"He hit Averill." Kade announced coldly.

"What?"

Kade glared and hissed, "Shut it. Ye'll wake the whole castle."

Will frowned but spoke more quietly as he asked, "How? When?"

"Last night," Kade said on a sigh. "Apparently he sorted out that she was dosin' the whiskey to make 'im ill."

"Was she?" Will asked with amazement.

"Aye," he said, but added in her defense, "She was tryin' to make them stop drinkin', but he thought she was tryin' to kill him and hit her."

Will was silent for a moment, then muttered, "Bastard. Though I suppose he had reason if he thought her trying to kill him."

Kade nodded reluctantly. "That's the only reason I'm no killin' him for touchin' her."

Will grimaced. "What are you going to do?"

"Wake 'im up, beat him senseless, and when he wakes up from that, ha'e a talk with him. He either stops drinkin' and refrains from takin' his fists to anyone here, or he leaves for good."

"Banishment," Will said solemnly, as they reached Brodie's door, and Kade pushed it open.

He immediately started into the room, but paused just inside the door with a curse when he saw that his brother wasn't in the bed. Brodie wasn't in the room either and it looked much as it had last night. Kade suspected the man hadn't even returned to sleep.

"Where could he be?" Will asked.

"Passed out drunk on the road between here and the village, no doubt," Kade said with disgust. He'd hoped to have the matter over and done with before Averill awoke, but it was looking like that wouldn't happen.

"Where are his furs?" Will asked, as Kade turned, intending to leave the room.

Pausing at his question, Kade raised an eyebrow and swung back to the bed, noting that the furs were gone.

"Mayhap he moved to another room to avoid you until your temper cooled," Will suggested.

"Nay," Kade said at once. "All the rooms are in use but Merry's, and he wouldna—" Pausing abruptly as it occurred to him that Brodie might very well take up residence in her room, he spun back to the door and hurried out of the room and along the hall to his sister's old room. But a quick glance inside showed it was empty.

"What about the room between mine and the one Domnall is in? It is empty is it not? He could have moved there."

Kade shook his head as he closed the door. "Nay. Averill and I slept in there last night. She said Morag spilled a food tray in our bed."

"That is unusually clumsy of the woman," Will commented.

Kade's eyes narrowed suddenly as he considered the situation. It was uncommonly clumsy for any maid to spill a tray of food on a bed, but Morag had proven to be a very capable woman, not the clumsy sort at all. Something must have distracted her or— Kade shifted his gaze, moving toward the door to their vacated room as it occurred to him that Averill had not mentioned the particulars of her confrontation with Brodie. Things such as where he had approached her. She had, however, said that Morag had knocked him unconscious. And Morag had spilled a tray of food on their bed.

He knew his friend was thinking along the same lines as he when Will asked, "Where did he confront Avy? He would not have gone in your room, would he?"

"He better not have," Kade growled, and moved on to the door to the room they'd had to vacate for the night. He pushed that door open and cursed when he saw that someone was sleeping in his bed. Kade started forward at once and would have ended up on his arse when his foot slid out from under him on the slick floor if Will had not grabbed his arm.

Muttering a thank-you, he straightened and peered down at the mess on the floor.

"I thought you said Morag spilled it on the bed?" Will asked in hushed tones.

Kade frowned as he thought back to last night, then admitted, "She didna actually say the bed, I just assumed so, else why could we no' sleep here?"

Will turned to peer at the man in the bed. "I am guessing because it was already occupied."

Kade felt his stomach churn with fury as he put it all together. Brodie was too heavy for the women to carry, so he lay where he'd fallen. And it didn't take a genius to sort out how Morag had spilled the food on the floor, Kade thought as he recalled Laddie hitting Brodie over the head with the shield to make him let go of Averill. Morag had probably done the same thing with the tray after dumping its contents on the floor. And the two women hadn't told him. They'd let him think the bastard was out of the keep to give his temper a chance to cool.

Shaking his head, he crossed the room, paused beside the bed, and glared down at his brother. The man lay on his side, facing away from him, his face covered by the furs and only his hair poking out, Kade noted, as he growled, "Wake up."

"He is dead to the world," Will muttered at his side.

"No' for long," Kade said grimly, and bent to give him a rough shake. "Dammit, Brodie. Wake up and get yer arse out o' me bed."

When that had no effect either, he pulled him onto his back, intending to slap his face, but stopped when the fur fell away and he got a good look at him.

Kade straightened abruptly, shock replacing his anger of a moment ago.

"He's dead," Will breathed, sounding as stunned as he felt. They were both silent for a moment, simply staring at him, then Will asked worriedly, "You do not think whatever Averill was dosing the whiskey with killed him, do you?"

"Nay," Kade said at once. "He had none last night. Averill was out of the weed she uses to make it. 'Tis what she was collecting yesterday when Domnall found ye. 'Twas untainted whiskey he drank last night. He got it from the inn."

Will sighed, then asked, "Then what do you think happened?"

Kade hesitated and bent to run his hands over his brother's head. He found a bump on the back, suggesting he'd been right in guessing Morag had hit him. Fretting over the possibility that the woman had hit him too hard and accidentally killed him, he turned Brodie back on to his side as he had been when they'd entered. He'd intended to get a look at the back of his head to see how bad the head wound was, but paused when he saw the edge of a bloodstain visible on the back of the dirty white shirt he wore. The edge of it could be seen just above the furs as they dropped slightly from all the shifting.

A sick feeling in his stomach, Kade pulled the furs down to his waist, then straightened abruptly again.

"He has been stabbed," Will said in hushed tones.

* * *

Averill's first awareness was a pounding head and a miserable tenderness around her eye. Grimacing as she noticed she was only seeing out of one eye, she tried to force the other open and sighed when it was too swollen to manage it.

"Averill?"

Frowning at Kade's tone, one that suggested it wasn't the first time he'd said her name, she rolled onto her back to peer at him out of her good eye and found him looming over her, his expression one she wouldn't care to have to see too often. He looked cold and grim beyond countenance.

"Tell me what happened last night?" her husband demanded the moment he saw that she was awake.

"L-last night?" Averill stammered, recollection rolling back through her head.

Kade sighed, some of the coldness seeping from him as he settled on the side of the bed. "Do no' stammer. I am no' angry with ye, but this is important. What happened with Brodie?"

Averill hesitated, then rather than answer, she asked, "Have you banished him, or has he agreed to stop drinking?"

"Neither. He is dead," Kade said baldly.

"What?" She sat up abruptly, as shocked as if he'd poured cold water over her in the warm bed.

"He is dead, wife," Kade repeated quietly. "Now tell me what happened."

"How?"

"I will explain after you tell me what occurred last night," he said firmly, his expression determined.

Averill frowned at his tone. Kade claimed he wasn't angry, but his tone said otherwise. Deciding that it mattered little to tell him now if Brodie was dead, she dropped to lie back in the bed, and said, "He was in our room when I went in after taking up the tray for Domnall. I was weary and Morag had suggested I eat in our room, that she would bring up a tray. When I entered, he was there. He covered my mouth so I could not scream and said he had come to ask me why I was poisoning him. That he'd suspected something was wrong when he kept getting sick, but had known for sure when he went down to the inn that night and drank whiskey without his stomach rebelling. He called me a murdering bitch, threw me on the bed, came down on top of me, and punched me in the face." She paused briefly then, debating whether to tell her husband Brodie had claimed he was going to rape and kill her, but then decided not to bother. Brodie was dead, and it would only hurt Kade.

Sighing, she continued, "And then Morag hit him over the head, and he slumped on top of me, unconscious."

"And then what happened?" Kade asked quietly when she paused.

Averill shrugged. "Morag helped me roll him off and we left him there."

"He was covered up with furs," Kade said solemnly.

"Aye. I decided you and I would sleep in here and had Bess help me make up the bed with fresh linens, but we had no furs for the bed, so we took Brodie's from his room, rolled him around to get our furs out from under him, then tossed his furs over him before leaving." She frowned, and said, "I am sure he was not dead then, husband. He was limp, but still warm. You do not think it was the tincture that did him in, do you?"

"He was stabbed," Kade said quietly, and Averill jerked upright in the bed again.

"Stabbed?"

"Aye. In the back," Will announced, drawing her attention to his presence. He was standing on the left side of the bed, in her present blind spot, and she had to turn her head a good way to see him.

Averill turned back to Kade to ask with bewilderment, "But who would stab him?"

"Any number o' people," Kade said wearily. "He was no' well liked here."

"If he was the target," Will commented, and when Averill and Kade both turned to him in surprise, he shrugged, and pointed out, "He was in your bed, Kade. It could have been someone thinking it was you. You have already had other attempts on your life."

"But those were all away from the keep," Averill protested quickly, not wishing to believe it had been another attempt on Kade.

"The stone that was pushed off the curtain wall onto him was not away from the keep," Will pointed out.

"But that was *outside*, not inside the castle itself. Surely a murderer would not risk creeping around the castle and . . ." She fell silent as Kade covered her hand with his own and squeezed gently.

"I ken ye doona want to believe our home has been breached, but Will is right, it could ha'e been meant fer me, and we must consider that."

Sighing, Averill nodded and lowered her head, admitting to herself that it might very well have been meant for her husband. And then anger washed through her, and she lifted her head again to glare out of her one good eye. "Have you not yet figured out who would be behind these attacks? Surely for someone to be so angry at you and determined to see you dead, you must have an idea why or who?"

"Nay," Kade said calmly, and added, "I've wracked me mind, but there's no one I can think o'."

"Mayhap it is not someone you have angered," Will reasoned, then asked, "Who would benefit from your death?"

Kade shook his head. "No one. Well, mayhap Gawain. He would be next in line did me father no' reclaim his title and position as laird."

"Not Gawain," Will said with a shake of the head, and Averill tended to agree with him. She liked what she knew of the man, so far. Now, had

Gawain been accidentally killed, she would have had no trouble believing Brodie behind it, but she just did not think Gawain the sort.

"Nay," Kade agreed as he stood. "I shall have to think on it some more."

"Where are you going?" Averill asked worriedly. If the person trying to kill her husband had brought his efforts inside the castle, Kade would not be safe anywhere, she thought, and said, "If you are correct, should you not arrange for a guard for protection?"

"Aye. I'll set two men outside the door while ye sleep," he said reassuringly. "They will follow ye throughout the day today, and another two will guard our door at night."

"Not for me," she said with exasperation. " 'Tis you someone is trying to kill. I meant a guard for you."

"I will not leave his side, Avy," Will said quietly. "And if I do, I shall ensure someone else is with him to keep him safe."

Kade grimaced at the words, but merely said, "We'll go below and leave ye to get more sleep. I ken ye had trouble droppin' off last night."

Kade and Will started across the room, but Averill called out, "Husband?"

Pausing at the door, he glanced back. When she hesitated, he quietly asked Will to wait in the hall. The moment her brother had stepped out of the room, he closed the door and returned to stand beside the bed. "Aye?"

"I am sorry about your brother," Averill murmured, and she was. She was not that broken up over Brodie's death, but she was sorry for Kade that his brother was dead.

He nodded. "Thank ye."

"Are you very upset?" she asked uncertainly, wondering how she was to comfort him.

"Nay," Kade assured her on a sigh, and tried to explain his feelings, something she suspected he did not often do. "He was me brother, but I hardly kenned him . . . and I didna like him. While I'm sorry he's dead, I feel no real grief at the loss. In truth, the news o' Ian's death saddened me more."

Averill nodded, supposing she wasn't surprised. She doubted if anyone but Kade's father would feel grief at Brodie's passing . . . and possibly Gawain and Merry . . . which seemed terribly sad, and yet the man had brought it on himself with his cruel actions. 'Twas hard to feel any real grief at the loss of a tyrant.

"Get some rest," Kade said, and turned away. This time she let him leave without calling him back, but she also tossed the bed furs aside the moment the door closed behind him and got up to dress.

There was no way she was going to be able to sleep now. Brodie was dead, and it was all her fault. Had she told Kade last night that the man was in their bed, he might have been moved to his own and still be alive.

Of course, then she and Kade would have been

sleeping in their room last night, and her husband would have been the one stabbed, Averill thought grimly. Perhaps she didn't feel so guilty about her actions getting Brodie killed. She was selfish enough to be glad it was him and not her husband. And, truthfully, this was probably the first useful thing the man had done in his life. Too bad it was his last.

Chapter Seventeen

"Wife." Kade paused on the stairs as he encountered Averill coming down as he went up. "I thought ye'd sleep a while longer."

"Nay." She grimaced, but shook her head. "I am awake now and have things to do."

Kade hesitated, his gaze sliding to the room at the top of the stairs. He'd just finished breaking his fast with Will and Gawain. The two men were convinced Brodie's death was the result of another attempt on Kade's life. He tended to agree with them and had decided that two armed guards should be placed in the upper hall at night to ensure such a thing didn't happen again.

Will had suggested a personal guard of two men for Kade himself as well, and while he didn't like it, he'd agreed for the sake of preventing an argument. He had not agreed with the Englishman's suggestion that they should be Will's soldiers, however. Kade was laird of Stewart now and had his own men to handle such tasks. However, Will and Gawain would not hear of it when he'd started to head out in search of Aidan to arrange it. They'd insisted on his staying inside where bits of the castle could not be thrown down on him and suggested he go apprise Domnall of what was happening while they fetched Aidan back for him.

That was where Kade had been heading when Averill had appeared at the top of the stairs and started down. Now he peered at his wife, and said, "Diya want me to keep ye company while ye break yer fast?"

Averill smiled as if he'd offered her the sun as a gift but shook her head. "Thank you, but no, husband. I can see you were on your way somewhere, and I was just going to collect something to eat from the kitchens while I spoke to Morag, then bring a tray up for Domnall."

"I'll tell him food is coming then," Kade decided.

"I suspected that was where you were headed. Is there anything you would like me to bring you when I come?"

"Nay." He leaned forward to press a kiss to her lips for the thoughtful offer.

Averill stood two steps higher than he, and it

put their faces on a level. Kade quite enjoyed not having to bend over to find her lips for a change. It meant he had no twinge of pain from his back wound, and he found himself deepening the kiss, his tongue slipping out to fill her mouth as his hands reached instinctively for her breasts.

When she gave one of her soft little moans at the caress, Kade was tempted to forget his present plans and hurry her back to their room, but then Averill slipped her arms around his back, her hand unintentionally brushing over his wound, and he stiffened, the idea dying a quick death. Another day or two of healing and perhaps he could follow up on the plan, but now was not the time.

A small sigh slipping from his lips, he broke their kiss and steadied her until she opened her eyes, then brushed a finger down her nose affectionately. She looked so adorable with her cheeks all flushed with color and her unwounded eye hot for him.

"I've things to do," he said in apology, not wishing to let her know she'd accidentally caused him pain.

Averill sighed, her gaze sliding to the great hall below and the door to the kitchens, and she nodded. "As do I." She glanced back to him, her eyebrow raised in question. "Did you say you wished something or no?"

Kade chuckled, pleased that his kiss could so overset her, but merely repeated his earlier "Nay" as he started past her. He heard her humming happily to herself as she continued down the stairs, and that made him smile as he continued on to the nearer door to Domnall's room. He opened it without knocking and strode in, reaching the bed before he realized it was empty. Kade halted then and glanced about, eyes landing on the figure by the window. Domnall was peering down at the bailey below like a king surveying his realm, but paused now and glanced his way, only to stiffen, something like surprise crossing his face as he breathed, "Cousin."

Kade tilted his head, one eyebrow rising in query at the reaction to his presence. It was enough to make Domnall give himself a bit of a shake and force a wry smile.

"Sorry," he muttered with a wry twist to his lips. "I feared ye were yer lady wife, and she would bullock me fer bein' up and about."

"Aye, she would," Kade said quietly, thinking he was lying. He didn't say so, however, but added, "Ye should lie down. Ye'll pull out the stitches Averill worked so hard to put into ye."

"In a minute, I'm sick o' bein' abed," Domnall said a bit shortly, turning to peer back out the window again as he said, "I saw Gawain and Will cross the bailey toward the stables just before ye entered. There was an air o' purpose in their strides."

"They've gone in search o' Aidan for me."

"Oh?" he asked, sounding grim. "Why? What's happened?"

Kade considered him solemnly, noting his stiff stance. "What makes ye think anything has happened?"

Domnall didn't answer. Something had caught his attention in the bailey, and he'd gone completely still.

"What is it?" Kade asked curiously.

"A lone rider just crossed the drawbridge into the bailey," the warrior muttered, leaning farther out the opening and squinting in an effort to see better. "He looks like—"

Domnall fell silent, and shook his head as if trying to shake out a nasty thought. He then turned his attention back to Kade. "So what has happened?"

Kade debated again asking what made him think anything had happened, but in the end simply said, "Brodie was stabbed while asleep in me bed."

Domnall's mouth tightened with displeasure. "What was he doing there?"

"I tell ye me brother was stabbed in me bed, and ye ask neither why nor by whom but what he was doing there?" Kade asked slowly. They stared at each other silently, sizing each other up, then rather than explain his brother's attack of Averill, Kade said simply, " 'Tis where he landed and where he was left."

"Hmm," Domnall turned and began to pace away from both the window and the bed, not to mention Kade. He was moving closer to the door at the far end of the room, Kade noted and started to tense, but relaxed a little when the man paused by the fireplace. Domnall leaned one arm on the mantel and peered into the cold embers for a moment, then asked, "Ye ken it was me, doona ye? I gave meself away when ye entered."

Kade felt the tension in his shoulders slip away as disappointment claimed him. "I suspected, but wasna sure until this verra minute."

The other man snorted and turned, a small blade in hand, but Kade barely paid it any heed. His healing was well along and Domnall's, while old, was newly reopened; one well-placed punch would incapacitate the man. So long as he didn't flee out the far door.

"Why?" Kade asked with bewilderment. While the two of them were not as close as he and Ian had been, Domnall was also his cousin. He was the son of Eachann Stewart's younger brother, a drunk and ne'er-do-well who had died quite young, shortly after Domnall was born. He, too, had been sent to train with Simon, and while Kade had always been closer to Ian, he had still counted Domnall as family and a friend. They had been through and survived a lot together, and it was difficult for him to understand why he would do all of this.

"Why?" Domnall echoed and grimaced. "I suppose I owe ye that much."

"At least," Kade said quietly.

The other man nodded, then shrugged. "After the accident that left ye unconscious for so long, when we were no' sure whether ye'd live or die, Angus said as how we'd ha'e to carry on fer ye and do what ye'd intended to do. We'd ha'e to come to Stewart and force yer father to cede the title and we'd ha'e to take over the care and runnin' o' Stewart fer ye. It was what ye'd want, he said, then he pointed out that as I was next in line after ye and yer brothers, it would be me job to do it."

He grimaced. "I waved the idea away at the time, but the seed ha' been planted, and I found meself unable to shake the idea. Me, a laird over me own land and people. The warrior who would deliver those downtrodden servants and soldiers from three drunken idiots who didna deserve their place as lairds over them." Domnall shook his head. "I didna e'en ken about the chest of coin then, but I wanted to be Laird Stewart.

"When ye didna wake up by the end of the first week, I began to think it might happen. Halfway through the next, I was sure ye'd ne'er recover, and I would be the one to force yer father to cede, claim Stewart, and take over ruling the lands." His mouth twisted. "And I liked the idea. I started to want it badly, and when ye suddenly woke up after so long asleep, rather than the joy all else felt, I was sorry as can be . . . and e'en angry that ye had. That's when I decided I'd ha'e to help ye meet yer maker after all, so that I could ha'e all that I deserved."

"All that was mine, ye mean," Kade said dryly,

and when he merely shrugged, asked with a sort of disbelief. "And ye had no qualms doin' it?"

"Ye were in me way," he said simply.

Kade's chin rose as if from a blow at the simple sentiment, then his mouth tightened, and he asked, "And Ian and Angus?"

"Well, once ye told us about the chest, I wanted it," he admitted wryly. " 'Twould have made everything that much easier, and while Angus had said I would ha'e to take yer place and tend to Stewart, that was before any o' us kenned about the coin ye'd been stashing away and counted on to help ye tend matters at Stewart. I didna trust he and Ian no' to suggest we should split it once I managed to kill ye, so . . ."

"They woudna ha'e wanted it, and even had they, there was more than enough to share," Kade said dryly. "Ye didna ha'e to kill them."

"Aye, but think how much easier it would ha'e been convincin' the people here to side with me against their laird and his sons with all o' it in me possession. Besides, after those three years as a slave, I yearned for comfort and the finer things for a change."

"Ye ha'e no conscience at all," Kade said with amazement, and wondered how he had missed that about this man all these years.

"Aye, me nursemaid used to say that, too, and she said it like 'twas a flaw," Domnall added with amusement. "But I've no' really understood the usefulness o' a conscience. If ye want something, why should ye no' have it? And why should *ye* be laird rather than me? Ye didna want it as much, else ye would ha'e argued with yer father and claimed it back when Merry wrote ye asking ye to." He shrugged.

"So ye killed Ian and Angus and came here?" Kade asked quietly.

"Nay. I headed for Mortagne. I thought ye still there and planned to show up with the sad story I told ye when I first woke here, then kill ye on the journey to Stewart. But when I stopped to camp a day's ride from Mortagne, I heard talkin' across the river and was amazed to see Averill in the water with her maid. And then when ye joined her and the others left . . . well, 'twas like a gift from God. Obviously he wants me to have Stewart, too."

"Ye shot the arrow," Kade said.

"Aye, but ye moved, and I nearly killed Averill by mistake." He grimaced, then continued, "I followed yer travelin' party after that, hopin' to get another chance, but the first arrow had made ye cautious. Ye ne'er left the others, stayin' always surrounded by soldiers. Ye didna even try to get Averill alone again."

Kade merely stared at him, and asked, "The stone that fell from the curtain wall?"

"Aye. I ken about the secret passages just as you do. Yer father told me while drunk one night years ago. They are verra handy."

"And the second and third arrows?" Kade asked, though he knew the answer.

Domnall nodded. "I thought sure I'd done it then. I was going to ride in with yer chest and claim me spoils, but thought I'd first just creep about and be sure ye'd died. I couldna approach anyone ere I knew fer sure ye were gone, else I'd ha'e to show up without yer chest and come up with where I came into money later." His mouth tightened with displeasure. "Yer the luckiest bastard I ever heard tell o'. I couldna believe it when I slipped into the castle through the passageway and overheard ye arguin' with Averill about goin' down to the woods with her to look for weeds. No' only weren't ye dead, ye were up and about as if naught had happened.

He shook his head with disgust. "So I slipped back out through the passageways and waited for them to leave the bailey, then followed them to where they stopped to gather the rushes. I debated goin' back and usin' the passageways to kill ye, but I was nearly spotted the first time when I threw down the stone on ye and thought it safer to do it from inside the castle. So, I reopened me wound and stumbled out to Averill, and she did exactly as I expected and brought me back here."

"And ye set about yer plan to kill me, but stabbed and killed Brodie instead," Kade said grimly.

"Aye," he said dryly. "As I said, yer one lucky bastard." A muscle twitched by his eye, and he ground his teeth before admitting, "I should ha'e realized somethin' was amiss when Averill wasna there, but I just thought ye slept apart as some couples do. Who would ha'e thought ye'd leave the bastard to sleep in yer bed and take another?"

Kade was silent for several minutes, but then asked, "Where did ye get your wound?"

"I gave it to him."

Kade turned abruptly to see a ghost in the now-open nearer doorway. His cousin, Ian, apparently risen from the dead, stood pale and grim, his hand resting protectively over his stomach. He would almost have believed him a ghost come in search of vengeance were it not for the fact that Will, Gawain, and Aidan stood behind him in the door-way. Kade smiled slowly. Ian lived.

"Nay! I killed ye!" Domnall almost howled the words.

"Nay! Ye tried," Ian snapped back with disgust, and turned to Kade to say, "I just arrived. I'd ha'e come sooner but was not well enough." He ges-tured toward his stomach and grimaced. "I took a sword in me belly."

"A gift from Dom?" Kade asked dryly.

"Aye. On the way back to Mortagne after col-lecting yer chest, we stopped to make camp fer the night, and I woke to a sword in me belly. I was so enraged by his betrayal that I grabbed up me own sword and returned the favor before I passed out. When I woke up, Angus was dead and Domnall gone with the chest. I figured he'd scarpered with it for France or something. I never imagined he'd have the bollocks to come here. I stumbled around for a day and passed out again. Next time I woke up I was in a castle, bein' tended by an angel. Her people found Angus when I told them where to look and buried him. They saw me back to health, and soon as I could walk, I mounted up and rode here to tell ye what had happened."

Ian turned to glare at Domnall as he finished with, "Had I realized he'd continued on here to cause trouble, I would ha'e sent a messenger at once and no' waited to bring the news o' his betrayal to ye meself. I'm sorry, cousin. From what Will and Gawain have told me, it would have saved ye a lot o' pain and Brodie's life. I just ne'er imagined he'd dare show his face here."

Kade saw the regret and guilt on Ian's face but merely waved away his apology. He didn't hold him responsible for a thing and was just glad the man was alive. Kade then turned to Domnall. "Give it up, Dom. Ye'll never be laird here now. And ye'll ne'er get out o' here. Yer only option is to drop yer weapon and give up."

Domnall hesitated, his eyes sliding between the men, when the worst thing in Kade's world happened . . . his wife came bustling in through the far door behind Domnall. All good cheer and happy smiles, completely oblivious of the situation she was entering, she hurried into the room, babbling, "Kade, Bess just told me Ian is returned,

I thought—Domnall!" she interrupted herself to gasp with horror as she paused beside the man. "God's breath! What are you doing out of bed?"

"Wife!" Kade barked, hurrying forward to try to stop her as she reached for Domnall's arm, no doubt intending to nag him back into bed. It was too late, however. Even as Averill paused and turned to glance toward him with surprise at his sharp tone, Domnall closed the short distance still separating them. He caught her about the waist with one hand to draw her back against his chest, and with the other, pressed the tip of his knife to her throat.

Kade froze, all the blood draining out of his face and leaving his mind numb with horror as he stared at his wife in the clutches of a man who had killed at least twice already and tried to kill several more times.

"Kade?" She peered at his stricken face with confusion, then back to the man who held her. "Domnall? What . . ."

Kade's heart ached as her words trailed off. Realization rose in her eyes, and his clever wife met his gaze, and said, "Domnall is the one who has been trying to kill you?"

There was no fear on her face, no hesitation, just the calm she had shown repeatedly in times of crisis. In that moment, Kade realized that he'd never loved anyone in his life as much as he loved this woman. Her good cheer, her passion, her courage, and her quiet calm in a crisis were beyond value. She had saved his life in the woods when he'd taken the arrows, not panicking and riding to Stewart to send back help, but getting him on his horse and getting him home. And she was not panicking now either. Her words were a simple statement of understanding, not a question, but Kade nodded confirmation anyway.

When he then glanced to Domnall, it was to find the other man smiling triumphantly.

"It would seem I have more options now," Domnall pointed out as he backed away toward the wall, dragging Averill with him.

Chapter Eighteen

Averill felt rage boil up within her at Domnall's betrayal of her husband but ignored it in favor of concentrating on keeping her feet beneath her as the odious man forced her backward across the room.

"Dom."

Kade's voice drew the attention of both of them, and when Domnall paused, Averill released a small sigh and glanced hopefully to her husband as he said, "Ye can live like a laird elsewhere with the chest. And yer welcome to take it and go so long as ye let Averill go uninjured."

"Oh, aye," Domnall snorted. "Ye'd just let me walk out o' here with the chest do I let yer wife go? Do ye take me for an idiot?"

"Ye ha'e me word," Kade said firmly. "Ye can walk right out o' here now, just let Averill go."

Watching out of the corner of her eye, Averill caught the way Domnall's head tilted and turned her own the slightest bit to see him peering at Kade with a marveling expression.

"I believe ye may mean that," the man said with wonder. "Ye'd truly gi'e it all up for a wench ye'd ne'er e'en met a few weeks ago."

"Aye," Kade said simply.

Averill turned to peer at her husband, her eyes shining with love. She had no idea what he was giving up exactly, but knew it was something he had been fretting over for some time and that was important to him. Yet he'd give it up for her. That was just about the most wonderful thing she'd heard in her life. Truly, she had the sweetest, kindest, most caring man to husband in all of England or Scotland, Averill thought, then Kade added, "But diya no' let her go, or hurt a hair on her head, I'll rip yer guts out with me bare hands and feed 'em to ye ere cutting off yer head."

Well, Averill thought a bit faintly, perhaps "sweet" was not quite the right word to describe him.

Domnall chuckled dryly behind her, his breath catching at her hair and ruffling it slightly. "Now there's the Kade I ken. 'Tis good to ken marriage has no' completely unmanned ye."

Kade stared coldly back. "What is yer answer? Say ye'll let her go and walk out o' here, and I'll ha'e the men lower their weapons."

"'Tis a truly kind offer," Domnall said dryly. "And I ken yer usually honorable about yer word.

Howbeit, I think this time I'll no' take chances. I'm takin' her with me to ensure me safe escape, and ye'll stay here to ensure I doona kill her. I'll set her free when I feel 'tis safe to do so."

Domnall began to ease to the side, forcing Averill to move with him by pressing the knife tighter to her neck, so that she either moved with him or sliced her own throat. She moved, her eyes searching out Kade as she went, memorizing him in case this was the last she saw of him in this lifetime.

Averill saw the way his hands clenched at his sides, his body stiff with helpless frustration and rage, then her eyes lifted to his to find them locked on her as if he in his turn were memorizing her. She tried to offer him a reassuring smile but knew it was a complete failure. She was scared, and the muscles of her face would not obey her mind's silent command to hide that.

Domnall came to a halt, and Averill felt the muscles in his chest shift against her back as he did something behind him, then a gust of stale air moved past her in a cloud. It reminded her of the night she'd crept through Mortagne's secret passageways to Kade's room, and she knew he had opened some sort of passage behind them. She wondered briefly why her husband had not mentioned that Stewart had them as well but supposed he would have in time. It also didn't matter much right then, she thought, as Domnall suddenly cursed.

Shifting her eyes to the side as far as she could,

Averill tried to see what had the man cursing and saw that he'd picked up a candle from the mantel . . . an unlit one that would hardly be of much use to him. She sensed his hesitation, then saw his eyes turn to survey Kade and the men by the door.

"You! Boy!" he snapped, and Averill noticed Laddie standing in the hall, peeking around the door, taking in the situation. The boy turned his attention their way at Domnall's call, however. As had happened the first time she'd met the lad, his eyes went wide, and he pointed to his own chest in question.

"Bring a lit torch from the hall," Domnall ordered sharply, tossing the useless candle aside.

Averill gritted her teeth and barely kept from jumping nervously as the holder and candle hit the floor and skittered across it.

She saw Laddie turn and peer uncertainly along the hall, but when he didn't move she realized the torches were too high for him to reach. Aidan seemed to realize it, too, and slid into the hall and briefly out of sight to collect one for him. He returned a moment later and presented a lit torch to the boy. Laddie immediately carried it forward, his eyes wide and worried, and Averill forced an encouraging smile for the boy. Whether it reassured him at all, she didn't know, but he puffed up his chest a little and forced the fear from his face as he reached them.

"Give it to her," Domnall snapped, when Laddie paused.

Averill held her hand out, but the boy hesitated, lifted his chin, and bravely offered, "I could carry it fer ye. Ye could let Lady Averill go then."

Her gaze softened on the boy, and her smile was a true one as she whispered, "Thank you, Laddie, but 'twill be best do I take it." When he hesitated, she added softly, "All will be well."

"I said give it to her," Domnall growled impatiently.

Laddie did not look pleased but handed the torch over. Averill had barely closed her hand around the flaming stick of wood when Domnall began dragging her backward into the passage behind them. She saw Laddie move forward as if to follow as was his wont, but Domnall suddenly reached out and slapped a lever beside them, and the passageway entrance slammed closed, locking them in the wall together and locking out everyone she loved.

Domnall wasted no time then. Turning them both, he forced her forward, hurrying her along the dark and narrow corridor behind the rooms.

Averill was totally unprepared when he suddenly came to a halt, and she winced as she felt the knife dig into her throat when she did not stop quickly enough, but had little time to worry about that as he suddenly withdrew the hand that held the knife to her throat and pushed her forward. Unprepared for that as well, Averill stumbled and fell forward onto her hands and knees on the dirty stone floor, the torch slipping from her hand as she tried to save herself.

"Pick it up," Domnall ordered, and Averill at first thought he meant the torch, but he was there before her, grabbing it up and gesturing it forward over her head, repeating, "Pick it up."

Averill turned back to look where he gestured and realized she'd fallen in front of a shallow, narrow alcove, just big enough for a good-sized chest. Rising onto her knees, she moved closer, eyeing the thing curiously and wondering what was in it.

"Hurry up, damn ye!" he snapped furiously, kicking her in the flank. "They'll no wait long before followin'."

Gritting her teeth against the pain shooting from her lower hip from the blow, Averill forced herself to her feet and bent to grab the chest by the handles on both side. She started to rise then, but the chest did not budge. Frowning, she squatted to use her legs in the lifting and tried again, but it was simply far too heavy, and her efforts were not shifting it at all.

"Pick it up," Domnall snarled.

"I cannot," Averill said quietly. " 'Tis too heavy."

"It had best no' be or yer useless to me. I canno' carry it and guard you, too."

Biting her lip at the threat in those words, Averill made another effort, but 'twas useless. She could not lift it.

Domnall had just started moving toward her, eyes cold and face mean in the torchlight, when the passageway door opened behind them. Cursing, he glanced wildly around, then moved close to the wall next to her, and hit something. He then hurled the torch down the passageway at Kade as he started into it. Darkness immediately dropped down around her and Domnall at this end of the passageway, but Averill saw her husband duck back into the room to avoid the torch. And then Domnall grabbed her arm in the dark and hauled her to her feet. She stumbled where he pulled her, saw another entrance had opened, then she was being dragged into a room. The entrance slammed closed behind her.

Before Averill even knew where she was, Domnall had her tight against his chest again, his knife once more at her throat, but his other hand now covering her mouth.

"Make a sound, an' I'll kill ye right now," Domnall warned in a harsh whisper, then eased them both closer to the wall to try to hear what was happening in the passage on the other side.

Averill glanced around as they waited, quickly realizing they were in Brodie's room. She didn't know if it was planning on the man's part or good fortune, but he'd chosen the one room least likely for them to be found in. With Brodie dead, no one would bother coming into this room until some-one ordered it cleaned, and she doubted if the men would even consider that Domnall would dare to stop to wait in a room, for they knew not that the all-important chest was in the passage alcove. Had Domnall not pointed it out to her, she certainly would never have noticed it, and Kade and the others would be looking ahead, expecting Domnall to follow the passage all the way to wherever it ended.

His arm tightened, his knife pressing painfully against her skin, and Averill became aware of the very faint sounds of voices reaching her. She supposed the entrance must have a sliver-sized crack either at the floor or where it joined the wall for them to hear it, but that mattered little. It sounded to her like the voices were almost directly on the other side of the wall and moving past.

Averill closed her eyes, trying to think. Domnall no doubt intended to wait for them to pass, and then . . . what? She considered the situation and realized with a sinking heart that her inability to lift the chest put her in a very precarious position. As he'd said, he could not carry the chest and hold the knife to her at the same time. Rather than a shield between him and those following, she was suddenly a burden and a risk.

With the men out searching high and low for them, Domnall could conceivably remain safely in this room for some time without fear of discovery. When things quieted down, he could slip out, collect the chest, and disappear with it . . . In which case, he didn't need her at all anymore. In fact, keeping her alive risked her screaming or otherwise making a sound that would jeopardize him.

Domnall would kill her, Averill realized grimly. It was the smartest move. He would probably wait until the men had passed by to do it, but she doubted he would wait long after. If she intended to save herself, she would have to do it very soon, she decided, like that very moment.

Holding her breath, Averill began to feel around with her hands for something that could be used as a weapon. She did her best to keep her back and upper arms as still as she could while she did it, in the hopes it would keep Domnall from noticing what she was doing. Her eyes closed and her breath eased out on a slow exhalation when she felt something leaning against the wall before her, and she eased her fingers over it, trying to deduce what it was and whether it would be useful. It took her a moment to sort out that it was Brodie's shield. A fine metal one that she doubted had ever seen even one battle—the one that Laddie had used on its owner their first night there, when Brodie had attacked her.

Still struggling not to shift her upper arms and back muscles too much, Averill slowly grasped the edge of the shield and managed to lift it. She then eased it over until she could grasp it with both hands. Averill paused then to decide the best way to proceed, but there seemed little choice in the matter. The only option open to her was to raise it straight up over her head and slam it down behind her onto his and hope she did so with enough strength to knock out the man, or he'd surely slit her throat for her trouble.

Gritting her teeth, Averill sucked in a breath

and did it. Ignoring the knife at her throat, she shot the shield up with as much strength as she could muster and swung it back over her head at Domnall.

Fortunately, distracted as he was listening at the wall, the man didn't notice what she was about until it was too late. She heard the gong of the metal shield slamming into his head and Domnall's startled grunt. She was suddenly released, and Averill immediately stepped away, raising the shield again and whirling to face him at the same time.

Domnall roared with fury as he saw the second blow coming and tried to raise an arm to shield himself, but stunned by the first blow, he was clumsy and too slow, and Averill was desperate and quicker. She slammed the shield down the second time with a furious shriek of her own, putting every ounce of weight and strength she possessed behind it, landing a damaging blow to the front of his head.

Averill immediately lifted the shield for a third strike, but Domnall was already falling forward, and she leapt back instead, keeping her shield at the ready should he dare move once on the floor.

She was staring at him warily when the wall beside them suddenly burst open, and men poured in. Kade was at the front and came to an abrupt halt when he took in the situation. His gaze slid over the man lying before her, then to Averill. Leaving Domnall to the others to deal with, he stepped over the man with indifference and moved straight for her.

Averill let the shield slip from her hands, ignoring the clang when it hit the floor as her husband reached her and immediately scooped her up into his arms. She caught at his shoulders and held on as he swung around, intending to carry her out of the room.

"Kade?"

He paused at once and turned them both toward Will. "Aye?"

"What shall we do with him?" her brother asked, gesturing to the man he, Ian, Gawain, and Aidan stood over.

"Throw him in the dungeon," Kade said coldly.

He started to swing away again with her, but paused when Will said, "Well, I suppose we could do that, but why you would want to hang a corpse in chains I do not know."

Averill took a closer look at the fallen man even as Kade did. Her eyes widened when she saw that Will and Gawain had turned Domnall over to reveal his own knife protruding from his chest. He had apparently landed on it when he fell.

"Then do whatever ye wish with him. I doona care," Kade said with indifference, and turned away again. This time he carried her out of the room without being called back.

"I am fine. You need not carry me," Averill murmured, as he carried her along the hall toward their room.

"Yer bleedin'," he said grimly.

"What?" she asked with surprise.

"Yer neck."

She felt worriedly at her throat and winced at the tenderness there and the length of the slice in her throat. It was long, but Averill had no idea whether it was from when she'd hit Domnall over the head the first time, or from when he'd been dragging her around before that. She didn't think it was very deep, though. At least she hoped not.

"'Tis all right," Averill said reassuringly. "It hardly hurts."

Kade ignored that and roared, "Bess," as he carried her past the stairs.

"Husband, I am fine. Really," she insisted, tempted to smile at his concern.

This had no more effect than her earlier reassurance, and he continued on to their room. Once there, Kade carried her to the bed then paused. Rather than set her down on it, he turned and settled to sit on the edge of it himself, still holding her in his arms. He then kissed her with a barely restrained violence that rather took her breath away.

"Yer ne'er to scare me like that again," Kade growled when he finally lifted his head. "I thought I'd lost ye."

Averill stared at him, a bit stunned by the depth of emotion she saw in his eyes, then glanced to the door as Bess bustled into the room.

"You called for me, my—" Her voice died as she spotted Averill. The maid blanched at the blood

Averill could now feel dripping down her throat, then turned and rushed back out into the hall, shouting for water and linens. Bess was back in the room in a trice and detouring for the chest where Averill kept her bag of medicinals. She paused long enough to retrieve what she thought she would need from the bag and moved over to stand before Averill and Kade.

"What happened?" Bess asked as she placed two fingers under Averill's chin and tilted her head up to better see the wound.

"Domnall cut her," Kade snarled, sounding like he'd like to kill the man, already dead or not.

"I hope you beat him for it," Bess said grimly as she leaned closer.

"Nay," Kade said, sounding unhappy, then added, "Averill killed him."

"I did not," she gasped, jerking her face from Bess's hand to glare at her husband. "I merely hit him with the shield. He fell on his own knife and killed himself."

"Oh," he said, then his lips spread in a slow grin. "Laddie, you, and Morag are proving handy with shields. I'm thinkin' we should hang some on every wall o' the keep. If we're ever invaded, ye can beat 'em back fer us."

"Morag used a tray," Averill reminded him, relieved to see some of the grimness slipping away.

"A shield is heavier," he pointed out. "And had there been one in our room that night, she'd ha'e no' spilled yer meal."

"Aye," Averill agreed. "Shields it is."

They smiled at each other and glanced toward the door as a rustling announced the arrival of Morag. She carried a bowl of water and the linen Bess had shouted for, and Bess took both with relief and quickly set about cleaning Averill's neck.

" 'Twill need stitches," Bess decided as soon as she'd cleaned the blood away.

"Nay," Averill gasped, lowering her head with alarm.

" 'Tis bleeding badly, Avy," Will said, making his presence known, and she turned to find that they had a good-sized audience by then. Will, Laddie, Aidan, Gawain, and Ian stood watching with solemn expressions, each nodding as she glanced at them.

Morag was still hovering nearby, and Lily and Annie were entering the room even then.

Averill bit her lip and glanced to Kade.

" 'Tis a nasty cut, wife, and in an awkward spot. Every time ye turn yer head, 'twill reopen. 'Twould be better were it sewn up," he said with regret, then glanced to the maids, and ordered, "Fetch her some whiskey."

"I shall get the needle," Bess announced, moving away even as Morag headed out to get the requested whiskey.

"But . . ." Averill began with something close to panic. She paused, however, before blurting the rest of what she wanted to say, that she didn't wish to have stitches. Averill had stitched up countless injuries since her mother had taught her to tend the ailing and injured, but had only ever needed them once herself, and that was for a cut on the palm of her hand as a child. It had only been two very tiny stitches, but in her recollection it had hurt like the devil to get them, and she knew this was a much larger cut and very much feared it was going to hurt even worse. Rather than blurt her desire not to have them, she tried, "But, husband, surely do we put some ointment on it and bandage it up, 'twill close on its own. I will just not turn my head for a while. I am sure 'tis not as deep as all that and will heal quickly."

"Ye canno' see it, wife. 'Tis no' shallow."

"But—" Averill paused as a small hand slid into hers. Turning, she found herself peering at Laddie as he squeezed her fingers reassuringly with his much smaller ones.

"I'll hold yer hand through it, me lady," the boy offered, solemnly. "'Twill no' be so bad, and ye can squeeze me as hard as ye like if it hurts. Me ma always held mine for me while me scrapes and cuts were tended, and it helps do ye close yer eyes tight and squeeze real hard on someone's fingers."

Touched, Averill let her breath out on a small puff and squeezed his hand gently in gratitude. "Thank you, Laddie. And I shall return the favor do you ever need it."

He smiled at the words, then glanced around as Morag reentered, a pitcher of whiskey in hand.

Averill grimaced at the sight. She'd never cared

much for the drink, and it did seem ironic that
she was now going to drink some when she had
worked so hard to stop her father-in-law and
Gawain from drinking it. But she had called for it
often enough in the past for men she was about
to take the needle or knife to, and suspected she
would be grateful for the effects of the liquid fire
once Bess's needle began pushing into her skin.

Straightening her shoulders at the very thought,
Averill held her hand out for the pitcher.

Chapter Nineteen

The click of the bedchamber door stirred Averill from the bored doze she had fallen into.

It had been three days since Domnall had died. He and Brodie had been laid to rest, Brodie in the family crypt with a priest to see him on his way, and Domnall without religious rites and away from the keep. Everything had settled down at Stewart since then. Kade's father was no longer moaning about being sure he was dying but had begun to dress and clean himself up and make appearances below stairs at the table for meals. He and Gawain were still not drinking, much to her relief, and while she knew they might slip back to their old habits, she and Kade would do what they could to prevent it. Ian was recovering nicely from the wound Domnall had given him and talking about returning to find the little English miss who had mended him. Will was making noises about taking his men and heading home and perhaps collecting his own betrothed and settling down, and most of the servants had come back to Stewart and were returning the castle to its former glory.

At least, that was what Averill had been told. She knew none of this for sure herself because she had been stuck in the bedchamber she and Kade shared . . . healing. Averill rolled her eyes with disgust at the thought. Kade was an even more stubborn nursemaid than she and insisted she needed to remain in bed after the wound she'd taken and the stitches Bess had placed in her throat. She had spent the last three days bored to tears, with only Laddie and Bess and the occasional visit from her brother or the other men to keep her company through the day. Kade came to sit with her in the evenings and read to her as she had once done for him, his deep voice rolling over her in soothing waves. However, Averill was heartily sick of the enforced rest and had planned all day to talk to Kade when he arrived that night and insist he let her up on the morrow.

Recalling that intent, she watched as he began to strip away his clothes. At first Averill was so distracted by the sight that she quite lost the thread of what she'd wished to speak to him about, then she noted the slump to his shoulders and the grimness on his face and frowned. The man was terribly depressed and had been since the night Domnall had died. At first, she hadn't been able to understand what was causing it. She herself was relieved he was dead, or at least, that the threat to her husband was over. However, then Averill had recalled that Domnall was his cousin and had once been a friend and comrade of Kade's and, despite his murderous behavior in the end, her husband was probably mourning his loss.

Averill waited until he had finished undressing and slid into bed beside her before broaching the subject, then said gently, "I am sorry, husband. I know that Domnall was once a friend to you. You must grieve for him no matter that he turned in the end."

Kade turned an askance glance on her. "Are ye mad? He killed Angus and tried to kill Ian and you." He shook his head. "Nay. I'm no sorry he's dead. It saves me ha'ing to kill him meself. But the bloody bastard went and killed hisself ere I could beat the whereabouts o' the chest out o' him. He must be sitting in hell laughin' himself silly at bestin' me like that." Kade ground his teeth together at the thought, and added bitterly, "The worst part is the ones who'll pay for it are the people o' Stewart. I counted on the chest to help get them through the winter this year."

Averill's eyes widened as she suddenly recalled the chest he and Domnall had seemed to find so important. It had not come up as a topic these few days, but now that it had, she had good news for him. Averill opened her mouth to tell him where it was, but curiosity made her ask instead, "What is in the chest that is so important that Domnall killed two men and would have killed you for?"

"Coin," Kade said simply.

Averill frowned, and muttered, "It must hold a lot of coin, for 'twas bloody heavy. I could not even lift it when Domnall ordered me to."

"What?" He peered at her sharply.

She smiled faintly, and announced, "'Tis in the secret passage, in an alcove by the entrance into Brodie's room. You probably walked right past it—"

Averill fell silent. Her husband wasn't listening anyway. He had launched himself from the bed and crossed the room. Kade was out the door before she could shout out to remind him that he was naked. Shaking her head, she tugged the linens out from under the furs and wrapped the soft cloth around herself over the thin chemise she wore as she got up to follow. She was at the door before thinking to grab her husband's plaid to cover him.

Muttering under her breath with irritation, Averill scoured the shadowy floor for the discarded item, then grabbed it up when she spotted it and headed for the door once more, only to have to struggle with it, trying to open it without losing her hold on either the linen wrapped around her or the plaid. She managed it with some time and effort, then stepped out into the hall in time to see Kade returning.

He strode toward her, a completely changed man from the slump-shouldered one who had entered the room moments ago. Kade was still naked as a babe, the chest the only thing covering his groin, but his shoulders were back, his stride confident, and a smile split his lips as he carried the chest toward her . . . as if the bloody thing weighed nothing, Averill noted, impressed with the strength he was exhibiting.

When he had nearly reached her, Averill stepped aside for him to enter the room ahead of her, noting as she did that Morag and Bess were at the top of the stairs, gaping after him like a couple of fools.

Shaking her head, Averill followed her husband into their room and closed the door.

Kade was already on the bed when she crossed the room. He sat cross-legged, the chest before him, and was fiddling with the latch to open it. She heard the click as it gave, then he threw the lid open, revealing the contents.

Averill came to an abrupt halt at the sight of the coin inside. The chest was full to the top, some even spilling out on the uneven surface of the bed.

"You are rich," she gasped with amazement.

"Aye," he said with a grin. "We are."

"But how—?" Averill asked with bewilderment.

Kade shrugged. "As soon as I earned me spurs I started workin' as a mercenary. A hired sword to help out any who could pay." He grinned. "Desperate men pay well."

When Averill glanced at him with surprise, he shrugged again.

"I had nothin' better to do. Mother wanted me

nowhere near Stewart and me father . . . and Uncle Simon didna need me help, so I gathered a small army of men together, and we worked for coin." He peered back to the chest as he added, "The men often spent theirs on women and drink, but I'm no' a drinker, and I've never had to pay for women, so I saved most o' mine. Plus I got an extra fee fer arrangin' everythin'." His eyes ran over the coins, and he said, "I always planned to use it to better Stewart. I just didna realize how much it would be needed."

Averill sank onto the bed, asking with bewilderment. "But if you are rich, why did you marry me?"

"What?" Kade turned to her with surprise. He frowned at her bewildered expression. "Why diya think I married ye, Averill?"

"For my dower," she admitted.

He snorted. "That piddlin' amount?"

She flushed hotly. " 'Twas quite generous."

"Aye," Kade said soothingly, and leaned to press a kiss to her cheek, then straightened again and scooped up a handful of the coins and let them rain back in. "But 'tis naught next to this."

Averill gazed at the chest as well and had to admit that he was right, her dower had been nowhere near this rich.

"Ye thought I married ye for yer dower?" he asked, distracting her.

Averill flushed but nodded. "Well, aye, that and because I am Will's sister."

Kade laughed at that. "By that reckoning, I'd as well have married yer father."

She smiled automatically, but then frowned, and asked, "But then why *did* you marry me, husband?"

"Avy," he said seriously, "why would I not? I liked ye from the start, enjoyed yer company, thought yer hair beautiful and yer birthmark adorable . . . and I soon came to love ye. Mayhap e'en before we married. I craved yer company every minute we were apart."

Averill stared at him with bewilderment, then pointed out, "But I stammer like an idiot."

"No' an idiot," Kade said at once, almost sounding angry. "Ye stammer when yer nervous, is all." He clucked his tongue with irritation, and asked, "Ye doona think Laddie an idiot, do ye?"

"Nay, of course not. And I know I am not one either, but others think me an idiot when I stammer, and—"

"Why do ye care what others think?" he asked with a shrug. "I'm yer husband, and I ken yer clever."

Her eyebrows rose, and she asked uncertainly, "And you do not mind that I am clever?"

"Why would I mind?" he asked with amusement.

Averill shrugged unhappily. "Most men do not care for clever wives."

"I'm no' most men," Kade said dryly. "And nay, I doona mind. In fact, I'd have it no other way. I love yer cleverness, Avy. I love you."

Averill bit her lip, then admitted, "And I love you, too, husband, and suspect I have done so since before the wedding, too. I could not help it. Will filled my head with so many stories of your honor and courage that I was half in love with you before you even awoke."

The smile that broke out on his face then was bright enough to light up the darkest night, but Averill got little chance to enjoy it. Kade suddenly leaned forward and kissed her, his mouth covering hers in a passionate kiss as if to seal the deal, and Averill suspected that was all he had intended it to be, but as always happened when he kissed her, their passion flared, burning bright and hot between them. Within moments, Kade was breaking the kiss, but only to remove the chest from the bed. He urged her to her feet, removed the linen wrapped around her, then her chemise, and ushered her back into bed. He followed, pulling her against his chest to kiss her again.

Kade's body pressed against hers as they kissed, one leg sliding between both of hers as he gathered her closer, so that his hands could slide up and down her back and cup her behind. And then he broke the kiss abruptly, and muttered, "Yer neck."

" 'Tis fine," she assured him quickly, reaching down between them to clasp his erection encouragingly. " 'Tis healing. Bess says she will remove the stitches in a few days."

Averill grimaced even as she said the words, for

receiving them had been an ordeal she would not soon forget. She had only managed to keep from weeping and screaming in pain because she'd had so many there looking on worriedly.

Kade's creeping hands distracted her from the unpleasant memory, and she sighed as one closed over a breast, squeezing and kneading the orb, then plucking at the nipple until she moaned at the excitement building in her. When he then pressed her onto her back, Averill closed her eyes and went willingly until he announced, "We must be careful. Yer no to move."

Her eyes popped open at the order, and she unthinkingly started to raise her head to peer down at him as he slid down her body, but a pulling of the stitches in her neck made her pause. Averill forced herself back to lie flat, remonstrating with herself to stay still, then clutched at the linens and gasped as he took one erect nipple into his mouth and began to lave and suckle it. Staying still soon become a challenge as his wandering lips and tongue left her breast to move lower, exploring her belly button, a hipbone, an inner thigh. By the time he urged her legs apart and dipped between them to kiss her there, Averill was atremble with so much excitement and pleasure that it was becoming impossible to control herself. Her body wanted to move, her head needing to shift and twist back and forth on the pillow.

"Husband, I prithee," Averill gasped when she

could stand it no more. "Do you not stop that and make love to me, I shall surely start thrashing my head about and rip my stitches."

Kade paused at once and lifted his head to look at her. Apparently deciding she was not jesting, he crawled back up her body. He paused then, holding himself still, his hips resting between hers and arms holding his weight as he peered down into her face.

"Raise yer knees for me," he growled.

Averill obeyed at once, making a cradle for him. He then bent his head to kiss her. His lips brushed across hers once, then twice, his hips shifting in time with the action so that his erection rubbed across the core of her in warm, firm strokes that made her moan. Averill reached up to grasp his shoulders, clutching at him as her hips shifted, her feet pressing into the bed as she pushed herself more firmly into the caress. His tongue slid out to urge her lips apart and thrust into her mouth even as his erection thrust into the center of her, and Averill gasped with pleasure at the exciting combination.

Shifting her hands to his head, Averill slid her fingers into his hair, nails scraping across his scalp and urging him on as she continued to arch into his thrusts, welcoming him with her body and heart until her pleasure peaked, and her body vibrated and clenched with her release.

Kade broke their kiss then, a shout slipping from his mouth as he threw his head back and thrust into her one last time, his warm seed filling her. His head then dropped to hang down, his eyes closed almost in pain, their bodies still joined together at the hip until a small sigh slid from his lips, and he eased himself out and shifted to lie beside her.

Kade then pulled Averill onto his chest, careful of her neck as he did. Once he had her settled comfortably, he released a second sigh, this one a long gusty one of pleasure.

Averill lifted her eyes to peer at him curiously, her eyebrows rising at the wide smile on his face. "What has you smiling like that, husband?"

His smile turned to a grin, and he glanced down, and said with a shrug, "I finally got to tup me wife again." When her eyebrows rose at the words, he pointed out, "It has been a long time since the wedding."

"Aye," Averill acknowledged softly as she realized that between all their troubles, this was the first time they had actually made love since the wedding. It would not be the last.

"I feel like I'm finally home," Kade murmured with sleepy satisfaction.

"You are home, my lord," Averill said softly. "We both are."

"Aye, we are." He kissed her gently.

HIGHLAND ROMANCE FROM
NEW YORK TIMES BESTSELLING AUTHOR

LYNSAY SANDS

Devil of the Highlands
978-0-06-134477-0

Cullen, Laird of Donnachaidh, must find a wife to bear his sons to ensure the future of the clan. Evelinde has agreed to marry him despite his reputation, for the Devil of the Highlands inspires a heat within her unlike anything she has ever known.

Taming the Highland Bride
978-0-06-134478-7

Alexander d'Aumesbery is desperate to convince the beautiful and brazen Merry Stewart that he's a well-mannered gentleman who's nothing like the members of her roguish clan. But beneath it all beats a heart as intense and uncontrollable as hers.

The Hellion and the Highlander
978-0-06-134479-4

When the flame-haired Lady Averill Mortagne braves an unexpected danger at Highland warrior Kade Stewart's side, she proves that her heart is as fiery as her hair. And he realizes that submitting to their scorching passion would be heaven indeed.

MORE DELECTABLE VAMPIRE ROMANCE FROM *NEW YORK TIMES* BESTSELLING AUTHOR

LYNSAY SANDS

THE ROGUE HUNTER

978-0-06-147429-3

Samantha Willan is a workaholic lawyer. After a recent breakup she wants to stay as far away from romance as possible. Then she meets her irresistible new neighbor, Garrett Mortimer. Is it her imagination, or are his mysterious eyes locked on her neck?

THE IMMORTAL HUNTER

978-0-06-147430-9

Dr. Danielle McGill doesn't know if she can trust the man who just saved her life. There are too many questions, such as what is the secret organization he says he's part of, and why do his wounds hardly bleed? But with her sister in the hands of some dangerous men, she doesn't have much choice but to trust him.

THE RENEGADE HUNTER

978-0-06-147431-6

When Nicholas Argeneau, former rogue vampire hunter, sees a bloodthirsty sucker terrifying a woman, it's second nature for him to come to her rescue. But he doesn't count on getting locked up for his troubles.

LYS2 1.009

At Avon Books, we know your passion for romance—once you finish one of our novels, you find yourself wanting more.

May we tempt you with . . .

- **Excerpts** from our upcoming releases.

- Entertaining **extras**, including authors' personal photo albums and book lists.

- Behind-the-scenes **scoop** on your favorite characters and series.

- **Sweepstakes** for the chance to win free books, romantic getaways, and other fun prizes.

- Writing **tips** from our authors and editors.

- **Blog** with our authors and find out why they love to write romance.

- **Exclusive content** that's not contained within the pages of our novels.

Join us at
www.avonbooks.com

AVON   *An Imprint of* HarperCollins*Publishers*
www.avonromance.com